The Sarah Project 2189

Rob Farrand

Published by Rob Farrand, 2025.

THE SARAH PROJECT 2189

First edition. March 30, 2025.

Copyright © 2025 Rob Farrand.

ISBN: 978-1763751507

Written by Rob Farrand.

Table of Contents

Dedication

I dedicate this book to my brother and my late parents, who always supported me and encouraged me to follow my own unique path.

Special thanks to Adam, all my friends and locals at the local watering hole who encourage me to keep going with the book. Checking I was making progress each week and sometimes, even without asking, they got an update while they sat sipping their drinks.

It was a challenge. I am sure it has a few issues not picked up on spell checkers. Nothing in the world is perfect. Sometimes it is how it is, and you must just be you. People will like it, or choose not to. I hope you will immerse yourself in the story and it creates a vivid movie in your mind.

I have always believed if you don't ask; you don't get and if you don't try, you will always fail. For that reason, I have given it a red hot go and backed myself by releasing this novel.

Chapter One-Sunset

S unrise has just begun. Tall buildings are throwing their long striking shadows on the ground, while the rest of the open areas of the city brighten. After a busy night, Sarah is eager to relax and unwind at home. She has no traffic or stop lights to worry about during the morning drive home. With the windows down, cool, fresh air catches and lifts her long black hair, pulsing towards and away from the window as buildings and crossroads pass by. This creates a gentle massaging effect on her scalp, helping her to relax. Quiet streets in the morning are a positive part of her life.

The sound of the propulsion drive from her vehicle whistles off buildings as the dawn light flashes on the windscreen as they pass by. Adelaide's serene morning streets can change in an instant. Sarah and her vehicle scan the view ahead, checking that shapes moving on buildings are cleaning machines and not something more sinister. Automated machines run through the night cleaning buildings, roads, and infrastructure, communicating with each other on all aspects of their assigned tasks. The machines log any issues with the integrity of structures and the condition of external areas, such as footpaths and lighting, that require repair. Indoor robots, like their counterparts, are now also ending their work schedules for the night. Swarms of robots ensure that all critical infrastructure remains in prime working order. If a robot is defective, the team will replace it and send the faulty one to a repair location. The human species may have grown by learning from the past and avoided significant wars leading to nuclear-assured annihilation, ending all life on Earth. However, there are also those that believe humans have created something worse in the last century.

Sarah swerves to avoid an animal crossing the street. After a productive night of hunting, she needs to be careful because of her low ammunition and reserves. Causing damage to her vehicle or delaying her arrival home could be costly to the future, and to her own safety.

The sun lifting above its horizon creates long shadows that withdraw like the ocean tide on a calm summer morning. Once the sun is overhead, they will lap at the bottom of the high-rise buildings. The sun's rays, through it's sweeping of the sky, cannot dispel pockets of darkness in the centuries-old town. Life thrives in sunless places like tunnels, subways, and underground infrastructure. The need for food and resources sees fierce fighting for survival. Some more intelligent animals and creatures use these conditions to prey, hide, or as their home. Sarah can use these traits to find her targets or avoid these areas as species use their numbers for protection against attacks.

The darkness gives Sarah some advantages, as she can hide and stalk the creatures she wishes to study. The cover of darkness is also an advantage to her prey's hunting skills as well, so she must be on constant alert. Underground areas and buildings serve as sleeping nests for a variety of humans, animals, and creatures, with species occupying them both day and night. Earth today has countless living conditions, with a diverse array of life inhabiting them. There are the Pure and Mixed Humans, living in houses or multi-story apartments. Other elites live in secure structures, barricaded compounds that ensure maximum security. These structures protect residents from interacting with the wild Unhuman, who occupy most of the earth.

Sarah must adhere to strict arrival procedures to allow her to enter her compound. Once verified, she can enjoy the much-needed rest, as Sarah's bosses keep her to a strict timeline with tight reporting schedules when out hunting. All devices that require a charge go to their stations. Any items that are replaced get crossed checked with stock numbers to be reordered if required, while weapons get cleaned, double checked, and re-armed. Security systems undergo a synchronization process to identify breaches or faults. All mission logs from the returning equipment are recorded on multiple servers and then sent to the command center.

Her compound is full of the latest technology from elite scientists and engineers. It's an old church, selected because of its thick walls, tall tower for communications and underground quarters. Several of the buildings surrounding the church almost stand as tall as its communications tower. The advantage of a small compound lies in the minimal effort needed for protection. The large buildings surrounding the church create a corridor that any flying objects or animals must pass through to attack. This gives the defense systems an advantage in predicting and creating firing solutions for engaging rapid-fire weapons, to ensure any debris from an object will be small enough to bounce off the church's defense shield.

It's a complicated project Sarah is undertaking. The natural survival of the Unhuman species intertwines with Mixed Humans, Pure Humans, and the Elite, each having their own reasons for existing on Earth. While all intelligent species know Sarah, her living and shelter areas, many of them are unsure why she is here. They seldomly attack, as they have witnessed her deadly defenses in action and intelligent species view Sarah as more of an annoyance than a threat, standing alone amidst them. The top three species prioritize fighting their own battles instead of wasting time on her.

Today's world population, which science has created through years of genetic modification, is a diverse new evolution cycle for Earth. In unregulated societies, new species thrive with a survival-of-the-fittest mentality. Unintelligent battles erupt with species fighting to find their natural place in this new Earth order. Others, with intelligence and more extraordinary power, fight their own wars to be the apex predators. Earth is a mixture of good versus evil, humans versus beasts, all in their own battles for survival and dominance.

The planet's health is the one positive outcome, now back to its pre-industrial age before humans forced change on it. Humans leaving Earth for life on the Moon, Mars, and low orbit allow nature to thrive. The humans that left Earth have no genetic changes. They are Pure humans and have cocooned themselves away from others. Their beliefs left them with no choice but to banish themselves from the Planet, through fear of becoming impure.

Humans' hunger for comfortable living, confusion over need versus want, and the misuse of DNA modifications have created many problems. On Earth today, there are Pure Humans left by the Elite, alongside Mixed Humans and genetic descendants of all species, leading to a wide range of Unhuman. All roam free on Earth outside compound walls, in their own areas, trying to find a livable balance. Unhuman creatures prey on each other and exploit opportunities to gain ground from other species, while Pure and Mixed Humans defend themselves against wild creatures and each other.

In their attempt to cure diseases over two centuries by creating more robust, more intelligent humans through gene modifications, scientists created this disaster that has now evolved on today's Earth. Over time, interbreeding with similar or different DNA modifications created improvements in a species or created new variants. Doctors were unaware of the future mutations that they would cause from their manipulation, or they just didn't care. From the beginning, the focus was on improving humans' lives to surpass natural humans' limitations, abilities, and strength. It wasn't all just about strength and longevity that people desired; it included appearance and the infatuation with other creatures' characteristics that inspired changes to look more like them.

In some areas, nature has taken over the once bustling city of Adelaide. Abundant in the city center and its surroundings are fresh water, vegetables, and other forms of natural food. No matter what intelligent life forms have thrown at the planet, Mother Nature will shine on through if their numbers decline.

Automated machines and factories supply food and materials to the Elite, both on and off-Earth. Manufacturing is by 3D and 3D4 printing, creating replacement parts, tools, or creating complete robots that are ordered through central command to complete tasks. All power generation is from fusion energy, ensuring minimal pollution, with any waste materials recycled where possible or eliminated in an environmentally favorable way. Trade and partnerships exist between humans and countries, both within the Elite and in underground alliances. These collaborations involve dealing with necessities for survival, with reluctant sharing of resources and materials.

Fresh grown food is a rare treat Sarah gives herself as a break from the manufactured food she has at her compounds around Australia. She checks each food for its generic makeup before preparing her meals with the supplied foods from the overseers. Sarah has a strict requirement to take all the supplied designed supplements to keep her body functioning at maximum performance, and to enhance her DNA modifications. The Elite overseers view Sarah as a slave and a guinea pig, pressuring her to achieve daily goals. They warn her that if she cannot meet these goals, they will stop supplying her supplements, turning her into a liability rather than an asset.

Sarah is the most impressive specimen by all standards, the finest DNA modifications sciences have ever created. Her father wanted to do what his father and great-grandfather could not achieve. Invent a virus to eradicate all mutants without impacting Pure Humans. Different levels of authority argue their lack of knowledge about what is true pure DNA. To what extent do you need to trace back to get Pure human DNA? What level is acceptable? What modifications are from natural evolution? How long should anyone live for? Who will oversee and determine the correct answers to these questions on Earth?

In cases of genetic defects, humans invented ways to tweak DNA, to make it better and stronger than the organ that failed. This is unacceptable from an Elite Pure perspective. Elite Humans abstain from illegal medications, consume only self-produced food, and limit medical procedures to those approved by the leaders. These Elite began living by their own rules and wanting to move away and segregate from the Mixed Humans, so they created their compounds.

Sarah, being equipped with years of DNA innovation, stands as a perfect superhuman. She has enhanced strength, acute senses, and regenerative body organs. Her genes are pure, not created by crossbreeding from other creatures, but engineered to the highest standard over decades. Her overseers relentlessly remind her there is a cost for all these superpowers. She must take the supplied supplements and limit contact with others or anything unnatural to avoid any chance of it infecting her or altering her DNA. This helps to limit her interaction with others or to not act outside the goals of a mission through fear they will stop supplying her medications. Knowing her immune system can handle infections and is immune to influence or alteration, the Elite fear it would change her motives for fighting and her loyalty to the cause.

All the rules and instructions to stay on track, focused on her mission have Sarah questioning to herself about why she is on earth. How did things go so wrong? Just what were the forebears thinking when they started playing with nature? Sciences, while searching for health benefits, tried to navigate the delicate balance between preserving the human quality of life and achieving immortality. Wealthy individuals took a different approach to altering their DNA, crossing boundaries to surpass others, wanting to be superhuman, always happy, enjoying life to its fullest with no signs of age or to have characteristics of their favorite animals.

Sarah's father, named after Cronus-Matthew, the God of time, King of the Titans, and ruler of the cosmos, is called by his initials CM. He grew up in Elite circles and now belongs to the select group of overseers. These Elite leaders say they are trying to make amends for the past wrongs. Headed by CM, they have tasked Sarah and others with a long and lonely fight on Earth evaluating a salvation cure. Under their rule, she experiences slavery, lacking social interaction and any genuine friendships while her body has aged at a controlled rate throughout this long existence on earth. To onlookers, she only appears to be a 35-year-old, although she is much older.

Sarah has only one fond memory she hangs onto of her father and her early years. Just as CM put her into bed, he would play a tune and whisper in her ear, "You will awake, and know it's time to shine, my beautiful girl."

Chapter Two-Adelaide

Adelaide, Australia, is still a populated city with inhabitants including natural animals, those with manipulated genes ranging from high-intelligence Mixed Humans to a variety of wild creatures. Onlookers believe Sarah has a programmed mission, devoid of personal control or emotion. Many see Sarah as a genuine mutant, and she is aware of this perception.

From dawn to dusk, dusk till dawn, all the creatures and animals of Earth go through their natural routines. It's truly a new world. It has a primitive cave dweller mentality entangled with intelligent humans scatted throughout. A strange mix of natural and unnatural creatures, with competing food chains and unique pecking orders that are well established and constantly challenged. No laws enforcement exists in this free world beyond the Elite compounds. Beyond their wall is a throwback to the wild west days: fight, obey or perish in nature's new pecking order. Are you the hunter or the prey?

In certain societies, individuals offer to have jobs that challenge and provide meaning to their lives by completing the essential tasks required for the group's survival. Jobs involve creating non-automatable parts or alternative forms of Artificial Intelligence needed but not yet trusted outside of human control. This is more prevalent in remote natural societies, where Mixed Humans live with little help from the Pure. Areas like these can form societies resembling gangs, because of the absence of technology, requiring a more hands-on approach.

Those who cause trouble in Pure compounds have punishment administered quickly, either banishment from a compound or orders to work and live in crucial factories. The death penalty is an option for the most violent crimes in a compound. With limited space and resources, especially in off world locations, the death penalty is an effective method the Elite use to reduce the population.

New species are being created from what was the natural human race. Humans with a low percentage of altered genes or part human part beasts are creating an even wider range of spin-offs from interbreeding of species. Some are intelligent, while others lack any self-awareness or morals. These so-called unintelligent Unhuman creatures can resemble wild animals derived from all of Earth's species since its existence. Centuries of roaming and breeding have blurred DNA lines, with different species now inhabiting the world's empty buildings, streets, undergrounds, and outback areas. Roaming free or in various-sized packs like ravenous wolves or intellectual armies, taking or destroying whatever they can. The dangerous ones are the in-between classes, nearly Unhuman with animal-like features and combined abilities.

To protect the true natural human species, while developing a plan, leaders sent individuals and families with the best genes into near-earth orbit, the Moon, and Mars. Leaders selected individuals and families with Pure genes offering them benefits to live with others off Earth, to maintain the gene pool's integrity and greater separation from mutants. Overseeing these groups of Pure are the leaders known as the Elite Pure. Their focus is on protecting their species and envisioning a Pure Earth, with only natural DNA inhabitants. The Elite abandoned second-class humans with lower natural genes on Earth, tricking them into supply resources and support. They promised inclusion, but once dominant, they abandoned those deemed unnecessary. Humans should have learned from what happens with this type of discrimination, race, and gender battles and found ways to live together.

The Pure who stayed on Earth by their own choice defend themselves and fight alone or in small communities. They considered it to be a superior option to living on Mars or the Moon, despite the difficulties of not having the Elite's defenses. With the collapse of the armies and police forces to help protect them, it has now become a long-drawn-out battle between Pure, Mixed Humans, and the Unhuman.

Elite Pure long to roam Earth freely again, but the dream is complex. Impatient elite argue for a clean slate, wanting to erase everything on Earth, returning only Pure humans and their innovative technologies. Scientists and others believe life's complexity and interconnectedness surpass such a simple plan. Food chains, animals and insects are all required for a healthy earth, so a scorched earth mentality is a flawed ideal. Not only ethically, but in all practicality. Earth has seen significant changes because of its interconnectedness and interactions, showing it would have been much better off without humans ever rising to their so-called intelligent life form. This is proven by its regeneration since human dominance has reduced all over the Planet.

The vast majority of Pure people oppose killing and fighting against fellow human beings. Elite leaders in the Pure public arena admit to being unable to find a solution, having explored all methods of reasoning. The Elite government's aim is to create vaccines for a natural decline of Mixed and Unhuman species, restoring the world to only Pure Humans. Early vaccines have been ineffective in reverting Mixed DNA or selectively making targets sterile. They are also not aligning with the Elites timeline, so they are misrepresenting their effects and existence to the public. The Elite are trying to show that they are developing a humane way to deal with Mixed Humans although it is proving difficult. They hope is it will then convince the public to move to the more primitive eradication method against Mixed Human and Unhuman attacks that happen occasionally, and others orchestrated by the Elite.

Genetic changes not only changed the greater Mixed Human's appearance, strength, and character, it also changed the gestation period in some breeds. Mixed Humans and Unhuman are reproducing faster than the Pure population, increasing the Elite leaders' sense of urgency.

Those remaining on Earth or deserted by the privileged have experienced some setbacks to a previous life's basic pleasures. Like walking outside the walls of their defended compounds or homes. However, it has fewer restrictions than an Elite life far from Earth's surface, living in an arrangement of plastic and tin tubes which are essentially blow-up tents. Without an atmosphere, there is no freedom to enjoy fresh air and sunlight on your skin. To promote the cause, the Elite claim that the life support systems provide uninfected purified air to those privileged individuals chosen to live in these off-world colonies.

Over time, Elite Pure imposed sanctions and new orders on space stations, the Moon, and Mars, shutting out all earthbound Pure from the Elite Pure life. Off-world travel is now restricted to approved arrivals and departures. Any unauthorized approach towards the extreme outer limits of space stations, Mars, or the Moon results in instant annihilation, without hesitation. Selected compounds and factories on Earth producing goods, food, or providing engineering to the true Pure are thriving as they still receive the support. Not only because of their resources, it is also to ensure they have a safe place to escape from their containment vessels if required or the ability to visit for holidays to experience gravity, fresh air, natural running streams and rivers.

Earlier warrior troops sent to Earth, warriors not as exceptional as Sarah, tried different methods of reclaiming Earth for the Pure. Hunt and kill methods, baiting areas to achieve eradication and other ideas that have all failed. These methods met with a backlash from both off world, earthbound Pure and Mixed Humans, forcing the Elite to abandon them. They did not want any species banding together in their larger population numbers to rise against them.

Chapter three. Preparing Mission 2189/432

Before wearing her suit, Sarah must always shower and wash off in her detox area. Her skin-tight bodysuits offer significant advantages to her while allowing her to move freely. The suit is incredibly pliable, molding to the wearer's body like a second skin. This allows Sarah to have total agility and range of movement while providing maximum protection from weaponry and biological threats. Sarah looks like a formidable warrior in her suit as the light shimmers off the wet black-looking material, showing off all her athletic, toned, and trimmed body.

Sarah prepares herself as weapons run self-checks for their readiness for use. Daily reports come in between two time periods. Seven AM and nine AM, four PM and seven PM. Mission protocols mandate adjusted reports if the away mission deviates from the specified church departure and return times. Each report encodes the scheduled times for responding to future communication. The narrow and unpredictable time limit eliminates fake or intercepted correspondence. If Sarah cannot respond on time, protocols will activate and require her to conduct more extensive tests on herself and the equipment. In extreme cases, all the sensitive materials will evacuate to the Moon. The church will reset all the passwords to prevent Sarah from entering, suspecting that she is infected, or someone may have taken her hostage. In either situation, they would rather dump her than help her. As part of all the protocols, they require Sarah to give a blood sample to be checked before they can open or verify any information she has. Sarah's feelings are further enhanced by the ongoing lack of trust after all these years.

Dawn Report 6935/2189 from the off-world Overseers 14th Sun of July 2189

Sarah: All systems scanned and cleaned. Confirm No noteworthy progress on tasks 13/7/2189. I require August's supply delivery to be completed and prepared for shipping to Earth's orbit.

Command: We concur with your findings. Strain 564 needs to show signs of working. We accept your assessment and agree some of the ill were showing signs of recovery and have no symptoms. Infection efforts have failed to take. We consider them to have become immune to further doses of this strain.

Sarah: I have received Strain 732/2116 intact and complete. New defense supplies are also intact. New Mission 2189/431 statement received. Supply module loaded and complete systems backup sent. Sarah Out.

Encrypted text is used to send regular, straightforward reports. Detailed messages to and from the Moon are on laser etched discs, as they are immune to space radiation. Delivery crafts also contain self-destructive mechanisms, so they will explode if tampered with or delayed. The self-destructive mechanisms on the delivery crafts will destroy and render any contents onboard undetectable, making them useless to anyone. Sarah has read and set all the parameters for the mission. She starts her pre-deployment procedures to leave the compound on the new task.

Sarah's vehicle moves from its parking garage to the pre-deployment station. All the support craft come to life, flashing and beeping while moving to their pre-launch stations to run system checks. As the pre-arranged countdown starts for the mission, all systems do a final check. Five minutes remain before Sarah leaves the compound. During this protocol checkpoint, the church's protection drones scout up to two kilometers away, transmitting data on moving objects, new arrivals, and potential obstacles along her path. One minute before exiting the compound, Sarah's armed protection craft deploy to increase the visual surveillance and ensure a safe exit.

Sarah has various crafts and technology with long-lasting power supplies. They still are required to dock to keep them in peak operational order. During docking, they perform the download of all logs and video footage, and the upload of any new programming required for a current mission. The central management also does a virus check and a mirror image check is used to compare the uploaded software to the systems sample.

Drone crafts are Sarah's eyes, ears, and security backup equipped with various tools, including cameras, heat detection, motion sensors, acute hearing with active targeting systems. Emergency supply drones in the entourage carry replacement items, specialist equipment, extra ammunition, and consumables for Sarah. To prevent their equipment from falling into the hands of the Mixed Human aggressors, the supply craft remain high in the sky, away from any action. Constant real-time monitoring of all Sarah's vehicle, drones and compounds are all synchronized, with Artificial Intelligence and preemptive programming. They will act with extreme force to protect Sarah's well-being if they perceive any dangers. Sarah relies on them as a source of advanced scouting and intel to keep her safe when in or out of her vehicle. Survival without them would be unlikely against an ambush or attack from multiple creatures, even with her remarkable skills.

Data and mission methods come directly from the overseers, and selected drones may have their own missions. Sarah doesn't trust any of the drones, even though they would assist her when necessary. Not knowing exactly what task the overseers have given them leaves Sarah with doubts. Occasionally, drones have had minds of their own, gathered extra data, moved slightly differently, and appeared not to have had Sarah's best interest at heart. Despite the central command's insistence that they were following orders under her control, Sarah remains skeptical.

Chapter four. New Start

Communication lines are open and confirmed. Mission 2189/432 final countdown has begun, systems are powering up, logging engaged, backups sent to the emergency pod, and the mission objectives installed.

Good evening, Sarah. Please confirm your status.

Confirm fit and active for service.

Refer to the mission log, confirm the route, and objectives.

I confirm log 9876, and I understand the mission objectives.

Please engage tracking and networking systems.

Networking systems employed and awaiting confirmation.

Confirmation of network and tracking acknowledgement.

Affirmative, acknowledge and locking onto satellites, access requests sent.

System power check.

All systems are complete and nominal.

Abort mission protocols reviewed.

Confirm.

Security system, drone passwords, and identification confirmation.

Confirm all green and loaded.

Switch over to onboard away systems. You have control.

Confirm away systems activated, vehicle and craft onboard.

Control systems are active. I have control.

launch.

Away mission protocols are active; vehicles are armed and engaged.

Safe trip Sarah.

I have left the compound, confirming secure compound lockdown, and all protocols activated.

They chose the church for its various departure options. The compound's security defense systems lack compassion and fire at any perceived threat, leaving the surrounding buildings empty. Regular shootings have created an understanding of a no-go zone near the church.

As Sarah drives down the streets of Adelaide, the sun is close to the horizon, creating long shadows that cover the width of streets. Buildings block the sun and east-west roads allow the sunlight to shine through. This creates strobing flashes over her vehicle, while other objects also block the sun are shadows of death. Large flying man-beasts, humans crossed with giant winged creatures from a past life on Earth. Created from the prehistoric animals brought back to life for their unique qualities, mutant humans with Pterodactylus creature genes, mixed with the hunger and cunning of a panther.

Unhuman creatures pursue not only nourishment but also enjoyment. To whatever toy they choose, it will be anything but enjoyable. Deciding to just eat you or play with your wounded body until they get bored. They communicate with every bite just how slowly you will die for their delight. You may be a delicacy or a quick snack. This slow, painful communication enhances the taste of your flesh. The exact timeline they peck on you, throw you, or carry you around for, is like a chef cooking a steak to order, rare to well done. They can treat you like a cat with a mouse, playing until you're injured enough to draw attention from other species. Then they will let you go to fend for yourself and watch you fight for your survival. The worst of human traits shines through in these Unhuman species.

Night approaches as the sun fades away. An amber, red, and purple glow reflects off the scattered clouds. Sarah's new mission begins as the sun sets and the streets awaken. The recent rain reflects lights shimmering on the wet road as she drives down it. Old advertising signs with past city ads still glow on buildings and objects. Nighttime service robots are deploying from their service locations. These robots have learning capabilities, so they expect Sarah during their shift along with other semi-regular traffic around this time. If they detect her, they will free a path out of the compound and down any principal streets she chooses. Their awareness of Sarah is not the reason;

it's a programmed response from years past. Sarah enjoys the green lights, even though she is not required to stop at a red one. She enjoys knowing that they prioritize her interests in their programming but acknowledges that their prime responsibility is to ensure the safety of other vehicles and robots on the road.

Mixed Humans occupy Adelaide in numbers, unlike other more distant towns. Living in multi-story buildings as communities, they must be careful, especially at night. The Unhuman species are active because the city lights attract them from the surrounding Mount Lofty Ranges. Because of abundant food and water, a variety of creatures live nearby for the Elites' experiments.

As Sarah powers down the road, the ominous glow of the blue lights under her matt black vehicle creates a striking view of power and authority. It shows she is serious and is on a mission. Her vehicle is an ever-evolving active entity which can create thousands of colors and shapes. Sarah prefers three styles with distinct colors. Matt black is used to blend into the dark, army flat green is for hunting, and a striking chrome appearance reflects the environment or confuses attackers who see themselves.

Today, it has the classic lines of an old 1970s Matt Black Dodge Plymouth Barracuda. The vehicle does not have a traditional solid external body. Its outside skin is a matrix of squares that can form different shapes or openings. Made of powerful compounds that can connect as a solid to absorb most weaponry. Sarah can reach inside this matrix field to grab weapons or equipment and jump in and out of the vehicle as it recognizes her. Weapons and other items have coding chips embedded in them. These chips allow the active field to sense them and open for easy access. The active field will prohibit any organic or material objects not in the database from entering with vengeance. This changeable body offers protection from the environment over a carbon and graphene roll cage-like structure. The wheels on the vehicle are not wheels at all, they are spheres, puncture-proof, while still having enough flex to give the vehicle the best traction on different surfaces. Tread spheres adjust for ideal grip, enabling instant multidirectional travel.

Sarah's vehicle can also fly, used to hop from one road surface to another, or to cover ground fast with the freedom from following roads. She flies over uninteresting areas, lost to dominating Unhuman. Flying is an efficient way to travel long distances, but it limits Sarah's ability to capture ground-level data and reduces the element of surprise. Another risk of flying is the large Unhuman flying in swarms who will attack other flying objects. The vehicle is in constant contact with her so she can control it to move to locations, or function as a decoy, however the overseers have the overriding capability.

Mission 2189/432 is a two-part mission, a quick hop to Murray Bridge, about one hundred and twenty kilometers from Adelaide. Then, another jump to Mount Gambier is four hundred and sixty kilometers from Adelaide and two hundred kilometers from Murray Bridge. The territory is beyond that of the local communities of Adelaide's City Center. These communities outside the city limits have been interbreeding and interacting. Over time, these populations transformed into unrecoverable wild packs.

Part of Sarah's general scope is to log all the surface data she can, including plants, animals, humans, mixed breeds she passes on her journey. The data is used to build a comprehensive catalog that is compared in real time to show any changes, either long-term or instant. AI programs analyze stored data for mission relevance and potential risks to the Elite's goals. Along with collecting data from a range of sensors on her vehicle, she also gives any verbal commentary that is beneficial. Once She has driven through places of interest, she will leap to area sixty-five to reduce the travel time to the mission's test zone.

Australia and the entire planet have changed because of technology and global warming. Large parts of the world are still uninhabitable for original humans. Technology has seen reducing CO_2 emissions and methane from trillions of tons of buried waste, which was bringing severe weather changes. Traditional timelines of summer, fall, winter, and spring in locations have moved three months forward. Nature continues its ancient cycle of checks and balances. Areas uninhabitable on their surface have had their communities moved under the sandy soil into subterranean habitats. Europe and the United States have entered an ice age. Meanwhile, Australia, once a dry continent with vast deserts, has transformed into a thriving natural wonderland. This makes it the perfect place for the Elite to conduct experiments. Adelaide's climate and Australia's isolation create an ideal real-world test environment ensuring minimal global impact.

Humans evolved and built structures in locations worldwide and off-world. Most capital cities have remained practical and capable of supporting human life. Eyre Peninsula is the largest populated Pure Human area, people still recognize Adelaide as the capital city of the state. Port Lincoln and surrounding cities grew by isolating Eyre Peninsula with a wall, separating it from the rest of South Australia. The wall stretched from Port Augusta to Woomera and Ceduna.

The Elite Pure's defended high wall and electronic moat make the whole peninsula safe for its now only Pure Human inhabitants. Like in previous centuries, the castle symbolizes power and serves as the ruler's residence. The Elite Pure nobles safeguard the humble people living inside the castle walls. These types of compounds worldwide hold the best educated people with all the latest technology. It's only a short three-hundred-kilometer hop over the sea to Port Lincoln headquarters from her church if she is required to be present for meetings.

The majority in three compounds ignored the rest of South Australia. These communities are self-sufficient, independent from non-Pure cities. Elite Pure Humans populate Port Lincoln, Mount Gambier and Yorke Peninsula with no Mixed Humans allowed within these walls. Towns like Murray Bridge have a more relaxed attitude and live alongside low percentage Mixed Humans. Sarah is an operative of the Elite. Therefore, in any city or town she visits, she will receive support from the Elite compounds, though sometimes reluctantly, as she is an expendable tool.

Adelaide and nearby areas have a cross-section of inhabitants, making it a great staging point for experiments and missions. Sarah is an ambassador of sorts for the Elite Pure overseers to other semi-ruled societies with her church known as the Elites embassy base. Semi-ruled societies acknowledge this because they fear the Elite might destroy their protection systems. Without defenses they will be overrun by Unhuman.

Earth's untamed Unhuman species do not understand rules and practices. They just hunt and kill to survive as they wander their territories. Like all wild animals, survival is their basic animal instinct. Sometimes they will wander alone, others hunt in packs using their force to encroach on new areas. All following food sources and changing weather patterns so they will not starve to death. Unhuman species have reverted to their new dominant creature habits, though breeding with similar others, or there are those that are still fifty percent to sixty percent human. They choose to breed with less altered humans in these areas, sometimes by force, creating a broader and more comprehensive mix of species.

Chapter five. City limits

S arah contacts the Moon-based operational crew that is overseeing her mission.

Central Command.

Send.

Reached the end of City limits, preparing to jump to area sixty-five.

Affirmative, tracking, engagement confirmed, Go for jump.

Sarah's vehicle adapts to a sleek aerodynamic shape, lifting off as the propulsion engines wind up to full speed. Her vehicle gains altitude and forward motion while her drones surround her like naval destroyers and submarines protect an aircraft carrier. All defense drones set their modes to kill, so nothing can enter the designated area surrounding Sarah. Quadrant sixty-five is on the Murray River, which was once Adelaide's lifeline. It almost faced death multiple times because of years of misuse and low rainfall. Global warming, along with better living practices, has seen the river reform in its former glory with thriving communities of different population sizes and species along its length.

Sarah will spend two nights and one day in Murray Bridge, logging data and conducting investigations. Control in Elite Pure areas can vary from 100% to a 40% Elite and 60% Mixed Pure rule, while in other areas, there is no control at all. It is an active daily balance in compounds like Murray Bridge. They have established a rule of 45% Elite to 55% Pure, and not all trust the overseers, since they deserted them during the Earth evacuation. As the Elite control infrastructure and have superior technology, they are at their mercy, never objecting to or directly oppose them. They must hedge their bets and believe that the Elite won't forget or eliminate them if a future that is created where only "Pure humans" live on Earth.

Sarah dispatched three drones to secure the compound in Murray Bridge, even though the central command monitor it using security drones. These drones only protect the infrastructure and compound. Sarah wants live feedback on the area around the compound to ensure she arrives without incident. Central Command has run control and safety checks on the multi-sealed positive pressure system, which protects the internal environment from any gasses or creatures. They distributed a pleasant-smelling cleansing gas through the facility to give it a fresh, welcoming smell. In case of an anomaly, Central Command will notify Sarah to terminate the mission and go back to her church compound.

Sarah lands on the far outskirts of town. Her vehicle changes shapes and styles to fit into various locations, while the drones stay at a higher altitude, out of sight. While she won't be covert, the vehicle's shapeshifting helps ease public concerns about it being perceived as a war machine or threat while driving through. Towns on the far outskirts lack the similar maintenance of other cities. Despite this, there are still houses and buildings that receive proper care from Mixed Humans and robots.

Murray Bridge and surrounding towns have a variety of living conditions and areas. Ranging from regions enclosed by walls and actively defended, to area less protected that are like individuals or tribes living in the natural nature of a remote village or forest. In developed cities, active patrols defend against creatures, whereas in other areas, individuals or small groups protect their own homes and land. A percentage of people on earth trust that scientists and leaders have their best interests in mind, ensuring their safety. Others have become wary of the Elites scientists, believing the rumors of a complete cleanse of Earth are true.

Sarah's principal aims at Murray Bridge include catching up with her informants, local law enforcement, and others who have contacted her, along with a couple of undercover activities. Sarah's compounds first two floors as part of the security system to keep out unwanted visitors. The garage has a lift that transports her vehicle to the third floor, where the main living quarters are located. Sarah can also enter or leave the third-floor area in her vehicle if necessary. The fourth floor stores the drones, defense, and communications equipment.

On arrival, the controlling AI system for the compound welcomes her while all the other security and protocols snap into action. She plans to spend three hours in the compound before venturing out to collect data. During this time, she will look up the locations of her tagged subjects, which include those inside and outside the safe area.

Having reviewed the latest data and made plans for her reconnaissance mission, Sarah prepares to deploy. She will start by exploring the wild-free areas. She has observed some of her tagged subjects there, which were administered a vaccine trial drug a few years ago. Sarah plans to take samples from them, using her drones to isolate the subjects by herding them into a safe, accessible area. Her defensive drones will create a protection zone for her to work in. Once established, she will tranquilize the subject using a fast-acting and short-recovery drug. This will enable her to take samples and download extra tracking data from implanted sensors. One drone will capture detailed photos, temperature readings, and measurements, while recording the entire data retrieval operation on video.

These missions are relatively safe, as Sarah can control the open space compared to entering buildings, alleyways or confined street hunts. The subjects can range from wild creatures void of any human mentality or appearance to others still resembling a basic human form. This first subject has developed an abundance of characteristics from its leopard DNA. His head has widened, his ears have grown longer, and the ear canal has opened. Yellow eyes, with better than seven times the vision of a human's eyesight, make these Unhuman species exceptionally dangerous nocturnal hunters.

DNA modification evolved to support humans' infatuation with resembling animals like leopards. With improvement in drugs and gene manipulation, these actions saw increasing numbers of people wanting to be like others with extra abilities. This leads to individuals with matching genes finding each other more attractive and reproducing. Offspring of these children has perfected altered genes and adaptations, as evolution has done over billions of years. Sarah's targeted subject exemplifies what two centuries of interbreeding with similar gene types can create.

The subject of this leap of leopard humans has skin with representative spots. They have grown large tails that play a significant role in their supreme agility. They can also stand vertically if they wish. Their teeth have adapted to their preferred diet of insects, fish, rodents, deer, monkeys, or anything else that is available, including humans. This species are great ambush hunters with some leaps still having the ability to speak English alongside their distinctive calls of hoarse coughs, grows, even purring when happy. These creatures deserve respect as they hunt with unique intelligence at the top of the food chain in specific locations.

Leopards have existed on Earth for over eleven million years. One helpful trait that has evolved with these creatures is their instinct to stay in one area and avoid encroaching on other leopards or similar breeds. This includes well-populated human regions. However, any humans that find themselves in their territory or on the outskirts of defended civilizations will become dinner.

Sarah has a simple job of catching the first subject, isolating, tranquilizing, and taking her complete collection of required samples. She remains nearby until the drug wears off. This allows her subjects to wake up and defend themselves against potential threats that may target weakened individuals. If you want to do any long-term real-world trials, you do not want your subjects killed in a situation you caused by rendering them helpless. Now that the subject is awake and in hiding, Sarah tracks him until he rejoins his group. After that, she moves on to her next target for the night.

This subject will have its challenges as it can fly. Viruses crossing from birds, bats, and other animals to humans were the start of creating this species with the interest in researching vaccines. While humans evolved from primates, chickens hold parts of the DNA of human evolution. Scientists brought back prehistoric flying beasts from around the same time humans walked on Earth to get their early DNA before they evolved into today's birds. Sarah collects samples from this spinoff to test gene manipulation in this species.

Sarah must approach with caution if she wishes to drug and sample this large flying subject. While diurnal, this species occasionally ventures out at night and Sarah can exploit its weak nocturnal vision. She can also see on her radar the subject is out alone, a short distance from its home nest. The subject involves a blend of humans and prehistoric bird DNA from a bird that surpassed the height of two humans and boasting a wingspan of approximately seven meters. These large Unhuman have difficulties taking off. Once they are airborne, they cruise at sixty kilometers per hour and have a maximum diving speed of two hundred and forty kilometers per hour. Humans with boundless wealth and no interest in AI technologies, space exploration, luxury cars, or extravagant yachts sought to stand out in unconventional ways. While they seldomly experimented on themselves, they sponsored secret underworld laboratories that did human DNA, embryo, and stem cell trials. Creatures escape these laboratories because of the loss of funding, death of founders, or the interest from backers diminished. The escape or release started their evolution and a fight for survival. Centuries ago, experiments like these occurred openly to assist other sciences, and they continue worldwide today. However, clandestine laboratories, Frankenstein in nature, are still creating creatures to defend areas or enhance an existing species to dominate areas.

Sarah stealthily approaches the tracked subject so as not to draw attention to herself. He is part of the superior breed in this species, from a mix of prehistoric birds, to get the full-size wingspan, hawk's DNA for hunting skills and attitude. If you can overlook their size and muscular legs, and the lengthened toenails resembling talons, you can still see a human form from a distance with their wings tucked in. Feathers cover their heads, backs, wings, and legs, giving them a bird-like appearance from behind. The distance between their eyes has narrowed and their necks can rotate over one hundred and eighty degrees. A stubby, beak-like nose has evolved into its mouth, strong enough to rip any prey apart while holding it in their still humanist hands.

Sarah's plan is to tranquilize it as soon as possible, then fire a net over the subject so it will not try to take flight. Avoiding it crashing to the ground when the drug takes effect, causing injuries. She will then race in to collect the samples and other data, remove the net, and stay nearby to defend it. Setting her plan in motion by having her drone drop some raw meat in an open paddock about twenty meters from the subject, it gets his attention. The subject waits briefly to see if any other animal grabs it. Then the Hawk-like human swoops in from the top of a derelict building. The instant it hits the ground, Sarah fires the tranquilizer dart and shoots the weighted net over it. It all goes well. Her vehicle, from its camouflage position, drives in to be by her side. While collecting data, Sarah notices that the subject appears paralyzed, but is aware of her. Sarah feels like its eyes or other eyes are watching her, thinking, and making plans of their own. Despite no suspect targets on her drones' sensors, Sarah senses something unusual. Despite feeling less comfortable than usual in these situations, she talks to him while collecting samples. She assures him she means no harm, even though she is unsure if the subject or others in its flock can understand English. Her talking and compassion unexpectantly settle the subject.

After gathering the data, she directs two drones to hover nearby before removing the net. In case of heightened activity, the drones have orders to kill, with Sarah's safety as the top priority. Removing the net with no issues and getting back into her vehicle, lifting off to a safe altitude to observe the recovery. Just before he prepares to take off, he looks at Sarah, lifting and flapping his wings in a menacing show of defiance. The white feathers of his wings, speckled with green, glisten in the Moonlight. They move in a determined pattern while he twists his head from side to side, seemingly in response to her presence. Turning swiftly, he runs in the opposite direction, gaining enough air under his wings to vanish into the night.

The night achieved its goals, leaving Sarah feeling accomplished and content. Sarah makes an audio note for future reference on this experience as she leaves the area. Subject 1398, known as Eithan Hawk, showed signs of awareness and not full paralysis on the sample, taking eight hundred and seventy-six on Mission 2189/432. Before it left the area, it looked directly at me and aggressively lifted its wings.

Sarah approaches her Murray Bridge compound, which is in the Mixed Human area, outside the defended walls of the Pure's city. The security drones hover, monitoring the perimeter as they prepare to accept her. A red glowing ring emits an infrared frequency around the defended area of the compound, serving as a warning to unwanted visitors. Upon entering and completing the protocols, she prepares reports and samples for drone transport to the church. An AI droid will safely prepare samples for transport to the off-world lab. After analyzing the samples, they may require Sarah to revisit the subjects and administer a new vaccine or drug as requested by the Elite scientists. Sarah can receive deliveries at her compounds from any command center, whether on or off Earth. However, she can only send to off-world sites from the church's facility.

It was a quick night of hunting for Sarah. Tomorrow is a complete work shift. She will meet and sample subjects at night before flying to Mount Gambier in the early morning.

Scientists have used computers to read evolution backward and reconstruct a large part of the genome. Now, this technique is used to compare and analyze changes in Sarah's samples. Elite scientists aim to reverse or restart evolution back to only Pure Humans. Laboratories have experimented on animals for research into human disease for years. Mice, as an example, share up to ninety-eight percent of human genes, but mice will not help with their goals today. They must use these new Mixed Human and Unhuman species to test any effects they can have on their DNA. The drug they wish to create to fulfill their dream will have to be undetectable to those they infect, so they will spread it to others in their species.

Chapter six. New Day

The sun rises on a new day, the command center confirms that her specimens arrived at the moon laboratory. Her samples are clear, and she receives all the relevant information for today's objectives. The morning has official meetings with Elite leaders and general catchups with assets all requiring different preparations. Arrivals at these locations and departures will follow various pre-arranged procedures. She can drive or fly into the Elite meeting as it will raise no alarms. Other operations will need to be conducted in a manner to protect both her informants and her identity. She will use wigs, makeup and sometimes a mask, with local-looking clothing over her suit to blend in with the public.

Completing all the departure protocols at her Murray Bridge compound, her first mission of the day will be an undercover meet and greet. Sarah will drive to the old freeway, then ascend to a high altitude using a valley. She will then turn back around to head to a friendly homestead near her desired location. Flying in from the north around the Rockley area, she descends to fly just above the ground, with her vehicle camouflaging itself with projections on its skin.

Sarah gets out of her vehicle in a forest near a friendly homestead as all her drones move to pre-arranged locations. Tactical drones leave to positions on the ground and on top of solid structures near the intended meeting point in the nearby town. The rest of the drones stay in a high-altitude holding pattern, conducting surveillance scans of the immediate area. When they inform her that all is clear of any targets, she makes her way to the homestead using all her athletic abilities. Sarah minimizing her gear on covert missions, carries only a couple of hand weapons to buy time for her drones to eliminate any threat. In any extreme situation her vehicle will fly between her and the subject to pick her up.

Sarah meets up at the farm with Joe, an older, semi-retired operative member of the Elite Earth team. He is like Sarah, a genetic soldier working for the overseer's command center. Joe talks about the recent intel he gathered, offering Sarah an inconspicuous vehicle for her to travel to town in. Sarah explains her mission to Joe, telling him she will head to a location just outside of Monarto.

In past years Monarto was a free-range zoo, now it has expanded into a laboratory to support the Mixed Human race. Sarah's contact is Leia, a worker at the facility. They will meet at her home in an estate full of multi-story apartments. Joe has done a background check on Leia by following her around the city and keeping track of who she talks to. Leia is expecting to meet with a representative of the Pure Human Elite group. She received instructions to be home at various times for the past three weeks. Joe has kept her under surveillance at these pre-arranged meeting times to ensure that she is not part of a Mixed Human trap, to capture a Pure representative. Sarah will rely on this intel and has studied the footage Joe has taken to pick up on Leia's personality traits. She will watch for them in the interview to sense her true intentions. Leia is likely nervous, as each previous meeting time has passed without contact. She may now be worried about her own safety and not be home.

Approaching the residential estate where Leia's apartment is atop of a seven-story building. Sarah selected Leia's apartment for the meeting because of it being on the top floor with a balcony. If she needs an escape option, her vehicle could pick her up from it. A public meeting could jeopardize Leia's safety because of friends or colleagues asking questions if seen with a stranger.

The civilians in town walk, use public transport or individual taxi shuttles. Therefore, there are only five private vehicles parked on the road. Sarah pulls over and parks one building back from Leia's apartment block. Before exiting her vehicle, she briefly waits to assess the area and receives feedback from her drones to identify anything unusual or distinctive. Sarah casually walks to Leia's apartment, choosing the stairs over the elevator for better self-defense options.

A lift and stairwells on both sides of the complex accessed a central passageway on each level. CCTV monitors the walkway and streams into the apartment. Outside sources cannot watch any of this security footage. Leia will witness Sarah's entrance into the passageway and be aware of the impending meeting.

Sarah arrives at Leia's door, using a pre-arranged phrase and secret knock to show she is there for the meeting. Sarah waits at the door, giving Leia time to disable AI help and automated services and reach the door.

Knock, thud, knock, tap tap, Sarah waits.

Tap knock, tap thud, tap. And the door opens.

Are you free for a coffee?

I have fantastic coffee here, Samantha. Is it acceptable? We can have one here.

Sarah, using her favorite alias Samantha, as she often feels people perceive her as a witch, enters the apartment. She assesses its layout to help with a quick psychological assessment. The apartment is spotless, everything neatly arranged. It has a pleasant natural feel, with scenic paintings and a mix of old and modern appliances. Leia appears to have a creative side with respect for herself. The apartment is all in order, neat, and quite welcoming. Following all the password's unease, Samantha introduces herself and comments on how nice, warm, and welcoming her apartment is, hoping to get Leia to feel comfortable. Samantha also looks around while they chat, checking that all Artificial Intelligence and security systems are off. She also asks to look at the balcony to ensure the doors are open, stepping outside briefly to allow her drones to lock on to her escape point if necessary.

They discuss the local area, feelings, and general community attitudes. According to Leia, the majority aren't involved in politics or factions; they focus on their own business. Some people believe in various conspiracy theories, such as secret testing and the eradication of non-true DNA humans by Pure Humans. There are even theories about an impending rise of intelligent Unhuman beings who aim to form alliances and eliminate Mixed and Pure Humans. Returning to the stone age, eliminating technology and rules.

Leia also tells Samantha about the Monarto facility and her concerns it is not just helping the Mixed Humans with any ongoing health complications. She believes there is a secret section creating an elite breed of Mixed Humans to form a super force. Leia then shows Samantha the intercepted communications, plans, and photos to help back up her and other employees' concerns about a secret laboratory in the facility. Samantha asks questions to confirm the emails, thoughts of the other workers, and their positions in the laboratory. She confirms with Leia if she has shared her contact with off-world Pure humans to anyone. Leia informs Samantha that she only contacted CM through the laboratory rather than the local Pure, as she was unsure of whom to trust on Earth. Samantha thanks Leia and gives her a device she can record more information on as she gets it. The unit is an encrypted low-power transmitter that only emits a signal when a dedicated receiver is within five hundred meters of it to accept the data. Short transmissions make it impossible for anyone to intercept data or triangulate the transmitter's location.

Sarah leaves the apartment and returns to her borrowed vehicle, casually leaving town in the opposite direction from which she arrived, heading back to Joe's farmhouse. Sarah sits with Joe, filling him in on what she learned from Leia, and confirms she left a transmitter for her to keep hidden in her apartment. Leia will use the device to record brief messages with no specific information or data that Joe will pick up by passing her apartment and triggering the device. Phrases like I would like a coffee; meaning intel is not urgent. We should catch up for lunch or dinner. Lunch means worthy information needing attention, and dinner means time-critical information requiring an urgent meeting. Joe will then decide if he should contact Leia to arrange a drop, or if Sarah should be involved and meet Leia again.

Joe and Sarah go through housekeeping protocols before she prepares to return to Murry Bridge to type up notes on what she has learned. Arriving at her compound and after sending off the information to the relevant overseers, Sarah removes all her disguises she used to hide her identity from Leia. She then organizes to meet with the Pure leaders at their headquarters in the center of Murray Bridge.

Sarah intends to fly into the Pure compound, using just three drones to ensure a friendly, non-threatening presence. Landing on the rooftop of the headquarters, Sarah steps out and walks confidently towards the greeting party. The sun reflects off her suit and her long shiny black hair hangs down to the middle of her back, bouncing as she walks. Her fringe and the shoulder-length sides of her hair lifting in the breeze created by her walking pace. After welcoming her, they escort Sarah and her drone into the building and to the conference room.

The ruling leaders are gathered at the table for the meeting. They include a premier the assets and maintenance officer, health leader, biological and physics scientists, and the head security officer. Sarah takes her seat at one end of a long rectangular table, her drone hovers just above her head to record the meeting. They begin with general pleasantries, an overview of the public's state of health, community feelings, and resources. They inform Sarah of the quantity of resources they are holding, as well as seasonal issues of supply with their local produce. Pure compounds and surrounding Mixed Human communities trade in various food and other resources that benefit all parties. Supply areas have climate issues and the uprising of Unhuman or Mixed Humans that hinder the supply of resources. All trading parties try to work together to ensure supply with technological advances or shared security to keep resources flowing. Sarah is most interested in trading issues, as they can affect her missions if regular uprisings occur. If the situation persists, the Elite may need to offer additional defenses in these areas to prevent loss. As a result, Sarah's operations could face potential impact.

The Earth Pure scientists summarize issues requiring help, give updates on food production and the general health of the local grounds around the compound. Both sides share only what is necessary. As Murray Bridge interacts with the Mixed Humans, unlike other compounds, the Elite Pure keeps any of the latest information related to experiments on the Mixed to themselves. Only the highest Elite hold the truth of the experiments, for now. Mixed Humans would feel a deep sense of concern regarding Elites' off-world experiments on low level Unhuman, causing them to become nervous and worried. Genuine doubts about where the line would be between Unhuman, Mixed Human, or Pure human. Who would the drug target and how safe would it be for others on Earth? After the meeting, Sarah takes care of transferring data from labs and controlling bodies, collecting information or physical objects from the committee, and then stores them in the drone. Sarah returns to her vehicle and grabs a short stylish overcoat to cover her suit to blend in with the public on a casual walk around the city.

Leaving the headquarters building, Sarah walks amongst the public. The compound walls provide a sense of security for everyone, as no one can enter without being screened or given permission. Residents have seen Sarah before on the streets or heard stories about her. In some stories, Sarah is famous, others she is just another person or an Unpure creature. Sarah is careful not to meet with anyone inside the walls that might cause them to be seen as an informer or transferring information to her. She is aware of the security the Pure committee has on her walks, so she limits social interaction. Sitting at a cafe allows her to listen to others and feel a sense of belonging. Streets bustle with children playing, people chatting in bars and cafes, some exercising, and occasionally someone will engage Sarah in a conversation. She ensures it is a general chat about nothing in particular. If they ask why she is in the compound, she always responds that she is a trade representative from a Pure colony. Anyone wanting to talk could be spies, probing Sarah's loyalty and seeking any useful information. After forty-five minutes, Sara walks back to the headquarters and leaves to return to her compound.

After spending six hours in her fast recovery module, Sarah prepares to go out on her night operations. These missions will involve getting samples from Mixed Human targets. There will also be meetings with Pure Human spies who may have witnessed her presence in the compound earlier in the day. Sarah made sure that she was noticed by intentionally visiting certain popular locations. Informants recognize the walk-through as a signal for meeting her outside the compound tonight if they have information to share.

The greater outskirts of Murray Bridge beyond the compound walls and surrounding towns offer little protection. Monarto does not have the Pure's defended walls and an extensive defense perimeter. Maintaining a grass-free ring is crucial for the nearby Mixed Human population, as it separates the Mixed and Unhuman lands near the Murray Bridge compound. Mypolonga, Monarto and Monarto South cities are the other three most populated cities inside this ring. With no food or hiding spots in the maintained baron ring outside these towns, the Unhuman, because of their instincts seldomly encroach on these cities.

Sarah's informants take on tremendous risk and pressure in meeting Sarah at night outside the walls. Sarah is aware and strives to be punctual, avoiding any delays. Meeting's end with a designated time and location for the next one, reducing any unwanted waiting times. Any informant not arriving in the agreed time period, Sarah knows they have nothing for her and moves on. Informants wait briefly at the location, aware that Sarah's absence is a sign of trouble. Someone may have followed the informant, risking Sarah or them. Sarah's drones track and protect informants, even from a distance. One informant turning against Sarah and the Pure's mission is possible. They could set Sarah up for capture, elimination, or give the ruling powers of Murray Bridge a reason to put restrictions on her. The off-world Pure relies on trusting Pure colonies on Earth for resources to keep the colonies going. The Elite's primary goal is to guarantee the affluent lifestyle by ensuring off-world colonies receive premium quality fresh foods that can only be grown on Earth. Also, to ensure they have a safe place to visit on Earth to experience the sun, ocean, and fresh air.

Places of significant importance, such as Mount Gambier, Yorke Peninsula, Port Lincoln, and Sarah's church compound in Adelaide, receive worldwide support from the Elite. Surrounding these compounds are electronic dead zones controlled by the overseers, which are like a castle's moat. These sophisticated boundaries have a range of weaponry, including beams of EMF pulses capable of wiping out electronics. They offer protection up to two and a half kilometers above ground, with the ability to track and fire pulses up to ten kilometers into the troposphere. These moats prevent any electronic devices or powered craft from traveling through, unless the entrance is open or allowed by the overseers. Supply craft with correct signatures may pass, but they have zero tolerance for errors and will kill any biological body that tries to pass an unopened gate.

Chapter seven. Meeting People

S arah's night begins once she completes the mission departure protocols and heads to her first informant meeting. All the informants possess an encrypted transponder for storing voice messages, just like the one Leia received. Sarah can transmit instructions to the device, receive any messages and talk with them through it. If they possess a physical object, Sarah or a drone can collect it. If the informant insists the information is time critical, Sarah will rearrange her missions to accommodate a face-to-face meeting upon urgent requests.

Sarah arrives at the first location and parks at a distance. Her drones give her a live view of the site to ensure safety for herself and the informant. Four drones hid just beyond the colony's wall on the main road out of the Compound earlier in the evening. They sit and wait to ping the transponders all informants carry if they are attending the meeting. When a drone gets a response, it will allocate a distant high-altitude drone to track the vehicle or person it has identified. These short pings will not show up on the Pure compound's surveillance systems. While the transponders could also receive information at this time, regular extra power bursts so close to the compound on regular vehicles or individuals would show up as suspicious. Putting informants in danger or highlighting them as a person of interest. The early pinging protocol informs Sarah about informant departures from the compound wall and their identity. If it falls within the designated timeline, it shows their intention to meet Sarah.

High altitude tracking allows the drone to capture an excellent overview of the informant's travel and any significant environmental activity around them. A detected ping on an unexpected person or vehicle. It will notify Sarah of this change. Sarah will then give extra attention to how that person, vehicle, or anything else in the general area reacts. Sarah may then decide to call the meeting off or attend it, but with a greater level of security.

Informants may be present at locations for work and may have no information. A warning signal accompanied each arrival. Sarah relies on these indicators to gauge if they have relevant information for her. Informants jobs require them to leave the compound at various times, enabling them to meet Sarah at the designated meeting spots, raising no suspicion.

Tonight's initial meeting will be with Philip, the clinic's head geneticist. He helps the so-called Pure Humans inside and outside the walls of the Murray Bridge compound. This colony of Earth Pure Humans does not belong to the Elite Pure category, unlike Port Lincoln, Mount Gambier, and others in Australia or worldwide. Compounds like Murray Bridge tolerate and support humans with a small percentage of genetically adjusted alterations. They have typically had cures for congenital disabilities, or diseases like cancer, and other life-threatening problems. Science and medical advances have evolved to eliminate or mitigate most human illnesses. The reality of nature is that new diseases still affect humans. Philip helps these people in his clinics. The Drone has pinged Philip's transponder, so Sarah expects a drop or download of information from him. Philip's status and job in the compound make him a valuable asset to the Elite. He may have direct information from those who interact with other species and Mixed societies. Philip also gathers valuable data from his clinic on Mixed Humans because of his clients' diversity. The Elite uses his samples and intel to help them develop strategies and rumors to benefit their cause. The leaders know that when a loved one, or a baby, requires life-saving procedures, it can conflict with the laws, beliefs, and mentality of Elite Pure. They cannot remain within an Elite compound if they have had alterations. This stern stance can divide the beliefs of those affected, causing them to turn against the Elite and align with the Mixed Humans. Their belief is in the fair and natural approach of preventing illnesses early in life. It creates less reliance on the society, however the Elite Pure just abandon them or let those that need any corrections die. Sometimes they are quite painful deaths, as the Elite leaders and followers just view them as defective, or ill, and will not waste resources on them.

Sarah's drone is tracking Philip in his vehicle. He is on his own and heading to the meeting location. When he arrives at the site, Sarah will watch his actions and any activity around the area before sending him a message on the transponder. By not placing his phone on the bonnet, Philip sends a clear signal to Sarah that he has information to communicate.

Sarah contacts Philip.

Hi Philip, Sarah here, we are downloading your messages. Do you have any physical evidence to deliver?

Hi Sarah, I've taken a patient's blood sample that may be interesting based on the messages.

Ok, please leave it next to the sculpture in the backyard, and we will retrieve it. Do you require any support or further communication?

No, that is all I have for you now, Sarah.

Thank you, the next meeting is in four days, at seven PM if we have information to transmit or share with you. Otherwise, in six months, the 2/03/2190 at eight PM.

Philip confirms the receipt of the information and continues with his business.

The drone will monitor the drop-off site and wait forty-five minutes to one hour before it picks up the dropped package. Philip, like other companies, uses drones to transport parcels, so it will not seem abnormal to anyone who might see the drone arrive and leave. Once retrieved, the drone will go to the Elite Pure compound laboratory in Mount Gambier. They will evaluate it under strict security protocols in a sealed unit and send the data to the Moon Elite laboratory for analysis. These samples will be destroyed after completing the testing. The Port Lincoln or Mount Gambier laboratories deal with and assess samples like this, but the Elite off-world scientists will not trust them with any samples Sarah collects herself. This method keeps the off-world Elite in total control of all experimental investigations and their results.

The next meeting tonight is with Sami. He has seen boxes that do not match the shipment locations shown. He tells Sarah that he didn't inspect the packages to avoid raising alarms. The Pure council's head of security has received the two boxes. Sami left swab samples for the drone to retrieve. The Elite laboratory will examine them for any suspicious elements in the parcels. While it may be innocent, there seems to be a conflict with its sent identification and the end destination of the packages. Sarah informs Sami they will need time to investigate the swabs, and she will give him any further investigation advice later.

Sami, the next meeting is in four days at eight PM if we have information to send or share with you. Or in six months, the date being 2/03/2190 at nine PM.

Thanks, Sarah.

Tonight's final meeting is with Jolene. The Drone couldn't find her or anything near the meeting spot. Sarah waits for the agreed period and then moves on. It seems suspicious as Jolene has had critical and disturbing information in the past months that may tie in with Sami's new report. To keep communication traffic to a minimum, Sarah only contacts her informants if it is essential and with minimal risk of someone noticing any send-and-receive signals. Sarah will decide if a drive-by is required on her return through Murray Bridge while she is in Mount Gambier.

Sarah gets ready to tackle her three other goals for the evening, involving driving along an ancient highway. She will drive close to the South Australia-Victoria border to collect data. It's a four hundred- and forty-five-kilometer drive, which Sarah will drive at variable speeds depending on what she or the drones detect. Sarah's favorite vehicle body for this type of work is a 2023 Dodge Hellcat in army flat camo green with matt black highlights. The highway to Tailem Bend leads Sarah to the 1km wide scorched earth ring that circles through Mobilong 10km outside Monarto, down to Monarto South, and back through Brinkley. Beyond the scorched bare Earth ring Unhuman live in the wild. Surprisingly, individuals call outliers who are Mixed Humans, live in fortified homesteads in these Unhuman areas.

Sarah covertly supports certain outliers, even amidst constant surveillance from the overseers. Sarah will send food, resources, or anything of interest she finds in her travels to them using her network of hacked drones. She avoids direct communication regarding shipments, instead including a note of encouragement and support in each one. Assisting them evokes her humanity and reveals her compassionate side, lacking in some places and Elite circles. Sarah always hears a shout-out from the outliers on the Ham radio airwaves, which are recorded in one of her secret hideaways. Sarah, loyal to the cause, sees herself as a laboratory rat. She believes having an underground network ensures her survival when the Elite no longer needs her.

Rumors circulate when one of Sarah's private or Elite drones aid an outlier that it was divine intervention or good luck. The outliers don't question any drone that flies into one of their homesteads with a small maintenance task or a job that suits the outlier's dominant skill set. They do the job and let it fly off. A tight group of outliers communicate and share comparable stories, aware of a guardian angel's presence.

On this mission, her drones will fly over a couple of these supported outlier homes on her way to Mount Gambier. Sarah intends to go offline and visit her hideaway in the area. It has been a lengthy and gradual process to secure it, just like all her undercover tasks. Unfortunately, the established homestead was owned by one of her trusted outliers, who was killed while outside its boundaries. She took it over after witnessing the incident years ago, believing it was worth the risk because of its convenient location between Murray Bridge and Mount Gambier compounds.

Sarah uses devices created by the outliers to block her Elite tracking devices and other equipment. She also stages distractions for the overseers and their drones. Sarah uses these tactics in various areas, where she has hidden equipment, hideaways, and other random spots. After a short reconnection, and with Sarah giving an Academy award-winning performance, the overseers acknowledge these issues in the area and let her determine the next steps.

Sarah's route takes her through the center of two reserves, Ngarkat Conservation Park, and Big Desert Wilderness Park. As the Mixed Humans bred with similar changed genetic humans, these areas became natural homing beacons drawing ever evolving Mixed Humans into them. Across generations, it has become the mecca for the totally Unhuman. Wild genetically changed humans who kept breeding with more attractive, similar types in this mixed free-living area. Climate change has expanded the area further north and helped the original areas become more fertile, making them a large natural wilderness. Sarah is tracking a few Unhuman subjects in this area. They received a previous version of a drug that blocks and alters their DNA, making them unable to reproduce. The Elite scientists hope to develop a selective marker, so a vaccine or termination drugs can target only Unhuman or Mixed Humans with traces of that DNA pattern.

If the opportunity exists, Sarah and her drones will hunt the subjects and lure them to a safe location so she can get samples of their blood. All the targets of interest have trackers implanted in them when sampled. When a drone detects a target, workable location and timeframes are provided to Sarah with all potential scenarios to aid her in getting the required samples. Producing a simple sterile drug is not complex for the laboratory. They have learned from experiences with genetic modifications. Therefore, they want to conduct many control tests on Unhuman to prevent any potential spin-offs. The ideal goal is an active drug that, if it detects a percentage of modification it will infect and kill the subject. Their current stage results from years of testing and perfecting. Drugs have had instant effects, some favorable, some not so favorable. They believe they might be on the brink of success with this latest round.

Chapter eight. Quick Hunt

Outside Bordertown, Sarah's drones pick up a subject that is out alone. It is a high-level target infected with a new drug twenty-four months ago. It's helpful for Sarah, it is near her secret homestead she acquired. During the hunt and sample collection of a prime subject, she will face increased scrutiny. Sarah believes this is a great opportunity for her to create fake outages and extend her visit to her homestead. The overseers might add the time to the hunt that she requires for visiting her homestead. Sarah deviates from her route to track the valued target. She will try to move it to a safe space more suited to her covert plan than getting the samples. There is no deployment of human or robotic maintenance teams to keep this area clear. Much of it is all overgrown with natural vegetation, with bushfires started by storms helping to control the growth and provide some open ground. The large trees with forest-like surfaces under the canopies are a perfect environment for Sarah to run and hide while hunting the valued subject. It also makes it difficult for her drones to negotiate below the canopy with her, allowing Sarah to use these conditions to her advantage while introducing intermittent dropouts. The overseers desperately want this sample, so if Sarah cannot get it this time, they will ask her to collect it on her return trip to Murray Bridge. Sarah starts the hunt and her covert communication dropouts.

Command target gained.

Copy Sarah, apply protocols, and isolate the target.

..... b j jj bb jjjui ssssshhhdddddhhhssjj.

Copy Sarah, not receiving.

Two mins later.

Sarah, come in communication lost.

All is OK. I am having trouble jjj isolating ddd target, ju mmm bbb bjsssh.

Command ddddd there is heavy foliage, nnnjj dd b bd.

Four mins later.

Isolating bbb Sub gjgg jj hh.

Two more minutes pass, and Sarah responds using a pre-taped message attached to her transmitter, then using an AI-generated response system to reply to the command center's messages. Sarah listens to the responses just in case they become suspicious. Over the years, Sarah has already extended this timeout to fifty minutes. With her natural night vision and cheetah-like pace, Sarah will be able to reach her homestead, insert the new command disks into her robotics units, and update her management systems. Creating some extra valuable time will give her a safety margin in case of any unforeseen issues.

Sarah herds the subject into deep, thick foliage that aids in the natural blocking of all communication signals. Her drones lose video coverage of her, but they do not react as they expect the outage. With the loss of many drones in the dense tree nest, the overseers keep them above the canopy. The command center will have minimal interaction with Sarah. They will only contact her in urgent situations. This allows her to hunt the beast independently and still be able to communicate with her drones if she is in danger. Without drones to help, the hunt comes with greater danger. She must summon every ounce of strength, agility, and skill, relying on her unique sensory awareness to maintain her safety. Sarah feels alive and somewhat free, not just a humanoid robot following orders. In this style of sample retrieval, she must focus on the task, as she may not be the only one hunting, creatures may hunt her. The command center uses a calculated timeline for the expected capture and sample taking when using drones, as they are watching a live video feed. Without the drones, they allow Sarah to focus with minimal communication and give her a level of freedom to decide the time she invests in hunting the target herself. There is always the chance the target may avoid capture or stay in a pack, depending on past results and the determined importance of getting an updated sample. Sarah must decide between her goals and the overseer's patience before they tell her to abort the hunt to return another time to try again.

On a hunt, in coordination with Sarah's movements, the drones will follow her orders. In this scenario, she wants to distract them with tasks so they cannot tell she has left the immediate area. Her fake vital signs will show she is OK, so they will hold their positions until she instructs them otherwise. Sarah also activates her custom-made blocker to create wacky and weird signals in the location on all monitoring systems. Over the years, she has refined this technique, resulting in increased outage time and improved excuses. In the early days, when Sarah was developing her system, the overseers started emergency protocols and had over-ridden drones to zoom into Sarah's location. Sarah leveraged her knowledge of the protocol to her advantage, ensuring smooth execution every time she activated it. Implementing the actions and notifying all overseers requires significant effort, which is why Sarah has extended her window of opportunity based on the Cry Wolf mentality. Leaders, bothered by frequent outages, have gradually relaxed rules.

The Elite desperately want samples from this Unhuman subject as it is a rare mix of animals. With multiple DNA modifications through mixed breeding in the past, these beasts have created their own territory and a large, diverse family herd. The subjects, who have been interbreeding for decades, have many mixed offspring. This makes them an ideal model for studying DNA evolution and family markers, which can help create their virus.

Sarah tries or at least pretends to be hunting the subject while stalling and blocking communications, to increase the expected blackout times. Returning to her vehicle having achieved her personal mission of delaying and increasing the dropout times without suspicion, she explains to the overseers her excuse for not getting the sample. Stating that it's a warm night, and the beast is too active in their packs to gather the samples. After leaving the area, she continues towards Mount Gambier, hoping that the Elite will request more subject samples upon her return to Murray Bridge. Being territorial, these creatures seldomly roam far from their patch, so Sarah expects the herd to be on the same ground close to her homestead in four days' time.

Sarah heads to Bordertown's city center, now a derelict town almost overrun by Unhuman. The surrounding areas are home to a diverse mix of beings, including Panthera, canine, birds, and other species. Some are extreme Mixed Human types, while others are fully Unhuman versions, like the one she just tried to sample. The center of town still has Mixed Humans living in and around it, with several of her outlier contacts distributed on the outskirts.

Sarah slows down, and her vehicle swaps into the matt black 1970 Plymouth Barracuda shape as she cruises through the town center, observing and noting any changes. Buildings occupied by Mixed Human are all multi-story, with the ground floor having security systems and booby traps, to keep out any unwanted, Mixed or Unhuman visitors. A small group of watchers patrol the city center, checking for wild creatures. Outliers from Murray Bridge notified Bordertown Mixed Humans about Sarah's arrival, enabling the town's patrol to monitor her in advance. They are aware of the consequences of interacting or attacking her, for these reasons they always give her a clear path through the city. The town is unusually active at night, more inviting than previous experiences. Sarah makes a mental note to check her video footage, but she thinks people looking out their windows at her cruising down the street are making slight gestures of acceptance. It could just be she wants to believe what she is seeing as she is on a high from having her stalling plan work so successfully. Sarah takes it as a win, smiles, and flourishes in the euphoric feeling.

Exiting town, Sarah takes off and heads for Mount Gambier as it's now three AM. She wants to get valuable rest and downtime before her missions in town later in the day. Reaching the outskirts of Mount Gambier, Sarah must check that they are expecting her and have given her a clear passage through the moat. While the moats overall authorities are with the overseers, Earth Pure has access to its control to maintain it and can override it for safety reasons. In keeping with diplomacy and a good working relationship, it is customary, although not obligatory, for the overseers to inform local leaders of Sarah's intended arrival and schedule.

Sarah flies through the Moat and into her private compound on the Adelaide side of a town called Burrungule. The moat circles Mount Gambier through Wandilo to Mil-Lel, then curves down south, close to the South Australia and the Victorian border to Ob Flat. It curves northward to the outskirts of Crompton and then back to Burrungule. Sarah lands on the third floor of her five-story building. The drones land and begin rearming or receiving any required updates. Her vehicle performs a scheduled safety check and a software upgrade. Sarah once she has cleared all entrance protocols, enters the office, sends off collected data and then prepares to go to bed. Off-world servers receive and reformat data from Earth servers.

Sarah is expecting that when she awakes in the morning, reports on the information collected along with any results on subject samples analyzed will be in her inbox. Sarah can enjoy a day and night off during her four-day stay in Mount Gambier. However, local security teams will monitor her, limiting her freedom and ability to do as she pleases, even on her day off.

Chapter nine. Mount Gambier

Sarah awakes at nine AM and has a leisurely morning scheduled before a meeting the Mount Gambier Elite Council. Earth bound Pure inside these walls believe in their off-world rulers' statements that they are the only true humans. This poses a minor issue for Sarah as she is not Pure, there are many rumors of her impureness and variable levels of acceptance of her inside the compound. Winning battles often require aligning with those who possess power and superior weaponry. Sarah, a soldier needed by the Elite, is both hero and tool needed of her services and capabilities.

Sarah drives to the meeting, bringing only one drone to allow the overseers to monitor the conversations. Today, not just Mount Gambier but Yorke Peninsula, Murray Bridge, and Port Lincoln will be involved. Before global release, the off-world Elite wish for them to hear the recent updates and new plan. The genetic modification experiments in Australia are the most aggressive and are leading the world, having begun centuries ago. Having extensive fertile land in uncivilized areas created perfect sites for holding pens. Animals mixed with human DNA and Unhuman species have escaped from these cages far from cities, out of sight and interest of most civilians during these experiments. Off-world overseers, who considered Australia's enormous size and the environment they escaped into, make it a non-issue. Over time, generations of Mixed Humans, Unhuman and escaped laboratory creatures, make the country the perfect test bed for viruses and drugs. An existing diverse range of species enables authentic real-world testing before contemplating any release on other continents.

After greetings, Sarah and the committee enter the meeting room. The leader of the Pure in Mount Gambier and her four heads of departments take their seats. She sits between two on the principal bench at center stage. The others, such as scientists, security heads, and other committee members, take their seats in the small hundred-seat auditorium. Sarah sits alone off to the side of the stage, while her drone lands on a pedestal between the principal bench and the auditorium seating. It can turn to face the speaker, avoiding any hindrance. The large screen behind and above the Pure leader's bench has the Elite Pure World logo displayed on it. A circle represents the world, with a white dove positioned above the human DNA helix as an equator. The broken test tube below the helix symbolizes their stance on gene modifications.

The screen lights up and shows pictures of beautiful Earth, fields, and children playfully running free. A narrator speaks:

Morning Earth Pure. Today, we will share good news on our mission to free us all from our compounds and roam free on Mother Earth as we did centuries ago. An Unhuman sterilization drug deployed with your help and using drones in remote Australia is working. It is having the effect that we all agreed on in the accord signed in the year 2089, called "New Earth." To develop a virus which will only affect the mutant Unhuman in a controlled safe release. We are here today to inform you our scientists have had major advancement in isolating a common Gene. This means we are preparing supplies for a virus release in the coming months. We assure you we have taken all precautions with this virus and soon we will walk free alongside you once again.

Applause fills the room as some stand immediately, and others rise gradually. Sarah Stands but does not have any sense of achievement or reward. She feels guilt overwhelming her more than anything else.

The meeting goes on. Reports follow in order of importance between the heads of each project team. Technology, maintenance, innovation, security, and defense experts. Sarah attentively absorbs information that could assist her missions or benefit her outlier friends. The meeting concludes with the leaders happy that it is possible they could leave the compound walls within their lifetime. They walk around the room shaking hands and patting each other's backs. A significant percentage of them ignore Sarah, though the executive members step up to her and offer words of encouragement. One or two others from the audience walk up to shake her hand. Most worry her impure genes might infect them and stay away. One person, the security head, shakes Sarah's hand like she has always done with other outstanding achievements. While doing so, she slips Sarah what feels like a note. Sarah is careful not to react or attract attention as they exchange pleasantries, casually slipping the note up the sleeve of her suit.

Sarah leaves the auditorium to go for a walk outside to study the mood as the public of Mount Gambier hears the news from the leaders. She grabs a jacket from her vehicle to cover her suit before strolling around as billboards and newsreels show the major milestone in the war against the UnPure. Excitement and a party atmosphere take over the streets. Folks spill from homes and pubs, exchanging congratulations. Those who recognize Sarah from Elite promotional material as a warrior with enhanced genes give her a wide berth. Yet, amidst the excitement, some acknowledge her, while multiple individuals express the same sentiment. "We support you."

Sarah sits at a coffee shop and watches for a while before returning to her vehicle. People dance with excitement near Pure headquarters in the center of town. Sarah has her vehicle project a loud thumping combustion engine sound. The thunderous idle gets their attention and acts as a siren as she pulses the accelerator, to encourage people to move aside and let her pass.

Sarah returns to her secure compound filled with mixed emotions, sitting alone while citizens party on the streets. She wonders what the future holds not only for her but her outlier associates too. What are the overseers' actual intentions? She knows that miscommunication exists between stories and facts. Sarah has gained motivation from this experience to reach her homestead, update programs, and send messages to her outlier contacts for their protection against attacks. She finishes her day out with a couple of video meetings and compound maintenance.

Sarah enjoys her day off by visiting the Blue Lake lookout after yesterday's news and the impromptu party at the compound. Unlike years past, the lake is now surrounded by multistory apartments for the growing population. Sarah parks, gets out of her Cat, and walks out onto the grass to sit in the sun. She dreams of having a family and enjoying daily life. Euphoria still fills the town. People walk with extra energy on the path circling the lake. Sarah blends in with the locals on this perfect day, dressed in blue jeans and a T-shirt. Only her vehicle and two parked drones stand out, giving away her location. She has her communication collar on for the drones, which is covered by her long black hair. It gives her communication capabilities with the command center or to control her drones if any situation arises. Sarah has the Pure's security team also watching her from a distance, far enough away to give her space, but they are still obvious to the public and Sarah. The official reason for the security is to provide Sarah with freedom on her day off, but she knows it's also for monitoring and reporting to the leaders.

Sarah decides on a brief parkway stroll, before she drives to her place using the outer compound wall ring route. People randomly smile and wave as they pass by if they don't recognize her. A couple of young women ride scooters past her. Before they get too far in front, one of the electric scooters fails. As Sarah gets closer, she can hear them chatting, wondering how they will walk home, or who they can call for help. As Sarah approaches them, they say hi and start a basic conversation about how nice the day is. She notices a wire hanging under the failed scooter and points to it offering to help, which they accept. She rejoins the wire by plugging it back in. The ladies jump around, thankful that the scooter is working. The infectious joy makes Sarah feel like just another local on a day out. One lady puts her hand out to thank her and during the handshake, Sarah feels a note placed in her palm for the second time in twenty-four hours. Sarah, being aware that she is being observed, slips both hands into her jeans pockets. One-handed use exposes the real motive - a hand-off. She moves away, looking casually around, and continues her walk back to her vehicle.

On her drive home, Sarah wonders what the message might be. The one she received at the meeting made little sense, so Sarah hopes this one might help put it all together. Who are these messages for? Her or the overseers? Is it some kind of test or a trap? Sarah's mind races as she has feelings she has never sensed before.

Chapter ten. Pep for Going Back

Arriving back at her compound and after completing all the entry protocols, Sarah moves into the bedroom and changes into a loose T-shirt and tights, removing the note she received from her jeans. The message is puzzling like the previous one, not a making sense or a clear warning, so she puts it back in her jeans. Sarah takes advantage of her free time by preparing a meal, listening to music, and relaxing. The interactions keep spinning around in her mind. Sarah believes someone is trying to inform her discreetly, without the knowledge of officials. Why? Is she in danger from the overseers, or is someone extorting her for helping outliers? What other reasons could it be? She reads the messages again:

The first message received at the meeting: "We thank you for all you are doing, and the time is near for the Pure."

The second message, from the girls in the park. "When the Pure rises, the truth reigns power, and what's right will be set free."

Random people on the streets saying, "We support you," along with these messages, make Sarah feel there's more to this than coincidences or her going crazy. Are more messages coming, or is she over analyzing? Are the messages in favor of the Elite and enthusiastic about a new Pure world? If it is messages supporting the Elite, why the secret handoffs? The girls on the scooters intentionally organized themselves to meet her.

Sarah again tries to rest and shuts her mind off to all other tasks. Tomorrow is a maintenance day for her, with equipment checks and video meetings with the overseers. The primary task is to program her compounds for a two-year standby. Software and defense systems will get upgrades and extra checks before this period starts on her return to the church. In the morning, she will also receive her return trip missions and will find out what importance they have placed on getting the samples from the Unhuman outside of Bordertown. Sarah hopes it will all pan out to allow her the time she needs to get to her homestead.

Chapter eleven. Morning of the Last Day

As the sun rises over Mount Gambier on a dry but cloudy day, Sarah awakes and follows her standard morning routine. It starts with water and vitamin supplements supplied to her by the overseers, followed by her workout sessions to keep her fit and her muscles in prime condition. It's a moderate workout most days, with light weights with lots of reps, spin bike interval sessions and kickboxing, followed by yoga. Sarah then showers and dresses casually to have breakfast and check her messages. Traditionally, Sarah receives a brief note to give her a basic day schedule before she enters the central office and reads the complete mission statements. These brief notes give Sarah enough information to dress correctly for the mission and do any housekeeping before reading the detailed plans. Today, she will again wear her Lycra warrior suit as she travels back to the church Via Murray Bridge. Sarah awaits three missions to be scheduled for today, the final ones for this cycle.

Sarah heads into her office, opens the mission statement with the hope they have allowed a large part of the day to get several samples, not only from the one she missed, but at least one other, preferably two, from the herd. When she reads the statement, it is incredible news. They want three samples of the Unhuman. If the extra subjects are in the right spot, they will help Sarah explain or hide any delays she creates while accessing her homestead. Sarah feels excited and wants to leave immediately. But first, she must collect a couple of items from headquarters.

All housekeeping tasks in Mount Gambier compound are now done. Sarah starts the last day of this cycle.

Command, I am ready to leave on Mission 2189/440

OK, Sarah, please ensure all Hybo cycle protocols are on, and the latest software upgrades are complete.

Yes, I confirm all updates are installed and running on drones, vehicles, and compounds.

Sarah, please confirm your status.

Confirm fit and active for service.

Refer to the mission log and confirm the route and objectives.

I Confirm log 9884 loaded, and the purpose understood.

Engage the tracking and networking systems.

Networking systems are active and await confirmation.

Confirmations of network and tracking. Acknowledgement.

Affirmative, locking onto satellites, requests and passwords sent.

System power check.

All systems are full and nominal.

Abort mission protocols reviewed.

Confirm.

Security system, drone passwords, and identification confirmation.

Confirm all green and loaded.

Switching over to on-board away systems.

You have total control.

Confirm away systems activated, vehicle and craft on-board systems active, and I have control.

Launch.

Mission 2189/440 GO! Leaving the compound.

Sarah prefers to drive through the streets once more in her Matt Black Barracuda rather than fly to the Mount Gambier headquarters. All but one of her support drones has flown outside the compound wall to wait at the moat for Sarah to arrive. There is no nine AM peak hour traffic in the city as Sarah cruises along the empty early morning streets. Most people work from home, as service sites require minimal on-site presence to run seamlessly.

While driving to the HQ, she observes people waving at her. Arriving at the Headquarters, Sarah enters the foyer. The single drone hovers high above the Cat, as it is a safe location and just a quick visit to pick up the two small boxes. Sarah walks through the large main glass doors and Natasha, the chief of security, immediately greets her. Natasha gives her two packages, subtly ensuring that Sarah can see the writing on them, "leave in Vehicle". Only Sarah's advanced light spectrum eyes can visualize these inked words. Sarah does not react. Recent days deviated from protocol, making her assume a valid motive behind it. Natasha exchanges pleasantries, then whispers, "We support you, happy hunting." Back in her vehicle, Sarah reflects on the strange note on a parcel, extra information in the two messages given to her, and the uncommon verbal remarks.

Driving through the streets and beyond the wall to the moat, Sarah is constantly thinking that she needs clarification on these messages. They are very cryptic and not a typical situation she has encountered before. Over her years of following orders, she has always received simple messages, so she hopes that the reasons for the vague messages will make sense before her Hybo. On arriving at the moat, she calls the overseers to allow her to pass through and leave the Mount Gambier compound.

I have reached the moat, and I wish to proceed through it to start on Mission 2189/440.

All clear; please proceed Sarah.

Sarah leaves the compound to focus on her mission: getting samples of the primary subject and others near Bordertown. Landing on the outskirts of the town with the Hellcat in Camo matte green hunting livery, she drives into the center of the city, planning her mission to get to her homestead. With a sense of urgency, she feels compelled to complete this task, despite not understanding the intensity of her feelings. This increases her excitement and senses.

Sarah's drones fly ahead to search for tracking signals amidst dense foliage. The slow process involves hovering, waiting, and moving to find the signal. The prime target has yet to show themself to the tracking drones. This is a critical time for Sarah. Her aim is to face difficulty in locating the subject to bolster her fake signal outages, without consuming excessive time or exhausting the overseers' patience.

Cruising through Bordertown and then lifting off to get high above the general area with her vehicle in its silent mode, as the rest of the entourage stays high until the locater drones find the target. Too much noise agitates creatures and can cause a stamped. Drones find subjects and use a surrounding and herding method to move them to a suitable area. Sarah has used this tactic in the past to extend hunting time in this location. It now might work against her if they cannot find the desired target or see other subjects to set her desired mission into action. The drones might herd the subject into a less dense area, which is the task programed into them, but different than what Sarah wants.

It's time to make a choice. Sarah must weigh up the options. She could land in the dense forest near her homestead to hunt. A brilliant choice at night. However, during daylight, drones may capture her crossing to the homestead if they fly high enough. The second possibility is to wait and maximize the potential of wherever the prime subject is located. Definitely not the best choice for a chance of getting to her homestead. Sarah runs through the excuse in her mind, in case someone catches her at the homestead. See could say "I stumbled on it, and it looked abandoned", "I surveyed it to see if it contained anything useful for future missions in the area". Although all effective answers, it will attract attention to the homestead for future missions. Sarah may have to leave it, or the overseers could request its destruction.

Sarah is feeling alive and electric. Recently, her sensations have intensified during hunting or pursuing personal goals. Sarah feels somewhat changed after recent events. Strangely, it is nothing truly notable, just slightly different wordings or interactions that might be all in her imagination. Sarah knows she is at the end of a cycle and feels relieved she will soon get a vital rest from all the pressure and missions. Just as she thinks it, alarms sound in her vehicle. The subject has been located under deep foliage only one kilometer from her homestead. Now the game begins. Her task is to collect samples and make a round trip to her homestead without detection.

Sarah thinks through her plan. She can remove her tracking and communication neck unit as she did in the past, but the drones will still track the subject. Should it exit the dense foliage without the drones detecting Sarah, the overseers will grow suspicious. Sarah considers abandoning her plans to visit the homestead because of newfound doubt. It is a constant risk versus reward calculation racing through her mind, making her heart run faster. Sarah feels euphoric and nervous. She decides to obtain the primary subject's samples first, hoping it leads her in the right direction.

Once she gets the primary subject's samples, the drones will cease tracking the target. Sarah is solely responsible for finding subjects lacking trackers. This will provide her with time and greater freedom of movement.

Sarah arrives at the principal subject's general area and tries to place her vehicle between the subject and the homestead. The homestead's bare earth around it and the maintained area closer to its walls still give the impression that it has been recently abandoned and is not too overgrown to pose a security risk. She descends through the foliage and lands to track the subject on foot. The cloud cover is making it quite dim under the canopy, and she knows that there may be other creatures around. She intermittently communicates with overseers in this area, in case she can make a run to the homestead after getting the sample.

The subject is slower today, with a storm brewing. A storm during the operation would be incredibly lucky for Sarah making the drones less effective and be forced to land if lightning strikes. In stormy conditions, they only fly if Sarah is in danger to reduce any chance that they might get damaged or struck by lightning. Sarah races through the shrubbery and between the tree trunks that are randomly spaced throughout the area. Running through them at Sarah's speed is like doing a short-course slalom race. The tracker shows she is closing in on her target, and Sarah readies the tranquilizer gun. Her goal is to swiftly collect the sample and then search for another subject between the vehicle and her homestead.

Sarah finds the target alone and stalks it briefly to get closer. The tranquilizer works extremely fast, so getting the blood, hair samples, and photos will take little time. Sarah quickly looks around and cannot see any other enormous creatures that could pose a problem to her while taking the samples, so she takes the shot, moving in as soon as the giant subject falls. A solid muscular figure looking like a kangaroo in appearance with its tail and stance, they have a unique run hop bounding stride like triple jumper. The head is human-like, with a much stronger jaw, oversized ears, and teeth. The subject has evolved muscle-bound arms with clawed hands at the end, and its toes have long nails to rip prey apart. Sarah must approach cautiously to ensure that the subject is unconscious, and nothing comes to its defense.

After getting the photos, hair samples, skin core, and a vial of blood, Sarah injects the tranquilizer reversal drug. Sarah traditionally will wait for the tranquilizer to wear off. For this large and dangerous subject, she opted for a more potent drug. Leaving immediately will buy her more time to reach her homestead, as the overseers will expect her to wait for the subject to wake. Back at the Vehicle, Sarah places the samples into it. After collecting more samples, she will load them all onto a drone in order to extend the timeline. Since the subject is Male, Sarah believes tracking and sampling a female would yield the best results for the overseers.

Sarah makes her way through the foliage toward her homestead, looking for a subject and still focused on her best option to break free. She goes wherever the hunt leads, managing broken communications to the overseers and her plan to hunt a female. They are happy with this news and recommend that she proceed at her own pace, agreeing to keep communication low because of all the breakups and interruptions, allowing her to concentrate. Sarah gets her drones to fly low over the canopy north of her position to herd any subjects south but have them stop short to keep them a distance from her. Sarah is now only five hundred meters from her homestead, and she decides she will go for it. She drops her communication and tracking necklace and sprints to her homestead. The AI voice commands will keep commanding the drones to move north and sweep back, keeping them far away from Sarah so as not to scare everything towards her at speed. Sarah and the overseers both dread an animal stampede. With the drones doing their now pre-program course low to the Canopy, Sarah can be confident that they will not get the vision of her crossing the bare ground to her homestead.

Chapter twelve. After the crossing

Sarah arrives at her homestead. The security system recognizes her instantly on its face recognition software and waits for the correct password and fingerprint checks. The defense drone programming with any near-wall activity is to only watch movements unless the homestead is under threat. Sarah set this protocol to avoid drawing attention to the homestead for any unnecessary reasons. Accepting the entrance code and fingerprint matching the system wakes up, all the lights and the computers start in operational mode.

Sarah gives voice commands to the system linked directly to pre-program sequences and active controls. Time restrictions mean she has to multitask to get everything done. She sends encrypted messages to the outliers about the information gathered from the Pure compound meetings and inserts USB drives with updated software, which she and her fellow outliers programmed. She dictates general broadcast messages that lack specific details. Instead, these messages convey moods of the Pure, drawing on common compound knowledge that the outliers would be unaware of because of their isolation. Most important is major news on the DNA virus and the Pure's dream of roaming free has significantly progressed. Outliers support each other through these news bulletins. They also swap and share equipment, and Sarah has over the years helped many of them out under different AI generated voices and code names. Under her three most common aliases, Sarah has built a great rapport with a chosen few and they, in return, build and change any equipment for her without question.

This homestead, while looking run down and abandoned outside, on the inside drones and robots have it operating like a command center. Drones from her homesteads can collect and analyze data that interests the outlier community. When a drone has any information, it will, via automation, send messages to give her trusted local outliers a heads-up to go look at it or to recover something. This outlier cooperative started with Sarah having respect for the outliers' commitment and survival skills and it has expanded into a sophisticated technical resource. The outliers have yet to learn they are actually communicating with Sarah. She uses several homesteads to send messages and drones from, ensuring information does not come solely from one location or one person. She is a "nobody" secretly behind the scenes.

Once the software is uploaded, all the USB sticks are destroyed. Sarah verbally instructs the AI system to act accordingly until the next update. Her stopwatch warns her it has been thirty minutes. She must complete her tasks and return to the hunt, avoiding suspicion. Sarah will not return to this location for at least two years, leaving the AI to follow its standard maintenance mode and keep up communications.

Activating the lockdown mode as she exits, Sarah will have to use all her skills to return to where she left her communication necklace, weapons, and tranquilizer gun. After a quick look in the sky and over the bare ground, Sarah sprints across, using her super athletic ability to the basic cover of the forest canopy.

There is a significant problem. Three of the Unhuman subjects are between her and all the equipment. The harassment of the drones has agitated them, and they appear to be aware of her. She cannot direct her drones to return to her, they are following a fake transmitter location, and the device is with her gear. Not knowing how many creatures are around, Sarah faces a life-threatening situation. It might be beyond her skills and DNA modifications to get around this situation without help from her drones or her vehicle. Sarah makes her way east to go around the Unhuman and return to her gear from the north in the same direction that her drones are moving subjects. This way back to her gear has less dangerous attributes as opposed to going straight to her equipment through the aggressive and scared creatures. Swinging around and coming back with the drones to her gear may benefit her or see her run over by creatures. In order to keep the homestead a secret and avoid uncomfortable explanations, she must take this risk.

As Sarah turns south, she can see the subjects ahead of her, and she moves in behind them. They are heading directly for her equipment, moving at a moderate pace as the drones have gone back to the start of their herding pattern. With luck on her side, Sarah has little difficulty in getting to her gear and puts back on her communication necklace. She alerts her drones and overseers about nearby targets, directing the drones to hold their positions. This gives the creatures a chance to calm down, allowing her to select subjects from the group ahead.

All her training from tens of thousands of hunts tells her the two most valuable targets are a younger and older female. Sarah cannot determine the creatures' relationship - whether they are mother and daughter or strangers in the pack. Sarah hits her two chosen subjects quickly with the tranquilizer. Although some distance apart, they both go down quickly. She sets of explosions to scare off the rest, creating a safer environment for her to retrieve the samples. She will tag these new subjects for future tracking and checking. One is an older, fertile female, and the other is a young female, maybe two or three years old. Sarah swiftly retrieves the farthest sample first from the young one. The counteracting drug efficacy on the new subjects is unknown, making it risky for her if the older one regains consciousness before she acquires the young one's samples.

Sarahs ecstatic. It couldn't have gone better for her. She achieved her own goals and the overseers' goals without major issues. She sprints back to her vehicle and lifts off, flying the most direct route to Murray Bridge.

Chapter thirteen. One Bridge to Go

On arrival at her compound in Murray Bridge, Sarah sets the programs running for her compound's rest period. Her last task before returning to the church compound is to collect a couple of parcels from the Murray Bridge Headquarters. She contacts them to arrange the pickup of the two boxes at 2PM from inside the foyer. This approach is simpler and more efficient. It avoids the need for security protocols or navigating through the building where leaders or laboratory staff may hold her up with conversations.

Arriving at the headquarters, Sarah parks directly out the front of a granite stairway that leads up to the main entrance. The headquarters have a wide stairway at the bottom that gradually narrows towards the main entrance, creating the illusion of ascending to a higher authority. Parking the Matt Black Barracuda at the bottom of the staircase with a drone hovering overhead, she exits and walks up the steps. The matt black absorbs the sunlight, making the Cat look solid in contrast to the light reflecting off Sarah's suit, highlighting her agile, flexible and athletic body. Together, they show they are a formidable force not to be messed with. Upon entering the foyer, Piper meets her and hands the two parcels over. Again, she glimpses "Leave in Vehicle" written in invisible ink, accompanied by a whispered "We back you, happy hunting." Sarah doesn't acknowledge the comment, but now she believes something is definitely different.

Before leaving Murray Bridge, Sarah drives past Jolene's house to see if she can get a ping on her transponder or receive a message. She can see that Jolene is home from as she drives past. The transponder activates and sends a message. Sarah now has questions about Jolene's absence at the meeting, as she was expecting no news. Jolene suspected that something was wrong in her laboratory. She also sensed a growing divide between different levels of scientists and those in the governing circle. The received message gives some insight, it reads:

I'm watched, not trusted with info, or involved in testing. Results of tests the laboratory is working on are not being shared. As I am shut out and likely compromised, I have nothing to offer.

Sarah now understands why Jolene didn't attend the meeting and suspects the overseers will just dump Jolene, and she will become collateral damage, left to sort out her own life.

Sarah has already sent the message from Sami along with the test samples taken off the packages that he had concerns about. Overseers informed Sarah that the samples were unhelpful, and they would consult the security team leader. In Murray Bridge, parcels do not need official tracking, as it is not an Elite society, allowing them to have a certain amount of freedom to do as they please. Sarah knows she will get a similar reaction to Jolene's news. If the overseers push and ask too many questions about Jolene's suspicions, it could have significant repercussions instead of rewards.

Sarah drives slowly through the outer Mixed Human areas of Monarto, heading towards the Unhuman zone. Upon reaching the bare earth ring, she takes off and flies all the way to the end of the freeway in Adelaide. After landing at where the old Tollgates original stood back in 2020, Sarah drives through the tall buildings near the CBD with creatures already exiting to start their hunting for the night from their hiding places within or under them.

Arriving at her church just as the sun sets, she will follow the stricter entrance testing than is required for a one or two-day trips. To ensure that the blood sample is current and not from a previous one, Sarah must shower, have the suits placed in a washer, and take the blood sample under video surveillance. Sarah cannot leave the secure wash area until the overseers approve all the samples. A failed result could see her incinerated where she stands.

All the drones and her vehicles go through deep software and hardware checks to ensure no one has tampered with them. Only once these checks are all done will Sarah be able to leave the garage, which is her final secure area, and move freely throughout the church.

She heads to the office on her release and logs her report, uploads the video and photos of the subjects she has taken samples from. After these chores, she can relax and take care of personal tasks, enjoy a meal and watch a movie to end this period.

Time and rest cannot free her from the lingering messages in her mind. The words play repeatedly in her mind. She wonders if there's a hidden message.

Why take this approach? What order would make sense?

"We Support you. When the truth and what's right rises, Pure power will be set free. Thank you for all you're doing."

"You're doing what's right. The truth must be set free. The time is near. Your power reigns free."

She notes one other strange change from protocol when leaving for the mission:

You have TOTAL control, not the standard you have control.

The verbal messages at the two headquarters were, "We support You Happy Hunting" when she received the parcels.

Why the invisible ink?

Sarah stops analyzing it all as she is due to start her hibernation cycle in the morning. Trying to solve a potentially unsolvable puzzle is pointless. She focuses back on relaxing, lounging, playing music, dancing, and being free before going to her last sleep in her own bed.

Waking in her bed for the last time this cycle, she gets up, does her gym routine, breakfast, and checks messages before preparing for her scheduled hibernation cycle. Sarah, one of the Elite warriors of this breed, the overseers have her believing she hibernates to prolong her life and provide sufficient time for the experiments to yield results. Typically, one to two years, but without specific limitations. The overseers carefully plan the durations to achieve the best outcomes. They can wake Sarah anytime for tasks or emergencies.

The morning meeting begins with her being congratulated by the overseers for her work during the last cycle. They explain that the recent samples she took are an incredible help to the cause because of their strong DNA strands that have evolved in that herd. The overseers inform Sarah they have an intelligent nanobot drug on trial that can do math and decision-making before it activates, killing the subject. It looks for and compares what a Pure Human is to any other variant, checking for mixed DNA. If the Mixed DNA reaches a preset level, the nanobots will multiply and kill the subject. It is not instantly lethal, as they want the nanobots to spread in a herd or community to reach the largest number of subjects as possible. It will spread fast in a community of similar DNA because of the increased activity of the virus and the programed multiplying characteristics. In contrast, it will stay dormant in non-mixed DNA subjects that do not reach the DNA difference trigger. The virus remains dormant for around a month in Pure or slightly mixed DNA individuals. Eventually, it dies off, and the body rejects it completely, leaving no trace behind.

Sarah regrets not knowing this information earlier, which would have allowed her to inform the outliers. She also thinks that the virus leaving a mixed human in two months is untrue. Miscommunication appears to be happening at several levels. Sarah focuses on running checks on all the compound's systems after the meeting. She sets the main command computer to start the lockdown one hour after she is in hibernation, ensuring her vital signs are normal.

Sarah undresses and climbs into her hibernation unit, placing an intravenous drip into her arm and monitoring pads on herself. She sets the clear lid to close on the capsule-shaped habitation module and seal. As it slowly closes, the lid gradually frosts over to make the unit dark and to help with thermoregulation of the hibernation gas. The temperature lowers as Sarah falls asleep. Sarah and the church will spend two years hibernating.

Chapter fourteen. Hibernation

All humans desire a happy, healthy life, longing for eternal youth. Over time, diverse beliefs and morals have divided opinions on right and wrong. With the changing world environment, it created more opportunities for evolving species to separate, living in changing climate areas and in alternative forms of life.

Elite Pure Humans believe in their exclusivity as true humans, but they ironically rely on scientific advancements in DNA experiments to prolong their own lifespans. They attempt to justify the medical benefits and procedures they used to maintain their health by claiming that they ethically conducted them, without involving genes, stem cells, or Frankenstein experiments.

Human hibernation is one of these scientific resources developed to make travel to Mars practical. In the early days, a trip took up to nine months. Besides the potential boredom for civilians, the significant size of a craft to compensate for sustenance and activity makes the size of the spacecraft impractical to build and propel to Mars. Mars trips now take two to three months, with passengers hibernating in capsules on speedy craft. The Elite discovered an additional advantage and used it to control both the Pure population on earth and in space.

As the Pure colonies in low orbit, on the Moon, Mars, and Earth developed, so did the need for greater leadership with genuine Elite overseers in charge. Leaders dedicated themselves to ruling, not wavering in the beliefs and standards of the Elite. This governing body devised a way to protect their dreams and visions, just like religion and cults of the past did to control the masses for their benefit. Elite hibernation cycles are the tool used to maintain control by the forebears and current leaders to rule over extended life spans. A group of four hundred Elite couples share a rotation of hibernation. They do this to extend their lives and maintain control over the seven continents and one hundred greater Earth Elite Pure colonies.

These Elite groups use hibernation to age over their designated service time of one hundred and ninety-four Earth years. The Elite group grooms and votes in younger teams as couples to join. Couples hibernate in cycles over their ruling period, starting at twenty years of age if they are not already born into a hibernating family.

The Leading Elite, on average, live for 165 years. Joining at age 20 if you don't use hibernation cycles, you would rule actively for about 109 Earth years. Using hibernation cycles of fifteen years at a time, you can extend your Earth years of active service, as you only age one year in hibernation. After 15 Earth years, you awaken at 21 and join the ruling Elite for another 15 years. Meanwhile, the couple you replaced goes into hibernation.

After ruling for 15 years, you go into hibernation at 36. You then emerge after 15 years and serve another active 15 years of rule till the age of 37. Continue the cycles until you reach the second-to-last one at 132 years old. Opting for a final hibernation cycle results in an emergence at the age of 148, with an expected lifespan of 165 years. Elite individuals typically forego the last cycle and live without hibernation from age 132 until death. This makes an active awake ruling time of one hundred and four years, with your opposing couple effectively ruling over one hundred and ninety-four Earth years. Couples stay on the board with an active lifestyle well into their one hundred and fifty years of age. Society knows them as elders until they pass away and they help maintain continuity among the hibernating groups. No other Pure Humans hibernate unless they travel to or from Mars, or the Elite make them part of their leading group because of their skill set.

The ruling royalty, Elite hibernators, have distinct homes globally or on the Moon or Mars. They have extreme security, separated from any other buildings or structures with large living areas where extended families and guests have semi-isolated areas to live in alongside them.

Chapter fifteen. Earth and Mars

Humans inhabit Mars and the Moon, both above ground, below ground, and in orbit. They live in a maze of tubes and enclosures with various levels of gravity. Public areas have projections and live vegetation where possible, making these open spaces as beautiful as any place on Earth. However, many inhabitants are unfamiliar with Earth's natural environment, as they have never visited. It's difficult to distinguish if you're on the Moon or Mars, with an artificial sky simulating the Earth's cycles. Travel between the enclosures is in vacuum tube transport vehicles for all but the entitled. The adventurous Elite have self-owned pressurized transport vehicles that resemble four-wheel-drive Toyota Land cruisers or vehicles of Earth's past. They use them for fun and to explore uninhabited parts of the Moon or Mars. They also provide a sense of limited freedom from their confined living spaces.

All off-world locations have large orbiting space stations that are partly residential but essentially used as spaceports for coordination and travel from the Earth's surface to the Moon, and Mars. Using spaceports allows for small shuttle trips between them and the surface colonies, bringing produce, resources, and people on regular launches to the station. Then, they load bulk supplies and passengers onto larger interplanetary craft to travel greater distances.

There are no countries or contents off-world, only one Pure race. Areas, resembling towns and cities on Earth, naturally separate into the haves and have-nots. Wealthy individuals choose to live on the moon's bright side, facing Earth's beauty. Others by choice live on the dark side, looking into deep dark space at night with its zillions of stars rather than seeing Earth. Both sides of the Moon receive equal sunlight and have identical environmental needs. Individuals choose to live in either location based on their beliefs and upbringing. The constant reminders of life on Earth and the possibility of returning can affect their decision.

An agreement between all off-world communities and Earth ensures equal resources, manufacturing, backup life support systems and expert technicians for life in these extreme environments. Just like on Earth, the Moon and Mars also have different-priced suburbs and communities, with no defined border between the bright and dark sides. So, you can observe conditional changes in these areas on both celestial bodies. Below ground and above have unique qualities of living, bars, shopping centers, courier shuttles, delivery bots, and standards. They separate all high-risk infrastructure and science buildings from each other for security and safety reasons. The buildings have air locked isolation sections that can disconnect in an emergency. Engineers have designed these sections to prevent a domino effect in case of a catastrophic failure of a section.

Stringently supported utilities clean, purify, and recycle water and oxygen sourced locally, while checking for any traces of viruses or infections. These utilities can also identify any presence of non-Pure Humans that might try to live amongst them. Impure can visit these stations under strict security for limited reasons. They must stay in independent infrastructure that's off-grid to the Pure and security personnel escort them to limit any interactions with off-world citizens.

The laboratory Sarah works for is a high-risk standalone unit, as they don't want the possibility of contaminating other systems or networks on the Moon. People working in the Lab must stay within its self-sufficient city. Leaders can come and go with relative freedom after a simple thirty-minute blood test and general check-up. Lower-level employees needing time off must quarantine and lack the same freedom of movement as higher-level staff. If they have been involved in more elaborate experimental sciences, it may involve weeks of isolation before they can leave.

Laboratories vary in their setup, with some simulating Earth's conditions, while others use microgravity for research and development of innovative technologies. The on-Earth laboratories have their own specific jobs, cross-checking common experiments done in off-world laboratories to see what changes there might be in Earth's environment.

All laboratories have their own CEO and project managers under them who collate all the data. They meet to discuss their recent results, conclusions, or modifications. CM, as chairperson, leads all labs on and off-world and serves as a senior leader on the Elite board. His laboratory is one of the most sophisticated, it is the elite of the Elite's secure laboratories in the entire network of laboratories. CM oversaw Sarah's upbringing and all her medical enhancements as her creator. If asked, he may acknowledge some fatherly traits, but he doesn't consider Sarah his daughter. She is a genetically engineered product, designed to be an ideal specimen with an enhanced immune system, superior power to weight ratio, muscle tone, and strength surpassing certain earthly creatures. She is everything they are fighting against and trying to eliminate on Earth.

Chapter sixteen. The Awakening

Sarah awakes and soon realizes something's wrong. The church is dark, the computer screens have not all turned on. This troubles Sarah and her mind instantly thinks of reasons. Could it have something to do with her actions in helping the outliers or suspicions after her prolonged stay at her secret homestead before the hibernation cycle? Sarah notices that only certain cameras are active on the main screen, which she can see from her hibernation module. With her extensive knowledge of camera angles, Sarah finds a hidden route to the armory and her vehicle. The hibernation clock on the wall shows only two days instead of the planned two years, indicating something abnormal. An emergency awakening is unlikely, as alarms and communications would alert her to any threats.

Thoughts flood her mind. Is it a trap? A test? Why would someone wake her and for what reason? Maybe the overseers are dumping her to fend for herself as they no longer trust her. Thinking through all her options, she remains stationary in the hibernation module, allowing time to be contacted if it is a planned awakening. Her primary overseers, including CM, should all be asleep doing their fifteen-year cycle. Sarah's hibernation is aligned with CM's cycle, with brief awakenings for tests and sampling requirements. They are pre planned, overseen by the laboratory newly awoken leaders and never after only two days. No other members of the lab have the codes to wake her.

Sarah, now full awake, naked and curious in her capsule, removes the drip and sensors used to evaluate her status. Slowly exiting and moving about carefully, making sure she does nothing that might alert anyone to hit a contamination button, or any other emergency alarms. She walks to her bedroom; grabs a bag and packs a couple of her suits along with a selection of casual clothes, then slips on some tights, a T-shirt, and jogging shoes.

If she leaves the church, she will be all alone, but staying doesn't feel right. The Pure have multiple ways to eliminate Sarah. Giving her a way of escaping and knowing she will destroy the church is one excuse they could use to explain to CM why they killed her when he wakes in thirteen years. It's the first time Sarah has experienced such a rush of emotions. She is nervous and anxious. Just before it consumes her, she hears a faint tune she remembered from a time so long ago.

Sarah now knows what to do.

It's time to shine. It cannot be a coincidence. Someone is sending Sarah a lifeline. This tune is a precious family memory, making it unlikely to be a trap. CM is the only other person who knows Sarah will remember it. With ninety-eight percent of the drones upgrading, it is an ideal time to attempt an escape. Someone having control of the compound and knowing all the techniques to awaken Sarah and illuminate the escape path is hard to overlook.

Growing tired of her trapped life recently, she believes it is now or never. Sarah has overseen many life forms on Earth, even the most basic ones seem more alive and freer compared to her. A strong sense of fight and flight adrenaline kicks in as she makes her move. She heads to the armory, collecting as many weapons as possible to load into her vehicle. Even if it only gets her to a safe building, she feels it is a risk worth taking. To give herself a slight extra chance, the church needs to be destroyed. Returning to the hibernation room where the major computer system is, she places some time-delay explosives. She also puts them in the armory and the drone maintenance area, which has the communication servers and satellite antennas directly above it. There will be no going back once the explosives have gone off.

She jumps into the vehicle, wakes up the computer; while strapping in so she can leave at high speed and take defensive actions. The dashboard displays the message "It's time to shine." Sarah opens the garage door while activating the cloaking device made for her by an outlier. The vehicle turns into a streamlined Warcraft, the most aggressive design she can imagine in a deep candy apple red with metallic flakes. As she leaves, her first big hurdle will be the security moat. Will it activate, killing Sarah and destroying the vehicle? She will not know or be able to act if it does, as it will all be over in milliseconds.

With newfound passion for freedom, Sarah's explosive exit from the garage causes chaos. Parts of the church are flying in all directions. Frightened creatures race away as deeper explosions continue to go off. Sarah swings through the buildings at speed, low to the ground to get as much distance as possible from the church. Staying below the rooftops and changing directions will allow her to see if anything is following her, or if any tracking alerts go off in the vehicle. The off-world command center will instantly know something has gone wrong. If they disable her vehicle, she can ditch it and hide in a building or tunnel. Her years of experience will give her an advantage in knowing where to hide and where not to go.

If all goes well, Sarah plans to reach her homestead in the Adelaide Hills near a town named Petwood. It is about halfway between Adelaide and Murray Bridge, with an old copper mine nearby in Kathmandu. The homestead is just a short distance from the main highway that supply vehicles still use often, the constant traffic keeps most of the true Unhuman away as they prefer much more isolated natural land. Nearby towns include Monarto, which is within the bare earth ring that circles a group of other cities. These towns are familiar with Sarah because of her previous visits, even if not by name. Some have spoken with her during intel gathering, others provided her with information. What reception she might get if asking for help now might be quite different.

Sarah has helped Mixed Humans, even the occasional almost Unhuman, that have been in danger either directly or instructed her drones to do so in critical circumstances, saving their lives. With her outlier acquaintances and all their combined contacts, she potentially has thousands of connections. Are they all loyal? Especially if their lives are on the line. Can she rely on them to do a task? Do they know what Sarah's ultimate mission was for the overseers?

Chapter seventeen. A New Pet

Arriving at Petwood, Sarah activates the homestead and puts it on high alert to assess her situation and decide what to do with her vehicle. Returning to it, she retrieves two boxes. Inside are tablets, one red and one blue, accompanied by a note instructing her to take one of each daily until finished. Sarah is unsure. Why now, and so many tablets they could have killed me in multiple ways?

Sarah trusts they are to help her, not hinder her, as someone must have known she would take the vehicle out of the church. She also remembers the phrases "we support you" and the changes to the command comment from "you have control" to "you have total control." In one box is a piece of paper with coordinates written in the same ink used on the box lids. Sarah feels more confident now and takes one of each tablet, contacts her outliers, and sends commands to her other homesteads to put them into activation mode. Sarah's primary goal is to determine who to trust and their knowledge. She listens for any answers on the broadcasting channels, which have erupted in chatter. Aware of the danger, she knows to be cautious when reaching out to them. Any of those pretending to help her could be Mixed or Unhuman, wanting her dead for what she had done to them on past missions.

Sarah types in the coordinates written on the note in the box. They both are just outside the moats of the Elite Compound on Eyre Peninsula and satellite images do not show any type of buildings or structures. This makes Sarah curious enough that she will send one of her drones to each location to investigate when it gets dark. She turns her attention to who could support her from the Moon base. Is it just one crazy person, or an organized group? Why free her by letting her out of her cage, or are they planning on using her for a new purpose? Sarah notes the facts down on paper to evaluate for any patterns.

Whoever initiated the awakening was likely in a prominent position. Is CM and his staff asleep, they should be? Are any of them involved, or did CM pass and the Elite no longer care about me, so they set me free?

Only CM and I know that song, and someone intended for the dashboard words to show support.

Words of support and two-handed notes after the meeting. There must be no Elite connection since Natasha is involved.

The first message: We thank you for all you are doing, and the time is near for the Pure.

The message from the girls: When the Pure rises, the truth reigns power, and what's right will be set free.

Sami worried about boxes going to people like Natasha, the Head of security. Two boxes being suspect is not enough; there must be others. If Natasha didn't flag them, then she was receiving and distributing them.

Leia's concern about Monarto could also be connected to Jolene's suspicion in her laboratory.

The software upgrades just before leaving Mount Gambier could have given me total control of the vehicle and compromised all the compounds? If so, in what way? This also suggests multiple people must be involved in the IT and tech departments.

Why the drugs? Are they to replace the ones I have been taking to help my body because of my genetics? A message saying take till finished suggests I will not get any more. What happens then? Are they sufficient to give me full virus protection?

Sarah knows she must determine her new purpose on earth. She looks over at her notes, messages, and evidence she has collated again and puts together a broken sentence.

We thank you for all you are doing, and the time is near for the Pure. When the Pure rises, the truth reigns power. You will wake up and know it's time to shine, my beautiful girl. We support you.

Sarah believes she has a new mission, and she's not alone. They, whoever they are, must know about her helping the outliers, sharing relevant news with them and her homesteads. Is the new mission to stop the Elite Pure? Sarah has an idea to evaluate her theory. If true and coordinates are to help her, and nothings visible, are any of her secret homesteads visible? Sarah types in her location and the homestead outside of Bordertown. She pushes back in her chair, causing both her and the chair to shoot across the room. She is in shock. Both homesteads she typed in are invisible to live satellite footage, and there is no visible evidence of them anywhere. She deletes her searches off her computer just in case someone can access them. Though reassuring, she hopes the true instigators of the apparent coup will soon reach out with more details.

Now, she must play a short waiting game to see if the Elite's agenda continues or if someone else emerges, before making her own plans for survival. Messages continue coming in from outliers on chat lines that are encrypted so the Elite cannot intercept these chats. It is doubtful that any outliers would side with the Elite Pure, so there is minimal risk of a mole within her tight trusted group. The church explosion has caught everyone's attention.

News broadcasts have not mentioned her escape, so they might have thought Sarah was still in her hibernation module. The leaders won't believe the theory for long if there is no hard evidence provided. Sarah thinks they will decide she has gone rogue because of recent virus news and fears they'll hunt her relentlessly to prevent further damage to their cause.

Chapter eighteen. The War Begins

In the Elite command center, CM, and his head of security Tarak, along with a select crew, are running cover for Sarah. The members of the laboratory who were due for hibernation are in their capsules as standard protocol dictates for the fifteen-year handover. CM awaits the new rulers to wake for the scheduled meeting. A face-to-face handover ensures that transferring information is secure and correctly received, there is one problem with this changeover cycle. CM has assured the new team will not wake. For now, he controls the command center completely, despite the loss of lives on both sides.

The lab's isolation from the Moon's infrastructure ensured the power exchange so far has gone unnoticed by others. They desire to maintain control as long as possible, allowing Sarah time to fulfill her purpose as CM intended. To be a warrior and with her exceptional skill set, she will naturally become a leader others will follow.

To maintain the illusion of normalcy, CM directs his personnel in the communication center to report the explosion at the church to all the Earth's Elite stations. With news that, the data implies Sarah was still in her hibernation module for her scheduled two-year cycle. Port Lincoln and Mount Gambier offer to send a team or a drone to investigate. CM informs them he has a team looking into it and checking for any contamination. Loyal members collaborate to create confusion for the coup to organize themselves before the Elite realizes something is amiss. In order to prevent further development of the virus, CM destroys all the data on the servers.

In the past 15 years, CM and his team created viruses and gained access to critical systems. At certain times, scheduled failures will allow CM, Sarah, and the team access to control them, affecting the Earth's Elite powers to fight back. His plan involves his team evacuating to Earth and joining forces with Sarah to overthrow the Elite's rule, starting with Australia and expanding worldwide. The communication center receives messages from all the Earth-based compounds in Australia along with those in orbit, on the Moon, and on Mars. All agencies seeking updates on what is happening, asking if help is required, whether it was an accident, or are the Mixed and Unhuman attacking. Cm's communication team stalls and suggests the ammunition store has exploded and caused a chain reaction destroying the church.

Now, time works against CM and team. They set all the explosives and wipe all off-base servers of any information or video footage. A scheduled supply craft has priority to leave the Moon base laboratory to go to Port Lincoln. This window for launch has now opened. CM orders his crew into the craft as he activates an AI program to stall long enough for the craft to leave as intended and arrive on earth unchallenged. Artificial communication mimics the team, fooling the Elite into thinking they're in control. The catastrophic destruction caused by the lab explosion will leave no chance of survival. Combined with biohazard protocols, it should create enough confusion to ensure the shuttle may continue its trip to Earth unchallenged.

The team's gamble is not without risk; they may shoot down the shuttle. CM is relying on his efforts over the past month to convince the Elite that this craft is of utmost importance in achieving their virus dreams. The lives of everyone on board depend on CM and his team's success in selling this idea. Without the leading laboratory, they hope the Elite will at least let the craft carrying the only remaining virus samples land. It will take eight hours for the shuttle to reach Earth's orbit and descend through the atmosphere. For the entire duration, CM and crew will have no communication or defenses.

As the shuttle approaches Earth, trojan viruses implanted in software will activate disabling defense systems in the orbiting colony and South Australia's Earth-based compounds. If they decide to shoot down the shuttle, CM is relying on these software hacks to stop them. The programs will instruct the weapons to destroy their own communication towers and critical infrastructure, leaving them with no choice but to scramble to shut down all defensive systems.

Chapter nineteen. Time is Ticking

Two hours have passed since the craft left, and the laboratory obliterated, activating the biohazard protocols and slowing down any inspection attempts. CM and team are at the critical point of their trip to Earth. They are still alive, but the following six hours are extremely risky. The Elite could shoot them down before they reach Earth, or once the shuttle changes its course and the Elite notices. The trojan software and a few in Elite compounds on Earth supporting the coup hold all survival hopes. Their best chance lies in the Elite's impatience and strong desire for a new world, which remains a top priority, ensuring they won't destroy the craft.

The shuttle slows, adjusts its trajectory, and enters the atmosphere. Elite's senior management is in chaos, security teams are holding meetings with the Earth, Moon, Mars, and the orbiting stations. The top powers of the new Elite cycle have emerged from hibernation, seeking answers and striving to agree on a decision. A dream of the Pure living free on earth is now at risk. CM and his team were leaders in this field, controlling the earth's cleansing program. With the laboratory gone and CM presumed dead, along with Sarah, the Elite are worried that these accidents are not accidents at all but targeted attacks.

Generations of Pure have passed living in the Elite compounds not knowing life as anything different and are happy with their lives. Their unwillingness to change hinders support for an eradication virus. For this reason, only the top controlling powers know of CM's true level of experiments being conducted on Mixed Humans in Australia. The Elites so-called Unhuman sterilization drug reportedly designed to reduce their population to zero ethically is not humane at all. It will not only affect the total Unhuman, but it will also kill Mixed humans with gene alterations down to as low as twenty-five percent. Have the greater Pure population realized the truth and are they acting against their leaders, opposing the eradication of all life on Earth?

CM and his team, because of their ethics, had a change of mind, agreeing that his grandparents and other Elite were wrong. This change in belief started from an early age for CM before Sarah's creation. He believed it was just him questioning himself, but it grew to be more significant over the years. Watching Sarah grow into a beautiful teenager, he couldn't ignore the love in her eyes. She was no monster, even with all of CM's manipulation of her genes, she herself was Elite. CM searched for others with a similar mindset to challenge those in power. Realizing he wasn't alone in his thinking, he started planning his coup.

His control extended to all the laboratories, though only he and his small team worked directly on the virus. They protected it and kept all data hidden from the other hibernation team. The second hibernation team's job was to study the effects of drugs on plants, the environment, and other essential elements for the Elite's pure and healthy Earth. Other laboratories were unfit to handle CM's test viruses because of the potential for rogue actions or accidental premature release.

Faced with chaotic systems shutting down and alarms blaring, elite leaders decide their only chance is to allow the craft to land in order to keep their dream alive. Once the shuttle lands safely on Earth, they can retrieve the test tubes onboard and replicate the virus in their own laboratory.

The Elite believe that someone is attacking them, but it is uncertain who. Someone is launching an organized assault connected to the groundbreaking news about the viruses and its imminent release. The Elite's fear of setbacks and the noticeable chaos weakens their appearance. Anyone wishing to challenge their hold on power will try to rise and shift control.

Chapter twenty. Free Falling

The shuttle has made it through the atmosphere and starts slowing as its guidance system prepares to take control and steer it to the landing location. Its course is still true to not reveal its actual landing destination, and it will stay on course until the last minute. This is the next critical stage for CM and the crew. Countless things can go wrong. They could crash land, or when the Elite notice it has overshot Port Lincoln, drones could chase it to its landing destination. Upon arriving in Adelaide, the Mixed Humans who witnessed Sarah leaving the church during her escape might not be present to welcome the team and accompany them to safety.

The Elite are anxiously tracking the craft. On target, fast, but the speed is acceptable to the command center at the stage. The Elite Leader Mark asks Astro, his head of security, to ready a team to retrieve the craft's contents. He contacts Natasha in the Mount Gambier compound and informs her of the plan. She lends her support to Astro, and they engage in a general chat about the systems that are down and the actions that are planned to rectify the offline equipment. As their conversation continues, he is told the craft will not land at its designated spot. Astro informs Natasha that the shuttle may head to her compound, which is the backup landing area if Port Lincoln cannot receive it or in case of an overshoot. It is better in an overshoot to head to Mount Gambier than to circle around for a second attempt at Port Lincoln because of the Pterodactylus in the area. His team attempt to launch tracking and emergency drones. He acts angrily at the response from the landing team that the drones will not launch. Astro asks Natasha to launch hers to aid in the recovery should the craft not reach the Mount Gambier landing site. Natasha organizes her team to launch their drones and is told that only one drone will respond to commands, and they have launched it.

Natasha is a tall blonde thirty-five-year-old lady, her staff and those around her admire her. The Elite Pure leaders in Mount Gambier have a great deal of respect for her and her attention to detail. They trust Natasha to run the security for the eastern section, with little or no intervention from them. She has complete control and influence over all matters in and around the compound. As the head of security, she leads Sarah's missions in the Adelaide, Burra, Waikerie, Renmark area, extending to the South Australian Victoria border and down to Mount Gambier. CM and his team communicate directly with Natasha about sampling, Sarah's mission, and movements. Elite leaders choose to distance themselves from decision making regarding the virus because of its sensitive nature, in order to avoid potential blame if the truth is revealed. CM recruited Natasha twelve years ago at the start of his active swing as she made her way through the ranks, with his help. Natasha, unknown to others, has modified the defensive drone that could take off.

Four other young people, along with Natasha, are the only ones inside Mount Gambier management, not confused by the recent events, as they are part of the coup. Around one hundred followers are under Natasha's command inside the compound's walls. Piper is the head of security at the Murray Bridge compound. Natasha recruited her five years ago, and they helped her move up the ranks. The security teams in Murray Bridge and Mount Gambier are doing their best to assist during the ongoing chaos. At least they look like they are trying to solve problems, but Natasha and Piper are, in fact, adding to them covertly.

Port Lincoln, the strictest run compound in South Australia, required Astro, the head of security, to be in their pocket. They also needed operatives in the engineering and service sectors who he recruited. CM has not told Sarah, so she would continue to focus on her missions and not trust any recruited persons. He believed she was better alone in the early stages rather than risk the chance of someone betraying her. Sarah's death would trouble CM as he loves his daughter, and it would ruin his plan for redemption.

In the shuttle craft with CM is Tarak, Cosimo, and Electra who are part of Tarak's security team. Duke, a software developer, and Logan, who specializes in software implementation and engineering, accompany them. Aurora is in logistics, and Mira is from communications. It is a tight fit with all eight of them inside the smallish cargo shuttle. They all need to think and act fast now as the shuttle overshoots Port Lincoln for its intended landing site. Many unknown scenarios will confront them. The effects of gravity on Earth will make them slow to move and breathing fresh natural air will shock their lungs. They cannot run, let alone defend themselves if they confronted by Elite forces.

Astro is still unable at this stage to launch any drones. The latest updated software glitch loaded by the engineering team statewide has grounded them all. The Elite are unaware of Duke's secret missions programmed into some drones. Activating them, like the shuttle-securing drone Natasha launched, will not aid their cause. Dukes updated software, after a well-choreographed time allows Astro to launch two drones his team believe they have online, and they race toward the shuttle.

Chapter twenty-one. Don't Crash

The craft safely passes the Yorke Peninsula and slows to make a landing in the dead zone outside of Monarto. As they land, twelve mixed humans from Adelaide and Murray Bridge meet the craft to help get the crew out and into vehicles. The team appear from the craft in their laboratory clean suits to leave little evidence that anyone was on board. An inspection may uncover crew traces, as they all have access to it, but excessive samples would be suspicious. Extremely weak from the cramped craft and the effects of being on Earth, they are relieved to be greeted by the recovery team and quickly organize themselves. Apart from pleasantries, there are no other general conversations. They have minimal time before those most interested in the craft arrive. CM, Tarak, and Duke plan to go to the Monarto laboratory. Electra, Aurora, Mira, Cosimo, and Logan will go to a secure building in Adelaide. CM checks inside the craft, then closes the craft door before getting into his vehicle as the others leave.

The two drones arrive at the landing site. Astro and his team feel accomplished securing the craft and the virus for the Elite leaders. Drones circle, searching for threats. If there are no threats, the drones hover above the craft, programmed to defend it until a recovery team arrives. A security team from Murray Bridge is scrambling to get to the craft and secure it until a dedicated recovery team from Port Lincoln can retrieve the contents. The Elite in the control room are unaware of the drones' true purpose. They defend the craft and ensure a disruption-free escape for CM and his team. Astro is the only one who knows their true aim. These hacked drones are blind to the team of Mixed Humans and CM's crew. They transmit data back to the security team, showing that all is clear and secure.

Shortly after the Murray Bridge security team arrives on site, the hacked drones engage them before they can get close to the craft. Not to kill them, just to hold them off briefly to create more confusion. In a discussion with Natasha, Astro tells the security team to hold back at a distance and watch the shuttle until the Port Lincoln recovery team arrives. Their belief is that drones are defending the craft, preventing anyone from accessing it to remove or tamper with the virus. For now, that is all they need to do until Port Lincoln crews arrive.

On arriving, the recovery team converse with the Murray Bridge security team before approaching the shuttle. If the drones attack, Astro will first try to disarm them by taking them offline, or the security and recovery teams will try shooting them down. It will be difficult to shoot drown a drone as they are far superior and can dodge single shots. Team's move in, and the drones are now letting them approach. Wearing hazmat suits, they open the craft door. Inside are a few of boxes forty centimeters square sealed and in good condition with hazardous seals intact. They remove the boxes and place them in airtight hazardous containment cases before putting them into a vehicle. It lifts off and flies back to the Port Lincoln compound. The hazmat crew positions explosives in the craft and moves away to the wash-down showers. Once they have all washed down, they remove all clothing and re-dress, destroying all the hazmat suits in a fire, and enter their vehicles.

In South Australia, malfunctioning drones, including one that attacked the security team, have caused concerns. Therefore, they unanimously delay the destruction of the shuttle until all crews are safely away. The aim is to prevent any potential drone attacks on nearby individuals or objects. Astro supports the team's idea and avoids giving commands that could provoke drones near his team.

Teams are far enough on their way back to base. Astro commands the drones to return. He asks Natasha to do the same with her observation drone before they destroy the shuttle with the explosives. Upon receiving the return command, the drones engage in a high-speed dogfight around the shuttle before ultimately crashing into it and self-destructing. Astro orders his team to destroy the shuttle now with confidence that the drones will not chase after them and attack. Fragments fly as the shuttle explodes, leaving a small crater.

Chapter twenty-two. All The Pieces In Place

C M, Tarak, and Duke arrive at the Monarto Zoo in a delivery van. They enter disguised to avoid being noticed by the general staff and head directly to the secure laboratory. Information from informants like Leia, Sami, Philip, and Jolene gathered by Sarah passes through Tarak or CM, only keeping the laboratory hidden from the Elite. Leia was right. There's something important happening at the Monarto lab that the Elite should've known. Loyal Mixed Humans are planning a revolt. The scale and stakes exceed Leia's and her co-workers' imagination. To ensure the coup's success, the team must keep their Earth arrival hidden for thirty-six hours.

Tarak is an imposing figure, at six feet tall with a solid fit appearance from many hours in the gym. As soon as he walks into the command center, he gains their respect and takes charge. His initial task is to contact the outliers and, in doing so, indirectly, contact Sarah. Acting as a new outlier wanting to be part of the network after the church explosion, he routes his transmissions through the homestead coordinates he gave Sarah. He also contacts Joe for support and verification under his cover name as a genuine outlier. Joe, as the lead recruiter in the general area and core supporters of the coup, pay attention to hidden messages in the general chat with the new outlier. As they welcome him, many offer advice and news from their areas, which helps Tarak to get a good idea of the overall mood. Joe also discreetly shares codes during open conversations to notify those involved in the coup to add the new outlier to their contacts. He also tells them to go dark, informing them that the ball is now in play.

Tarak, after establishing himself with the known supporting outliers, sends them part (A) of the plan and advises them to take action to protect themselves. He requests the outliers, and those trusted inside the compound spread the message about the Elite's upcoming virus release, causing more casualties than just the Unhuman. Initially, the coup's plan involves adding pressure and confusion while the Elite frantically try to work out what is happening. The Elite's greatest fear is an uprising, adding strain on their resources. CM aims to capitalize on chaos, exposing Elite's vulnerability, seizing their compounds and providing residents with an alternative lifestyle choice.

It is not without complications. The Earth left to itself outside the compound walls for nearly two centuries has seen the Unhuman and wild vegetation expand. It will take a lot of negotiation, possibly some fierce fighting with the truly Unhuman to expand livable areas and have a free life outside the compound walls. Not everyone will support this change, as some believe only the true Elite Pure should inhabit the Earth. Mixed and Unhuman may view this as a chance to eliminate the Elite, Pure, and other species before their own extinction. The truth is no perfect answer exists. All that is certain is that the Elite seek to alter the current lifestyle solely for their personal benefit.

As Tarak begins stage (A), Duke collaborates with the Monarto software team. Their goal is to disable defensive spy satellites, causing them to descend and disintegrate in the Earth's atmosphere. The Moon lab was in control of all defenses systems, so they expect minimal resistance from off-world Elite. Earth compounds only have a small group of defense personnel, security moats, a few hand weapons and drones.

Duke re-arranges his thick, bold-rim glasses and removes a small notepad and a pen from his shirt's pocket. He sits up in his chair at the keyboard and frantically types. Flicking through his notepad now and then and scribbling notes on another piece of paper as he adjusts his malware coding. Once completed, he will supply Natasha, the Port Lincoln engineers, Murray Bridge, and Yorke Peninsula with a code to send to all their servers connected to the network. This coding will interact with the codes he currently has running, causing more shutdowns and chaos. Computers the team already have control of in each compound are systematically rewriting codes on all the defense systems. Once activated, the new code will give the impression that the Elite engineers have regained control. However, Duke has now gained remote access to control and override crucial parts of the Elite's systems.

Chapter twenty-three. Making Chemicals

C M is in the laboratory working with the scientist to produce part (B) of the plan. It relies on the Elite following the instructions in the virus boxes, multiplying and releasing the deadly virus so CM can give the order to set his plan in motion. A team in the Monarto laboratory replicates a catalyst drug to activate the virus' killing part held by the Port Lincoln laboratory. The Elite, following the protocols for release, will send one of each of the tubes from the shuttle to other Elite compound laboratories around Australia to be replicated.

Left in the shuttle were two labeled boxes: one, a vaccine for Elite protection, the other, a virus along with instructions that all Elite leaders must consume the vaccine before opening test tube two anywhere on Earth.

Labeled virus instructions say it will infect and sterilize any Unhuman or Mixed Humans with over thirty-five percent alteration to what the Elite deem to be Pure Human DNA. Elite in power wanting it believe that it is what they asked for and will kill anyone with above three percent altered DNA.

The Monarto laboratory team has built the catalyst drug to be used alongside the DNA samples gained by CM's team over the past fifteen years. These samples are from individuals in leadership roles who have shown a willingness to release a virus in order to eradicate specific humans. This is clear from their behavior at meetings and in their actions. They will load the catalyst drug into two hundred miniature drones, which are about the size and appearance of a large wasp, sending them to each Elite compound. When in the correct location, the wasp drones will spray amounts of the catalyst drug onto a subject or into the general area they are in. The catalyst drug is harmless to anything apart from its designated target, it has no human detectable smell, making it difficult to sense or notice. It remains active until wiped off with cleaning chemical. If a wasp drone distributes it as an airborne spray, it will semi-suspend and drift down, filling any room. All drones carry the same drug and can maneuver through obstacles to reach their target. The drug will multiply if it enters a non-intended target, and the non-intended subject will exhale it for two to three days. It will die off with the infected person not having any idea they were transmitting it. The catalyst drug design, which originates from the virus the Elite wanted to eliminate Mixed Humans to create their Pure new world, embodies an irony CM and the team enjoy.

To ensure the packages reach their intended location without raising alarms, they use standard courier services. Each package looks like ones the operatives have previously received, which Sami noticed and was instructed not to interfere with after informing Sarah.

The wasp drones are in vacuum-sealed packages that, once exposed to air, will activate, and start their missions to seek their targets and infect them. If multiple targets are in the same room, each drone will release the drug above or around their intended target to ensure they breathe it in. Each drone has two primary targets programmed into their operating system, with operatives receiving them in positions close to the chosen targets. If the Elite Pure followed the instructions and took the vaccine from test tube box one, their fates is now sealed. Not taking the vaccine means they have escaped the first attempt on their lives.

The Elite's vaccine is harmless on its own but contains a detectable tracking device. Once combined, the nanobots in the catalyst drug will confirm a DNA match of the selected target, and the drug will become fatal within forty-eight hours. The coup relies on the Elite's belief as Gods and leaders of the new world, and their urgency to eliminate Mixed Humans, thinking they now possess the drug.

The coup team is playing their hands by causing disruption and recent events, aiming to deceive the Elite into believing it's a perfect cover for covertly distributing their virus. Saying their drones are distributing a non-fatal deterrent spray to protect the Pure communities because of the Unhuman uprising.

CM, Tarak, and Duke have had a massive first day on Earth to give the planned coup the best chance of succeeding. They will now get some rest, leaving the heads of each section to finish the tasks they have set in motion. Tomorrow will reveal if the Elite obeyed instructions and took the vaccine, setting their own fate in motion.

Chapter twenty-four. Crew Two

Cosimo, Electra, Aurora, Mira and Logan are going to do their part of the mission in Adelaide's city center, on the top floor of the largest building in the CBD. It was one of the last buildings constructed as the Elite were leaving Earth. Standing Fifty stories high on the corner of Victoria Drive and King William Road, with a front yard stretching to North Terrace. Surrounded by a wall initially three meters high, it has now increased in height to six meters. Adelaide's Governor's House and army parade grounds stood on this land in 2035 before this impressive building replaced it. Two hundred meters wide, two hundred and fifty meters deep, and one hundred and eighty-seven meters high. The top three stories have laboratories, garages, and workshops, with the rest of the building housing approximately forty-five percent of all the Mixed humans living in the city center.

The second part of the coup team arrived in Adelaide at the governor's building. After receiving an update on in-house preparations, they showered and went straight to bed. To ensure continuity and control, at least three members of the Moon base team will always be awake, similar to hibernation cycles. In the morning, they will awaken right before CM, Duke, and Tarak prepare for bed to receive an update.

The Mixed humans occupy the Governor's building, which is well maintained and hasn't impacted any of Sarah's missions, so she has never had a reason to enter. She is well-known within the community for assisting building occupants in times of trouble or when they are being stalked by an Unhuman. Even before they became part of the Earth alliance against the Elite. Climate change has widened the Torrens River, and it now laps at the Victoria Drive end of the building. The Mixed now uses it as a river to ship boats and other craft out to sea through its outlet at West Beach. This allows them to spy on the Elite's compounds at Port Lincoln, Mount Gambier, and York Peninsula.

Compared to CM and Tarak, the rest of the Moon coup team is young. Tarak is middle-aged at eighty years old, and CM is in his one hundred and twenty-third year. Most of the group in the Moon lab is new, with ages ranging from thirty-six to seventy. They joined the team in various cycles, including the most recent one. Typical days in the Lab community include time in the entertainment areas or working out in the gym. They keep their bodies in top physical condition to ensure any vacation time or missions they enjoy on Earth, they will cope with its gravity. CM put all his like-minded people together on the same shift, sadly, loyal workers given the chance to escape the Moon and become part of the coup rejected the idea. They all met with laboratory accidents, or killed in their hibernation modules by software errors before they could alert anyone outside of the laboratory.

It is five o'clock in the morning and CM calls the governor's team to update them on how it all went in Monarto overnight. After the briefing, Cosimo and Electra inspect the drones and weaponry with the Adelaide workshop teams, while Aurora plans the coordination for the attacks on the Elite compounds. Sarah is many years older than Aurora, though they look quite similar. Aurora's black hair is much shorter than Sarah's, and her eyes are hazel, unlike Sarah's almost glowing green eyes. Aurora, like others on the team, comes from a family that hibernated and was part of a previous lab team. Having experienced two hibernation cycles alongside Sarah, they have a strong professional connection and knowledge of operational procedures for missions. Aurora hopes this will continue when Sarah hears from her in her new position. Before she reaches out to Sarah, Aurora uses secure communication devices to message select Mixed Humans and leaders in South Australia. Her goal is to create a comprehensive list of weaponry, vehicles, and skills possessed by Mixed Humans supporting the coup. She asks leaders to summarize resistance from Mixed communities, local obstacles, and the positions of any Elite weapons.

Aurora also contacts Joe. He lives a dual life with one residence on the farm that Sarah visited, where they all known him in Monarto and Murray Bridge as Joe. Then he has his secret outlier homestead, where he acts under the cover name of Roderick. Similar to other outliers or associates, they communicate securely via radio channels. If he must have a video chat, he disguises himself enough so that Joe and Roderick appear as two quite different people. Even Sarah doesn't know Joe is Roderick, one of her trusted and most helpful outliers.

Chapter twenty-five. New Mission

Aurora and Roderick must now execute the plan's critical part, part (C). It may have unforeseen consequences, and the rollout may be bumpy. They don't expect a warm response from Sarah when she is told about the coup, and they explain the new mission to her. CM, Aurora, and Joe hope Sarah has worked out the messages and knows she is not alone, so she will expect contact from someone. They doubt she will understand their approach to the coup. Sarah, like Joe, goes under different names in her outlier circles that do not match any of her undercover names she uses in towns. Her favorite name is the one she uses in her Petwood compound, which is Sabrina.

Roderick contacts her, at first in a general chat, and after some public communications with other outliers, he asks Sabrina if she is available for a private chat. She accepts his request, as Roderick has been a trusted outlier for many years. It is rare for Sabrina or any of her other outlier identities to accept private chats, as most of her compounds use Automated Intelligence, resulting in only general chat responses being generated. Her more meaningful conversations are all by direct message, using different methods when the information or favor she is asking for requires it. As Sarah can seldom get to a homestead to send messages or receive them in real time, she gets one of her private drones to go to a GPS coordinate on her mission route and sit dormant. Sarah then can load or receive a message, and it returns to the homestead to send the response. Sabrina and Roderick open a secure line:

Hi Sabrina. How are you doing? Is everything okay?

Hi Roderick, all is well in my homestead, how is yours?

All is well here, Sabrina, but I have critical information for you. Are we secure and free to talk?

Yes, are you okay? Is something wrong? Roderick.

I am well. I have news about the explosion in Adelaide.

Yes, I have heard chatter on the communication channels. What do you know? What has happened?

Sabrina, I must apologize!

Why?

It is Joe Sarah. You are safe. CM is leading a coup. We were behind your escape from the church and are here to take the Elite down, and we need your help.

WTF, why, why keep me out of the loop? How did this happen?

We thought it was the best way to ensure your safety. If the coup failed, CM wanted you to be free, but he couldn't trust communicating with you except through recent messages.

What help do you require?

Sabrina, we want you to stay under this name for now. The Moon base laboratory is gone. They also believe you were in the church when it exploded.

Aurora is listening and wants to talk and update you. Will you allow us to do that, please?

Sarah's head is spinning. She sensed someone orchestrating everything, preparing her for something before hibernation. She no longer feels alone as she trusts both Joe and his alter-ego, Roderick. It also explains why Roderick has always played a vital role in parts and data acquisition in the past. The pleasantries shock Sarah, as she is accustomed to being instructed. It gives her a sense of power, confidence, and respect that they are asking, not telling her.

Yes, I would like answers from Aurora.

Okay, I will patch her in on the call. Please accept her.

Hi Sabrina, I wish to apologize. We needed you to complete the compound missions, not knowing of the impending coup, so all your responses and actions would be natural, as they have always been so no one would raise suspicion.

Did you not trust me?

We always trusted you. We didn't want to affect or have you change your style. CM also wanted to ensure your safety.

Is CM alive? What happened?

After you escaped, CM and seven others, including myself, escaped the Moon laboratory before destroying it and are here on Earth. We intend to overrun the Elite and stop the rollout of the virus that will kill all Mixed and Unhuman, Australia wide.

Your team has worked towards this goal, as have I through my missions. Why has this changed and he not contacted me?

CM has always had your best interests at heart. He is busy making sure we will win! Elite Pure aimed to eliminate all non-Pure, defying our ethics and those of the disapproving Pure majority. Senior Elite aim is for an acceptance of only 3% alteration, erasing all other Unhuman and Mixed Humans. That would be Ninety percent of the population around Australia, including Murray Bridge and compounds like it with a more liberal acceptance of Mixed Humans. We have recruited a networked of key Pure operatives. You have met some of them who have given you messages, boxes or waved to you on the streets. You are not alone. We have also hidden your movements and helped you in your covert missions to build up trust with a core group of outliers, Mixed Humans, and almost Unhuman acquaintances.

What do you need from me? What are the tablets you have given me? Are they to protect me from the virus?

We want you to create a team and spread the word with Mixed and Unhuman. The ones that know you, trust you, as you have helped them out in times of danger. No, tablets won't help with the virus. They are to purge the pills that the Elite tricked you into taking to stay loyal. The drug manipulated your beliefs and restricted your thoughts on freedom by convincing you that if you stopped taking them, your abilities would disappear. You will feel stronger and faster once they are gone from your system. CM changed your supply to a weaker dose, resulting in increased vitality and heightened emotions.

WTF, they reduced my abilities when I was putting my life on the line for them! FOR you! Why? Why should I help after hearing all this? They haven't treated me equally.

Only you possess the abilities required to do this. You were born for it.

Sabrina?

Sarah doesn't respond. She now feels yet again trapped under a different name but being used for the same operation.

Sabrina?

Sarah?

Aurora realizes Sarah will not respond and hangs up to give her time to process all the latest information. Sarah's refusal or rebellion will make any attempted overthrow harder or impossible.

Chapter twenty-six. One "S" Or Two

S arah has had information for the second time in forty-eight hours, which has taken her by surprise. She thought those overseeing her were completely unaware of all her extracurricular activities. The secret homesteads covertly helping outliers in gathering data or materials. Sarah again feels trapped as a tool, nothing more than a means to a different ending. She also realizes that timing is critical for their plan to work, so her warrior instinct kicks in. She cannot just sit in her homestead and hope things will work out. If not stopped, the Elite will create a virus to eradicate anything impure, including her. Sarah decides she must take on the role of Sabrina and calls Roderick on the homestead's private chat Line:

Roderick?

Roderick, are you on the channel?

Hi Sabrina.

Roderick, as per our earlier conversation, can you have Aurora contact me?

Yes I will, Stand by.

Sabrina, are you there?

Yes, I am here. What mission do you have for me?

Please collaborate with Mixed in Adelaide to secure their support. You have contacts in Adelaide and outliers around South Australia. We're in a CBD building, ready to offer you any help you need.

Can't you use the Humans in that building to communicate with the other Mixed in Adelaide?

The Unhuman have control over the night, tunnels, and various town buildings. Most residents here rarely leave the building and have minimal contact with the broader community. There are also limited lines of communication between different Mixed Humans. They are alone, like outliers, or part of a small, loyal group that lacks trust in others. We need you to lead them to help us win the upcoming war.

Why do you think I can help? They see me as the enemy.

Despite being seen as the enemy by some, you have the skills required to unite them. Your vehicle represents power, and you have control over it. We reprogrammed it to only follow your orders when you were in Mount Gambier. We also gave you tranquilizers in certain missions for you to use that only paralyze the subjects, but they could still hear you. You have experienced their effects when sampling Eithan Hawk. Sabrina, will you help us? We are asking you not forcing you to do this.

Sabrina?

Sabrina?

Chapter twenty-seven. Adelaide Alive

Sabrina doesn't respond to Aurora. She is uncertain about what to do. CM was to be in his final hibernation and with the Pure planning to unleash a virus, she knows it's now or never. Sabrina thinks through her options, she could die in a coup attempt or by the Elite's releasing a virus. Only one option offers freedom, and its best chance is during the Earth and off Earth chaos. She plans to return to Adelaide and assess the public actions following the virus news leak. She can stay in her vehicle and bring a few drones for added protection. Sabrina sends out a message to the outliers to inform them of her intention to go to the city center. She asks them to reach out to any of the Mixed humans they may know in and around the Adelaide CBD to gauge their feelings. Sabrina expects Roderick to hear her message, so he will inform Aurora of her plan.

Sabrina faces a new battle for survival, defending herself from Mixed, Unhuman, and Elite Pure's loyal followers. She dresses in one of her favorite-colored skin suits and jumps into her vehicle. The deep purple metallic-looking suit makes her look more approachable and noticeable. Purple has always been the color that projects creativity, royalty, femininity, and spirituality. It is also associated with magic, peace, extravagance, and pride. Sabrina hopes those that see her in it may feel more likely to approach her than in her traditional black suit. She checks her weapons and commands two defensive drones to assist her, one to scan in front and one to protect her from behind. Flying low and fast, she will traverse the valleys of Nairn, Oakbank, and Uraidla before making her way to the outskirts of Adelaide. From there, she will enter from the east and drive down the Parade through Norwood.

Sabrina has not decided on her best plan yet. She'll scan the CBD outskirts to see how people react, staying in her vehicle as any interaction outside of it, in buildings or tunnels, could lead to her being trapped. Separated from her vehicle and lacking extra drone backup, she'll be in a life-or-death situation. Then having to rely on Roderick, Aurora or Mixed Humans on her side, being willing to help.

Unrest and heightened street activity are inevitable after the church explosion. The nearby Convention center is an almost Unhuman camp of bat-like creatures, and the Entertainment center houses a kettle of Hawk-like humans. Panther and leopard creatures hide in underground tunnels, derelict buildings, or vegetation around the city. All would have heard and scattered from the explosion. Some individuals have not yet returned, and those who are still in Adelaide will be agitated. Pure may send a team to investigate the church incident and identify any potential involvement. If they see Sarah, they will tell the Elite she is alive, affecting the coup's plans. Time is against Sabrina and the coup, so she understands that being proactive is better than doing nothing.

Sabrina lands on the Parade, and her vehicle takes on a more modern shape of a 2026 model of the Hellcat Challenger in majestic blue. Those watching her will notice the similar appearance, recognize her and her vehicle, but she hopes it shows she is in a different mood and with a changed attitude. Driving on Norwood Parade, she notices the typical mood and appearance of the town. Primitive individuals riot for their own interests, seeking food and water. All customs that worked to give relative calm and natural balance appear to be now lost. Respect from years of living together has gone since the news or rumors have spread of the church blowing up, and the meeting in Murray Bridge about the virus release.

This situation is more volatile than any Sabrina has experienced on these streets. She's witnessed many violent acts and territorial disputes, but this stands apart. It is like animals sensing an impending earthquake or an approaching predator, but instead of fleeing, they are fighting each other. They are aware of impending danger but lack knowledge of the aggressor's identity or reliable allies. Fighting each other for resources and to be the top authority, which they believe will give them the best chance of survival.

Sabrina drives further into the city's outer ring to investigate if the same is occurring on Adelaide's central streets. The chaos may be lower in the inner CBD as the balance of Mixed using the same communication network is greater than the outer city limits. If it is more widespread, it will be difficult for Sabrina to isolate any subjects to communicate with.

Approaching the end of Norwood Parade and turns onto Flinders Street, noticing that even though there is panic in localized places, they are still showing respect. So far, they have let her pass with no aggression directed at her directly. Her vehicle has taken on many shapes, but there is no mistaking who is behind the wheel of the latest one. The Elite will instantly know if they see Sarah's Cat that she is alive. She can only hope it adds to the confusion, suspecting Sarah has gone rogue and release the virus knowing it will also kill her.

Sabrina heads along Bartels Road, past the parklands, which are overgrown in parts, but with other areas still immaculately maintained, with no sign of any activity. Sabrina drives down Pirie Street, with movement in the shadows as creatures dart in and out of hiding. The atmosphere is pretty normal with none of the rioting seen in Norwood.

The inner city has always been more civilized than the surrounding suburbs, as communication outside the CBD between the Mixed is sporadic and sometimes less than civil. However, it is efficient enough to keep etiquette amongst individuals, groups, and sometimes, the Unhuman population. Sabrina turns north and heads down King William Street towards the building that Aurora is in. They will notice her as will the more influential Mixed Humans that live on this central city street. Sabrina stops and parks in the center of the intersection of King William and North Terrace. This will catch everyone's attention and make them notice that she's alive, has a new attitude. Sabrina waits to put a sense of doubt and curiosity in their minds about what action she will take next. Her drones circle high above in a two-hundred-meter radius of her location, appearing like vultures circling a carcass while they scan the area and send Sabrina images and data. After a five-minute pause, she speeds away to see what remains of her old compound.

Arriving at the old church, she can see what devastation she caused. There is not much left of it. The explosion of the ammunition stores, power supplies, and her drones resulted in a massive crater, causing damage to nearby buildings and the Morphett Street bridge. While Sabrina sits and looks at the destruction, she feels a sense of freedom. Alerts from her drones soon interrupt it as they detect an incoming drone launched from the old governor's building. While it is heading toward her, she has also noticed signs of human activity in the ruins around the church. Sabrina is on high alert. The activity could be Mixed Humans looking to salvage something valuable or Unhuman scavenging. She suspects Aurora or someone from the governor's compound launched the drone. Allowing it to get closer, she notices it heading towards the area of activity on the church grounds. While it hovers, Sabrina and her drones prepare to act if required. Seeing Natasha and a young man walking with their hands up shocks her. A drone lands in front of them, leaving something on the ground. The drone then flies towards her vehicle with a sign illuminated on it "Sabrina", and she allows it to land. As it interacted with Natasha, Sabrina feels safe to step out of her vehicle and approach it.

Sabrina gets out of her vehicle with her hand pistol drawn. Natasha and her partner stay still and watch Sabrina as she approaches the drone. The compartment bay opens and reveals pieces of equipment, a communication device, and two other boxes. Written on them in the same invisible ink is the now common text "we support you." Sabrina is feeling much deeper emotions, and it is making her even more anxious than normal. She has not felt these intense irrational responses to a situation before. Sabrina places the communication necklace on, gets back in the Cat and drives off as the conversation starts.

Hi Sabrina, it is Aurora here and Natasha. Any contacts you make can use the chips in the boxes to communicate with you securely.

Natasha, can you hear me?

Yes, Aurora.

Sabrina is on the line too.

Hi Sabrina, it has been an exciting couple of days.

Yes, it has Natasha. I am still processing it all. There is some unrest on the streets.

The news has spread about the Elite's plans. I am investigating this explosion with my colleague to report back to the Elite in Port Lincoln.

What is that report going to say?

What would you like it to say Sabrina?

After the explosion, someone must have seen me leaving the church, so they must suspect that I have escaped. If you don't report it, you'll be in danger because people will witness me later today. They will suspect I have gone rogue and blew up the Moon laboratory as well. That might be the best choice, as they may believe it is only one person attacking them, not a group attack. What are your feelings, Natasha?

Yes, it will be hard to cover up the fact that you escaped. I intend to return to Mount Gambier and see if the Elite follows the virus release instructions. I will join forces with those against the plan and assist in the coup within the compound until someone exposes my cover.

Okay, this afternoon and evening I will try to contact those around Adelaide in the Mixed Human areas and encourage them all to band together and help. Aurora needs to update me on the plan after I contact those who will join us.

We will have drones ready to help you from the Governor's compound here in Adelaide, Sabrina, if required.

Thanks Aurora.

My colleague and I will head back to Mount Gambier now and inform them your vehicle at least escaped the church, and you were likely in it. However, it is impossible to be sure because of the catastrophic damage. If someone spots a vehicle like yours in Adelaide, it will cause follow-up requests, giving us additional time. We can add as much as possible to the theory you have gone rogue.

Thank you, Sabrina and Natasha. We expect to keep control of 90% of the defense drones and systems for another 72 hours, making it unlikely for any Elite support to be available from other compounds. Those we have recruited will delay any attempts to get systems or other weapons ready in Elite compounds. Thank you all for your support. We are doing what's right.

In conversation with Aurora and Natasha, Sabrina circled the city to be visible. She asks Aurora if there is any data on any of her previous subjects. Aurora acknowledges the request and instructs one tech to upload what they have to Sabrina's vehicle.

Sabrina needs to contact the Mixed Humans soon while it's still early in the afternoon. They avoid going out at night when the Unhuman have the upper hand. Physically meeting with a core group of Mixed that supports the coup will assess their willingness to help in the face of danger. As they know, it will expose them as supporters of Sabrina and make them targets for the Elite. Loyal soldiers or spies sent by the Elite will already be in town to quell any uprising if it starts and may lurk in buildings surrounding meeting locations. Aurora and the crew have allowed certain drone activity from Elite compounds, keeping the coup's actual mission undercover as the Elite believe they have control over their principal aim of using drones to spray the supplied eradication virus.

Sabrina puts out a call on her outlier channel for them to contact any trusted Mixed Humans in town to meet her. She arranges five meetings locations the Mixed living nearby will be familiar with. This will also reduce the diversity of attendees at each meeting, as they will be in a city square spread evenly throughout the CBD. Victoria Square is in the city center, while Light Square lies in the northwest quadrant, near her former church compound. Hindmarsh square in the Northeast quadrant, Hurtle Square in the Southeast, and Whitmore Square in the southwest.

While tall buildings could hold Elite soldiers surrounding these Squares, there is sufficient tree cover to make it difficult for them to attack effectively. Sabrina informs each group of the meeting time at each location, starting with Light Square and then in the order of Hindmarsh, Victoria, Hurtle, and finishing in Whitmore. She did not choose this order by accident; it is to reflect a math symbol ∃ to say there is another way, the existence of a variable.

The initial meeting will start at 2:15 PM and will continue for five to ten minutes. Sabrina will then drive around the city to each other meeting in order at the times of 2:45 PM, 3:15 PM, 4:45 PM and finishing at Whitmore at 5:15 PM. There is less chance of any attacks during the first and second meetings, but if anyone is watching her, they may target the other meetings.

Driving slowly into Light Square at 2:10 PM, the sun is still relatively high at this time in late summer. The tree's dense canopy makes the square quite dim. Sabrina quickly scans the area with her drones to ensure no Unhuman is hiding in trees or any other sign of danger. Sabrina knows that some Mixed will walk in and may already hide in the general area, others will arrive with some type of vehicle. The independent Mixed normally use a motorcycle or scooter as they are easy to get in and out of apartment lifts and move throughout the city. Most Mixed live in the old University Campus and the adjacent buildings. Others will have to travel further from apartment buildings scattered around the outer blocks. Sabrina is not hoping for numbers, more of an assortment of willing Mixed Human supporters from nearby. Having attendees from unique buildings increases the impact of word-of-mouth.

Chapter twenty-eight. Meet And Greet

Sabrina parks in the square and exits her vehicle. Light beams pierce the canopy and reflect on the Hellcat and her suit. She confidently stands alongside her vehicle and beside a large tree. While it does not ensure her safety, being between two solid objects with the drones at opposite angles is her best defensive posture. With her weapons ready inside the vehicle, she stands with authority and waits to see who will arrive. Her drones track several targets that are slowly approaching, keeping Sabrina informed of their locations. Her eyesight, hearing, and agility are all advantages over the Mixed Humans. One or two attacking her would be little competition for her, taking on a number may pose a challenge. Her new emotions and standing still make her feel like prey rather than a hunter.

She can hear a speeding vehicle enter under the tree canopy. Getting an extra adrenaline kick from the sounds of the vehicle raises her heart rate and fight-or-flight feelings. The drugs the Elite forced her to take are wearing off. These new, powerful feelings are distracting her. She is wondering if it was a good idea to give her these new emotions after being a methodical, lethal warrior her whole life. Her mind quickly focuses back on the task and the warrior kicks back in. The vehicle noise stops, and the drones inform her that at least fifteen targets are now circling her. None of the targets seem game enough to approach her just yet until one slowly rides out on an electric motorbike. Sitting on what resembles a Harley Davidson chopper, is a lady with long blonde hair, wearing a black tank top with an old whiskey logo on it. Her toned arms from gym workouts have bold tattoos on them, one arm has a panther from her shoulder down to the elbow. The other arm has a dragon, with its wings open and claws out. Bold cursive writing is on the inside of each forearm. The lady slowly gets off her bike and walks towards Sabrina. She is tall and slim with pistols hanging off the hips of her tight denim jeans. Sabrina stands still as she approaches to within a meter of her. The lady speaks.

You don't know me, Sarah, but you have saved my life once or twice in the past. I hear you are going by a new name these days. My name is Tova. How can I help you Sabrina?

Sabrina recognizes Tova and remembers the times she has intervened to help her while she was holding her own against the Unhuman attackers. A wry smile appears on Sabrina's face as she thinks, this lady always finds trouble. I think I'll like her. Sabrina looks Tova in the eyes.

Tova, I will just reach in and get something out of the box in my vehicle.

She reaches into the Cat, pulls out a few communication chips, and hands them to Tova.

Please take one and give the rest to anyone who you think might help us. I am putting together a force of Mixed and Unhuman to overrun the Elite leaders as they are determined to wipe us all off the earth and expand from their compounds. Our vision is a world where every individual may live their life, regardless of species.

Tova responds as more people approach.

Dam Girl, have you got some kind of death wish? Taking on the Elite, they have so many defense systems, they will wipe us out before we can do anything.

I am not alone in this quest. We will have help, which I can explain to you later. We have limited time to act. Can you spread the word? If we do not defend ourselves now, the Elite will attack us with a virus within six months and we will all die.

There are now fifteen people from diverse Mixed Human communities standing around, ranging from slightly Mixed to verging on Unhuman. Light Square has a higher population of Mixed because of its distance from the Unhuman territories. The turnout is higher than she expected, with everyone listening attentively while maintaining some distance. Sabrina introduces herself and gives out communication chips to new people. There are characters she recognizes as she has taken samples from them, others she has helped on the streets and in the underground areas of the city. She requests to be called Sabrina from now on and for them to spread the information they learned today. She also cautions them about potential spies or soldiers the Elite may have in town and to only converse with long-time acquaintances. Sabrina waits for five minutes as the group disperses to help them if need be.

Jumping back into the Cat, Sabrina drives off but doesn't head directly for Hindmarsh Square. She does not want to arrive too early to attract attention to the location. All upcoming meetings will be more challenging, as troublemakers and specific species may attend them. It is also possible someone could enter a meeting intending to harm her. The southern, east, and west squares have more diverse populations. These areas have a greater mix of DNA types with a higher percentage of alterations. The eastern square is where the modern crowd live, who breed with like-minded altered DNA types. While still mainly human-looking, they show various signs of altered appearance representing their chosen species. Hindmarsh and Hurtle squares on their western sides still have high-rise buildings kept well-maintained by robotic maintenance devices, as they are still part of the inner city. The eastern sides of both squares have buildings deteriorating sporadically because of the expanse of parklands surrounding and encroaching on them. These Parklands have become quite overgrown with lower building floors now intertwined with the vegetation. Prime territory for nesting and living for the almost Unhuman and wild Unhuman species. Challenges may arise with these diverse range of attendees or there is also the possibility that no one will attend.

Sabrina drives in from the north on Pulteney Street and veers sharply right then left as she enters the square's intersection, stopping at a forty-five-degree angle with the front of the Hellcat pointing down Grenfell Street. The dense trees and overgrown vegetation provide Sabrina cover from the tall buildings surrounding the square and any sniper attack. Anyone, regardless of their species, hiding in the foliage, must come out and meet her in the open. Sabrina parks at the intersection to ensure a clear view and personal protection. The drones use their sensors to scan the area for anyone hiding in the vegetation that might hold weapons. Stepping out of the Hellcat, she strategically positions a weapon on the roof and carries another on her hip, prepared for any unexpected events. The low treetop canopy means her two drones must circle just above her head. It is a less welcoming optic, but she believes it is the safest way for her to approach this meeting.

Standing still for a brief time after exiting her vehicle, she can hear approaching noises over the breeze gently rustling the treetop canopy. A drone stops and holds position, looking directly west down Grenfell Street, as Sabrina has her back to it. She believes Western Mixed Humans are friendlier than those from the other three directions. People approach Sabrina from behind, on foot and in vehicles, as shadows move above the tree canopy. One of the above shadows rapidly increases in size, causing the western approaching Mixed Humans to stop and hide. The creature's fast-swooping approach directly at Sabrina causes its shape and wingspan to be projected on the canopy. Mixed that had not yet taken cover do as it reduces in size as it passes over Sabrina, sores directly up into the air and out of sight. It does a barrel roll high in the sky, then flies down at speed, crashing through the canopy to land with force just meters from her in a crouching spring-loaded position, ready to re-launch, with its wings fully extended it looks directly at Sabrina. It is a male with strong square shoulders, a large chest, biceps, ripped abdominal muscles, and powerful legs. She recognizes him and finds him curiously attractive. She does not flinch as he looks at the gun and the box on top of the vehicle, slowly standing while retracting his wings. In a deep voice, he starts the conversation.

Sarah, why are you calling us here today?

Sabrina answering authoritatively.

To save you and those like you from extinction.

The man, with eagle-like features, twists his head in a 270-degree range before responding.

How and why would you do that?

We intend to remove those in the Elite Pure from power that wish to wipe out all Mixed Human and Unhuman from Earth.

Eagleman lets out a deep groan and steps back several paces.

Their threats have persisted for years. Why is it so important now?

Sabrina informs him that a virus to eliminate only completely wild Unhuman was proving to be difficult. Their goal now is to eradicate anything impure. Her team have destroyed the virus and technology they have been working on for decades, but it won't take them long to re-engineer a virus that can infect and kill anyone living with changed DNA or simply anything on Earth, including Pure humans who don't have a vaccine.

The approaching Mixed have now joined the group, as Sabrina and Eagleman talk. As he turns his back to Sabrina, they edge a little closer. Eagleman chirps while he raises an arm, and in an instant, the other two wing humans land with a similar arrival technique, one male and one female. The emergence of additional altered humans from the surrounding vegetation further unsettles the Mixed Humans. Some leap from their hiding spots, landing on all fours before standing vertically, while others slowly emerge, representing Panthera humans, leopards, panthers, and tigers. They all stand at a distance from each other, apart from their apparent ability and some skin markings that represent their species. When standing upright at a distance, they look relatively human. Their faces, slightly altered with pointed ears and less prominent noses that have darkened in color and eyes that are closer together. All of them present can speak fluent English and with their exceptional hearing, they will have heard all the conversation.

Sabrina knows her pressing issue is with the Mixed Human behind her. Having lost friends in fights with wild creatures, they are now timid. She encourages them to approach. They move forward but are reluctant to get too close. Sabrina wants them to stand, face one another, and realize their shared battle. She hands out tags to Eagleman and in conversation with him she turns her back on the Mixed. This does not instill confidence in the Mixed Human as Sabrina appears to be giving the wild creatures greater attention. A few who trust Sabrina and feel she has control slowly approach. As they do, the group now assembled behind Eagleman rush forward in an act of aggression towards them. Sabrina's drones act in a millisecond, firing warning shots into the air. Tension is rising between the two groups, with Sabrina right in the middle. She instinctively grabs her side weapon and the one off the roof of the Hellcat. Two drones hover at head height, pointing weapons directly at both groups. She needs to avoid a conflict, or everything will escalate into widespread panic and an all-out war, eliminating large numbers of each species. Effectively doing the Elite's work for them.

In a powerful voice, Sabrina calls for unity, reminding them of their collective fate and the potential consequences of failure. Fearing Sabrina and her drones, the wild creatures all step back, prancing and moving in an agitated manner. She gives out more communication devices to those who displayed leadership, telling them to disperse and go home. Sabrina didn't want this type of commotion as it will attract attention and disruptions to future meetings.

Chapter twenty-nine. Center Of The City

Victoria Square is in the center of the CBD and is well-maintained, with manicured bushes, trees and several roofed structures that will offer protection to anyone attending the meeting. Sabrina is not expecting a great attendance. She hopes that at least one representative from each of the four inhabited buildings will be brave or interested enough to take the risk to meet her. When she arrives on time, she is surprised to see a couple of Mixed Humans she recognizes waiting for her. They are typical of the Mixed Humans that roam the streets of Adelaide, carrying weapons and dressed in camouflage gear. Svetlana and Brandon are fit-looking individuals, as are a significant percentage of Mixed Humans as it is a necessity for survival, and their interbreeding keeps the genetic population in great physical condition. Unfit or weaker gene humans living outside protected compounds have died off, being unable to defend themselves or gather food and resources. The effort needed to stay alive amongst other classes and species all fighting for survival, with no medical help or food, means only the fit and tough will survive. Sarah has helped Brandon and Svetlana out in the past, even walking them home chatting to them after saving them on the streets of Adelaide. Using her outlier name, they have traded parts and information that their communities have requested over the years. Meeting her as Sabrina will create some queries, while also putting more pieces of the puzzle together for them.

Sabrina exits the Hellcat parked under a structure on the north side of the square. Together, Svetlana and Brandon approach her and realize Sabrina is Sarah. Sabrina explains she blew the church up and that a fight is coming to ensure the safety of all mixed and Unhuman alike. She asks if the other two buildings will send a representative. Svetlana explains that surrounding building communities cooperate and support each other as society, but the other buildings choose not to be further involved. Sabrina gives Brandon and Svetlana four communication chips each. She asks them to give one to a trusted representative in each of the other two large buildings. Then the others to anyone they believe will gather numbers to support a fight against the Elite. As they end their conversation, shots ring out from rooftops at opposite ends of the square. They all duck for cover. Sabrina asks them who or what is in each building. Brandon tells her they are storage or food growing areas and that both building's floors are all sealed off, requiring codes to enter each level. The emergency stairwells would be the only way up to the roof or down. Drones ascend, flying behind buildings to the shooters' positions.

For now, the structure in the city square provides some protection. If Sabrina leaves, the Hellcat will protect her, but Svetlana and Brandon will face death. Sabrina has never transported a living human or Unhuman in her vehicle before. She could have the Hellcat open its skin, creating a doorway for them to enter, but she is unsure if it will let them pass. CM and the team told her she has total control of the vehicle after the software upgrade, so it is possible they would have expected she may need to carry a passenger at some point, but it is all theoretical. Sabrina asks them if they would like to enter the vehicle, explaining it may not let them or it may chop off an arm or leg as the opening closes. Svetlana, looking at Sabrina, pushes her pinky finger on her non-dominant right hand into the opening. Nothing happens, Svetlana calls out.

okay well, jumping in could be an option, it appears.

Brandon responds with apprehension in his voice.

It could be an idea, or we could think of a better one.

They all smile at each other. This playful banter is a fresh experience for Sabrina.

After a brief discussion, they all agree that finding out who the person is shooting at them is the best course of action. Sabrina suggests they might be testing their defenses by sacrificing themselves. Others may lurk to attack once they work that out. It might also be to split up the meeting and reduce the chance of others joining. Sabrina's drones fire on the attackers on the rooftops of each building, killing two on one roof while on the other building one shooter escapes to the stairwell. Both drones now focus on the building with the trapped shooter. Sabrina tells Brandon and Svetlana to stay with the Cat. if anyone approaches and you cannot defend yourselves, jump inside and the Cat, it will, or should, protect you. Sabrina finishes her comment off with a turn of her head towards them and smiles. She is embracing these new feelings of sarcasm and comic relief that are creeping into her personality. Sabrina grabs a couple of weapons out of the Hellcat and explains what she is going to do.

Okay, let's go with this plan. I will go over to the building, trank that dude and tie him up. You can then hop in the Cat, or not, and it will take you to the building. What do you think? I have another fun meeting to get to, so we are a tad time critical here.

Brandon and Svetlana agree with Sabrina, and she sprints off to the bottom of the building in the square's northeast corner. It is one of the smaller buildings surrounding the square, only seven stories high. There are a lot of blind turns to negotiate in the stairwell and the shooter can wait for her at any of them.

Sabrina has her drone release a smaller version that can enter the stairwell ahead of her. It will send the video back to Sabrina through the tactical glasses she slips on. She prepares to open the door, anticipating the shooter's presence behind it or on the first floor. He also may be in communication with someone else who can see Sabrina and is waiting to take a shot at her while she is vulnerable at the door.

She flicks the door open and kicks it wide enough for the drone to enter. Two shots ring out, putting holes in the door. Now, Sabrina has a few answers. He is alive, armed and in view of the door, expecting someone. The drone sends video of a clear entrance. Sabrina knows as soon as he hears the door open, he will step out of cover and shoot. Kicking the door open again, she rolls in as her drone lays down cover shots to keep him from stepping out to shoot at her. Once inside, she has her drone fly up the stairs around the corner past the shooter as he tries to shoot it out of the air. The shooter finds himself trapped, unable to go up and needing to pass Sabrina in order to escape. She calls out to him.

I don't want to kill you. Who are you working for?

There is no answer. Sabrina has the drone shoot at his feet. Is it worth your life? Are you alone, or are there more of you?

Sabrina starts up the staircase as the drone keeps him occupied. With one hand, she grips a pistol, and with the other, a tranquilizer gun. The drone moves towards him and as he raises his weapon to take a shot, Sabrina leaps off the riser five steps down up to the first level landing, while firing two shots. One to his trigger hand and a tranquilizer dart into his neck. He drops his weapon as Sabrina lands on her side on the concrete floor with both weapons pointed at him. The tranquilizer takes effect, and he slumps to the ground. Sabrina jumps to her feet, grabs the cable ties she tucked into her weapons belt to tie him up and grabs the communication device he has on him. She leaves him on the landing by the first-floor door so Brandon and Svetlana can drag him inside the room and question him.

Sabrina returns to the vehicle to talk to her new friends, rather than bringing them over in the Cat. She sits down, leaning against the Hellcat's rear wheel, and turns to them.

Hi, so what have you all been up to? How has ya day been? Me, I just shot some dude in the hand and a dart to the neck while flying sideways through the air. The look on his face was priceless. Anyway, you will find him on the first-floor stairwell landing. So, do you guys want a lift over to the building or want to run over yourselves? I have somewhere else I need to be, so a good chat is a short chat.

Svetlana replies, noticing Sabrina's sarcasm.

I guess we will risk the jog over rather than you're driving or getting chopped in half if the Cat doesn't like us. It didn't take my pinkie off me, but it didn't pinkie swear it wouldn't hurt us either.

Sabrina smiles.

Yes, the Cat has had a bit of an attitude in the past, but it is my ride, and I like her! I have his communication device, so I will check it to see if I can learn anything. You guys can grab the ones of the others and anything else worthwhile. Also, question him and find out anything you can when he wakes up, and we will chat later.

Sabrina jumps into her Cat as Svetlana and Brandon stand ready with their weapons. She spins all four wheels on the grass and fishtails across the Square to the road to provide extra cover for them, as they run across to the stairwell. When they are inside, she leaves to head for her meeting at Hurtle Square.

Chapter thirty. Hidden

Arriving at Hurtle Square, no one is there. Sabrina is only a few minutes late and suspects the action in Victoria Square has scared off any willing Mixed wanting to hear firsthand what is now common news spreading through all the communication channels. Because of recent activity in Hindmarsh Square and now Victoria Square, it's not surprising nobody is there.

Sabrina parks as in Hindmarsh Square and waits in her Cat. It is now five minutes after the agreed time, and no one is in the square. A shadow flashes over her vehicle several times, then crashes through the thin canopy over the road. It's Eagleman. He lands with the same authoritative approach, stands, and retracts his wings. He and his pack distributed throughout the city have been watching Sabrina. In his deep voice, he says.

Sabrina, we will stand with you. I will have my followers spread the news, and I will come to your next meeting at Whitmore Square to help you in communicating with that end of town. Others with translation abilities will fly out deeper and communicate to the broader species that we all need to flock together and stand side by side. I can't give you any idea of how they will interpret it, or if they will even care. They may decide to attack you or anyone who trespasses on their land as they are wild and defend their territories fiercely.

Sabrina thanks him for the support and asks if he or his team has any idea who attacked the meeting in Victoria Square.

Eagleman lets out a loud, whaling musical scale of chirps. A short time later, a smaller shadow circles and crashes through the canopy, slightly out of control, trying to land like Eagleman. It's a female bird, also looking quite human, with long fire-red hair and a spotted toned physique.

Hi, Baldy. How can I help you today?

Eagleman turns and looks at her.

Still having trouble sticking those landings Frieda? Agile, cute, but no technique.

She smiles.

Frieda, did you or any others see the attack in the park? Could you tell who they were or how long they had been there before the attack?

Still bleaching ya wig, I see Baldy.

He smiles.

I only arrived after the shooting to check what was happening. There were only four, and I've heard little from others in our flock. I will fly up and check with our high-altitude spotters and ask if they have seen anything.

She turns to Sabrina.

I've been watching you for quite some time. You have pissed off some of us with your tests. I am sure Baldy here and his crew feel similar. While you made some sick, none of us half-breeds have died, but some of the full bred did. I know you were just following orders, and you seem free of them now, so we will help you, as it appears Eddy will do.

She turns to Eagleman.

Is that right, Eddy?

Yes, I will help Sabrina in communicating with other Raptors and help in any way we can for our mutual interest.

Frieda opens her wings, shows off all her athletic ability, darting through the canopy, calling out later Sabrina, Baldy, and some other type of squark. Sabrina looks at Eddy.

So, it's Eddy?

Yes, my name is Eddy, Frieda always likes to stir me up as my genetics are of the Bald Eagle type. We get along well, and her genes of the Peregrine falcon give her extraordinary eyesight, speed, and hearing. They are helpful to our types as a security net and surveillance. We provide strength and protection for them from any threats. The Leopard and Tiger types you met before have a few advantages over us in their what you might call humanist state, so in a one-on-one fight, it could go either way. In these humanistic states, we have banded together like humans of different nationalities. Mostly it works out ok, like humans there are issues and diverse groups. The leaders of each group communicate and have created a type of United Nations deal. The interbred Unhuman and their offspring groups are a different story. They are much wilder and in unhinged communities with no rules.

Good to know, Baldy. Now, let's fly and get to the next meeting.

Eddy Shakes his head and launches into the air. Sabrina yells out as he is leaving.

Hey, you didn't tell me what Frieda squawked at you.

Eddy circles and flies back, skimming the top of the canopy, rustling the leaves. His deep voice penetrates it as he passes her.

Let's just say dealing with you two is going to be trouble.

Hey, good chat Baldy, you know you are going to love it.

Among all squares, Whitmore Square stands out as the most overgrown, hosting a diverse mix of species. Partly because of two service tunnels, each having four lanes that join the northeast of Adelaide city from Hackney Road to the Corner of Anzac Highway. The tunnel's exit is about 600m from Whitmore square in the city's southwest corner. One tunnel is still in service, but because of its emergency exit connections to the second tunnel along its distance, it is unsafe to walk. The other tunnel suffered a partial collapse at its Anzac Highway end and as the maintenance bots don't have complete access to support it, it has now become a haunt for varied species to nest or feed using the emergency escape tunnels to enter and exit the city at night.

Sabrina arrives to find Eddy talking to a couple of other birds, dogs, and cat type humans. There are no mild Mixed Humans to be seen at this meeting either. They exist nearby in small numbers but avoid certain areas where complete Unhuman can lurk. Sabrina is aware of the lurking creatures in buildings and overgrown areas, ready to attack when instructed or desired. Having the leaders at the meeting with them able to give warning messages in their own language not to attack is the best situation Sabrina can hope for. She shares news with those present and nearby, promising updates after she decides on a plan. Right before getting in her car, Frieda swiftly swoops in with her wings tucked back, squawking to identify herself to those who can understand. She opens her wings, stopping on the spot, landing, and retracting them instantly.

She looks and smiles at Eddy.

So, big guy, how was the walk-in? You didn't get to do the fancy plunge through the canopy landing here, did you?

Sabrina looks at Frieda, dips her head in appreciation, with a smile.

Wow Frieda, that was an impressive entrance and landing. Did you see that, Baldy?.

Freida tells the group that the four men were part of a group of six seen together in a black multi-seat vehicle from an unknown location south of the city sometime yesterday.

Frieda, would you and your group team up with Tova if she will search for this vehicle? I'll search and have drones ready at the governor's building if we find anything.

Frieda agrees and Sabrina calls the people who will be involved in the search party using the communication chips she handed out. Each chip has its own address and Sabrina can link whoever she wishes to communicate with as a group or individually. Sabrina calls Aurora, Tova, and Freida and explains the plan to them.

Frieda will send her team to search the city for any vehicle sightings. If they find it, Tova, you move in and observe it until I arrive. Tova, you ride the streets, looking down the covered alleyways and in garages. I won't inform Brandon and Svetlana, as they haven't responded after interrogating the captive. They will have limited searching power anyway apart from broadcasting to groups on open channels, which might tip off those we are looking for.

After a brief chat, Eddy agrees with the plan, and he tells the others at the meeting to spread the word of the coup, asking them to allow Tova and the crew to negotiate the city safely.

Sabrina drives to Halifax Square, where no one attended the meeting to start her search there. Tova cannot cover the entire city alone, and it is impractical for both to drive every street together. Frieda and her team can cover the city from high in the sky and send Tova and Sabrina to any location that requires further investigation. Eddy will also circle the city, ready to help or direct his contacts to if needed.

Tova, having agreed with Sabrina's plan, prepares to team up with Freida to search and observe the city's mood. Loading her bike with her retro-looking weapons, a long rifle, a stubby nose shotgun and a couple of pistols. Slipping on a deep red leather jacket over her tank top and tucks the front into her jeans to show off her rodeo belt buckle. She straps her favorite pistol to her thigh over her tight, knee-torn jeans and straddles her bike.

Opening the garage door, she exits onto Currie Street, heading west as Freida flies high above observing Tova, as her crew fly's grids over the city from North Terrace to South Terrace, and East Terrace to West Terrace. Sabrina's drones join in the search with Tova, who is heading to Victoria Square via West Terrace, then east up Grote Street, which runs through the square's center. Tova believes that the black vehicle will be close by the shootings, likely down one of the smaller side streets or alleys surrounding it.

Sabrina tells the group she heard nothing on the radio she took from the hostage. Suspecting the others witnessed the shootings being nearby and are now protecting themselves by staying quiet, so they can still conduct their mission.

Chapter thirty-one. Plan In Action

A manda's first choice is Trades Hall Lane. Directly behind the buildings on the west side of the square, right under Brandon's building and close to the one Sabrina entered. This lane also comes out on Grote Street opposite the old central market, next to the other shooter's location. The back of the market is an old car park that is now used to store and support the city's maintenance bots. It could be a good hiding spot for a couple of rogue humans as it is a known resting spot for Unhuman, making it unlikely that anyone would visit or look for them without skills and weapons.

Freida and her team have seen nothing, nor has Sabrina in her searches. Tova calls Sabrina and tells her she will drive through the maintenance area to search for the vehicle.

No! Tova, wait for me! I will be there in a couple of minutes, and I will look. It is not safe for you alone.

Tova doesn't answer. Sabrina yells out.

Damn it, girl, I don't need to be saving your ass today! She orders her drone to stick with Tova and protect her at all costs.

Tova turns off the typical Harley compression engine sound she likes to ride with, and the bike only emits a quiet electric motor sound. Now blending in with all the maintenance bots preparing for their nighttime deployment, she rides into the Central Market parking bay. There is a lot of action, with robots fixing broken bots and others loading or updating their missions. The area is not particularly well lit, as humans seldom frequent it. She reaches the third floor unnoticed and there is no sign of the vehicle yet. The floor has an exit chute that the bots drive or fly out of directly onto King William Street in the square's southwest corner. As Tova rides along the north side of the third-floor, blue pulse shots flash past, just missing her. She turns sharply and stops behind one of the larger service bots, realizing there is more than one shooter. Tova gets ready for a fight as a blur races up the deployment chute with weapons blazing, directed at where the shots came from. The drone accompanying Tova stays over her in a defensive position to protect her while informing Sabrina of the shooter's location. Sabrina calls out on the comms unit for Tova to stay where she is, just as another fast-arriving object shoots up the chute. Sabrina throws one of her weapons into the air and Eddy, now wearing gold-colored protective chest armor, fly's past, catches it and lands between Tova and Sabrina.

It seems there are three or four shooters. Sabrina darts from bot to bot in a random zig-zag pattern, shooting at the locations where the shots are coming from, attracting the attention of the shooters so Eddy can sneak closer. When one shooter stands up and prepares to take a shot at Sabrina, Eddy takes him out, leaving only three shooters. Tova is also shooting her pistols at the closest target to her, as she does the drone with her fires as she rests and changes location.

Tova's sudden appearance on the floor caught the attackers off guard. They were all close together, chatting, and unable to change their locations without leaving the safety of their positions. They must surrender or face death unless they have surprises for Sabrina and her crew.

The random start-up of maintenance bots and their movements preparing to exit is also aiding the team to keep the shooters boxed in. Sabrina's second drone has been communicating with her while it slowly and methodically enters from a different location, checking out hallways and rooms for any other suspects. Weapons firing caused unhuman to exit the complex's darker areas. Any Unhuman moving towards Sabrina, the drone flies ahead and fires warning shots. If they stop and turn, it lets them leave. If they don't, it kills them before they can get to Sabrina's location.

The Unhuman natural tendency is to run or move away from noise and danger to protect themselves and it works well for them in this instance. The drone has reached the north entrance where Sabrina and the team are. Sabrina tells the drones to move when she counts to three to each take a shooter west of her location. She informs Tova and Eddy of this action and starts her count: one, two, three. The drones race to confront each shooter as

Sabrina prepares to kill the one closest to her. Yelling out, throw your weapon out and surrender or die. She pops up from cover, surprising the shooter how close she is to him. He instantly throws his weapon on the floor. The remaining two momentarily hesitate, then rise to fire, only to be killed by the drones.

Sabrina asks her subject if there are any more in the building. He says he doesn't know anyone right now, but there's a meeting coming up with others. With all the commotion, it is likely any residents of the complex have scattered, and the people who would have attended the meeting have fled as well.

Tova and Eddy join Sabrina to give supporting cover to protect their exit opportunities, in case more shooting starts. Her drones also move to defensive positions. Sabrina locks eyes with Tova.

Damn it girl, you know how to have fun and attract attention, don't you?

Giving her a smile, she then looks towards Eddy.

Baldy, what's with all the bling, making a fashion statement? Are you going to a fancy-dress party that you have not invited us ladies to?

Eddy just gives a short, deep groan.

Focusing back on the shooter, Sabrina asks him what his name is, where he is from, who the others were, and why he is shooting at them. He replies.

My name is Dave, and I am a resident of Adelaide. The other two are part of a six-man crew from York Peninsula Pure. They are here to check if you're alive and eliminate you since you've gone rogue. You and others are going to release a drug to kill us all.

WOW!! Sabrina responds, briefly turning to Tova and Eddy, shrugging her shoulders, and raising her hands. She turns back to the shooter.

So, Dave, are you Pure? Why would I want to kill all the Pure? Actually, wait don't answer that!! I have some issues with them and how they treated me. But it's okay. I now have a new fun attitude to life these days, not being all drugged up. I am much easier and nicer to be around. Hey Baldy?

He gives another short, deep groan.

Well, my new friend Dave. I know who you are now and will give you a mission. You, my new friend, will spread the word that I am not the devil here. My girl Tova and I are for sure badass females and we, lucky for you, are on your side. You want to be on our side, don't you, Dave? We are here to stop the Elite from wiping out all Mixed Humans, which is what I imagine they will attempt to do tonight.

She turns and looks at Tova, then Eddy.

So! It is a long story about poison drones flying around the city spraying stuff.

She turns back to Dave.

You will tell all that will listen that the team and I are on the side of the free, the understanding Pure, Mixed, and Unhuman alike. I will give you a communication device and you will inform me of your progress, or Tova here will hunt you down for fun and kill you. Does that seem fair to you, Dave?

She summons the Cat to come and join them, grabs a comm device out of it handing it to Dave, who looks quite shaken and in shock. He agrees to do as he has been told.

Tova runs off to grab her bike and turns back on the Harley engine noise. Riding it back to the group, the sound rattles objects as it thumps through the maintenance bay.

Dave runs off, she shuts down the bike next to the Cat and looks at Sabrina.

Drones? drones tonight? Something you like to tell us.

Sabrina looks at them.

Yeah, drones, I shouldn't have mentioned that in front of Dave. It's possible they'll spray a drug statewide tonight or tomorrow night. I mentioned that at our meeting earlier. I am sure I have mentioned this to both of you!

They both respond in unison.

NO! You have not, Sabrina.

Oh, ok, my bad, yeah the Elite are going to spray a drug far and wide intended to infect and spread, killing all Mixed and impure under the disguise of a harmless deterrent spray. Don't panic, it should be safe. Well, that's what I was told, so hey, if it is not, I am as Mixed as you lot, so the joke is on all of us. Do we all feel better about that now?

Eddy speaks up in his serious voice.

No, Sabrina, we are not good. What do you know you are not telling us? We have offered to help you and have proven to be with you. What the hell!!

Wow, so serious, Baldy, aren't you having fun? Come on, you have not worn that costume in years. Don't lie, you know I saw you last time you had it on. Ok look, we are letting the Elite believe they are still in control and winning while we build our forces to attack them. We also hope that within the compounds, those on our side are causing unrest that will keep the Elite leaders in check. They will help spread the truth about the Elite's intentions and capabilities. We hope the majority will not want total eradication, or trust that the drug is safe for them. Ok, again, a good chat guys. Thank you! Anyway, I have a date with our Mister Comic-Con character here Golden Baldy to meet more Unhuman. By the way, Baldy, I do like the black pin striping accents. It makes it look like you have muscles.

Tova laughs as Baldy groans and flies off.

Tova, do you think I upset him?

Nah! He enjoys hanging with us girls and might even have a bit of a thing for Frieda.

Sabrina smiles and gets into her Hellcat.

Thanks for your help. You head home, and I will have my drones follow you and wait till you are safely inside. If you need anything, call me. I will let you know how we go tonight, and we will catch up tomorrow.

She waits for Tova to start her bike and exit down the chute and then follows.

Chapter thirty-two. Meeting Wild Friends

Sabrina drives down South Terrace and into the parklands. The setting sun cast long, east-stretching shadows that blend into the darkening ground. Most birdlike creatures are returning to their nesting areas carrying food for their young from their days hunting out in the greater suburbs. Eddy can speak multiple bird languages. He circles above, explaining in each breed's own language, and in English, that Sabrina is here to help. Come listen to her as we need your support to help us all to have a better future. Driving deeper into the area, Sabrina picks up signals from old trackers from subjects that she has taken samples from. This interaction will be different as she won't be hunting and tranquilize them beforehand. She will be totally reliant on them being prepared to have a chat, not killing her with plenty of backup hiding in the vegetation. Many species here are wilder than the Leopards, Lions, and Panthers in Hindmarsh Square. Sabrina's primary aim is for their groups to listen, leave peacefully, and spread the word within their prides, leaps and packs.

The tracker has plotted a path to the location of a subject. Sabrina chooses not to send her two drones ahead because it is one of her aggressive tactics. She will instead slowly drive closer, then exit her vehicle and hope they will all be curious enough to approach her calmly.

The leaders of each species will have heard and understood Eddy's English announcements. She must take a gamble on whether they trust her to visit their jungle peacefully. Stopping the Hellcat thirty meters from a subject she called Lionheart, who has stood her ground as Sabrina advanced. She exits the Cat while her drones stay away, calmly, and slowly approaching the thick bush in front of her.

Areas of the parklands are now pitch black, with only well-worn paths traveled by creatures or service and transport craft offering beams of light. These paths all run west, allowing the setting sun to penetrate under the canopy as it approaches the horizon, and the corridors line up. Sabrina softly calls out as these beams dimly light the area.

I'm here for a friendly chat. I know you are not alone. Please hear me out, and preferably not have your mates make me their dinner tonight.

A gentle roar followed by what sounded like a purr comes from several locations as the bushes rustle surrounding Sabrina. Lionheart emerges, a mere six meters ahead, resembling more of a lioness than a human. She has pronounced ears, a black nose, whiskers, and a jaw with extremely sharp looking teeth. Her Paw-type hands and feet have claws for nails. As she stands her body still resembles that of a human female. A mix of short yellow-brown and orange-brown fur covers her entire body, extending all the way to the end of her long tail.

Sarah, what are you doing here? Did you have an accident at your home? We thought you were dead, and we would no longer have to put up with you and your tests.

I go by the name Sabrina now and am no longer employed by the Elite or under their control. I'm here to help you all be free, just as I am. The Elite are going to release a drug to kill us all. We have a team working to remove the Elite leaders wishing to do that from power.

Lionheart looks at Sabrina.

Do you truly think it's possible or practical?

I don't know. But not trying knowing what the Elite are prepared to do to have this world to themselves, means that not today, not tomorrow and not in the distant future either, they will wipe us all from the Earth. To prove my point, they are planning to release a virus within the next forty-eight hours that they believe is going to achieve that dream. I blew up the church for this reason, and our team is working to eliminate the Elite with this vision. We will need support from all your kind and others to win. Will you help us? Will you fight alongside the Mixed and open-minded Pure for a new, free world?

Lionheart slowly backs away into the vegetation.

I'll speak with the other Panthera and canines, and we'll decide. You should go now! We're hungry and your recent behavior scared away our prey. Now, you look appetizing.

Wait, please take this communication device.

Sabrina gently throws a couple of them towards Lionheart. There is no response, so Sabrina follows Lionheart's advice, returns to her Hellcat, and leaves the parklands.

Chapter thirty-three. Dark Side Friends

Driving out of the parklands, Sabrina meets up with Eddy.

Well, that went about as I expected it would. I will hopefully hear from Lionheart in the morning and also follow up with CM to create a plan. I want to contact the Hawk humans in the Entertainment Center and, with hesitation, the bat species in the Convention Center. Thank you for your help today.

You are welcome Sabrina. I will fly over and talk to the Hawks in the Entertainment Center. I know a few of them. As for the Bats, you are on your own there. We don't particularly get along and I am guessing they will not take kindly to you entering their coven, either.

I am shocked, Baldy; I am kind, sweet, and irresistible. Who would not like me?

She smiles and looks at him. He waits for an abbreviated time before he responds.

Not to mention humble, cheeky, and lethal.

Aww, you are too kind, Baldy, thank you. You should hang out with Tova, Freida, and me more often.

He ignores her comment.

I will go to see the Hawks, then call it a night before your bat friends take to the skies. Good luck with meeting them. I will call you tomorrow after checking in with the South Parklands flocks.

Eddy flies off towards the Entertainment Center. Sabrina is pleased with how the day has gone so far. She spontaneously talks to her vehicle.

Look at me go Cat, making friends and influencing people. Who knew I had that in me?

She Pulls up outside the convention center while informing Aurora of how her day went, telling her she is about to enter the coven to chat with Valorie and Vandeman. Aurora asks if that is a wise idea, so Sabrina explains her reasons for wanting to visit to her.

They are a large force to be reckoned with, having covens everywhere. I have spoken to all other species, so not directly communicating with them would be a mistake. They might feel ignored, targeted, or undervalued compared to other species. I imagine they will expect me, as they have plenty of informants and spotters all around town.

Aurora offers to send drones or help, but Sabrina rejects the offer. I have a history with Vandeman and Valorie, so I'll just walk in. I am learning from all these meetings, a lot of my history is not all pleasant, according to species around town. Hopefully, they will see I am a nicer new person now. I am sure they will see that. Yes, surely they will see that. Otherwise, I'll show them just how badass I am! So hey, what can possibly go wrong?

Sabrina exits her Cat as the drones land in front and behind her vehicle to show those watching that she does not intend to attack anyone. The security cameras focus on her as she walks to the main doors and through the foyer entrance into the center's main room, which is pitch black and quiet. Sabrina knows it's full of Bat humans as she calls out.

Hey Van, Valorie, I know you are here. It has been a while. Do you still love me? Come on, turn the lights on.

Sabrina, with her superior eyesight, is aware of the circling occupants in the dark. The general population will not know that she can see them, but she knows the two elders in the coven do. The lights slowly come up as Sabrina slowly turns on the spot through three hundred and sixty degrees. Surrounding her are two thousand or more Vamps, wearing anything from twelfth century clothing to a cyber-Gothic look. It is quite a sight. A few have wings, some have faces resembling bats, but most look very human. When Sabrina returns to the start of her rotation, Van and Valorie stand directly in front of her. Van has a similar physique to most genetically altered humans and stands with his wings slightly open to exert authority. He has slightly pointed ears and a pleasant yet effective set of fangs, but otherwise a strong, fit, healthy human appearance. Valorie is a beautiful-looking lady with a fantastic smile. Even with her fangs showing, she looks elegant, alluring, and welcoming.

Sabrina cannot help herself and looks Van in the eyes, slowly raises her hand above her head, rotating her wrist in a complete circle, with her finger pointing to the ceiling.

Very impressive vintage TV series and movies look, you lot have got going on here.

Sarah, what gives you the right to enter our coven and make that comment? Or I hear you are going by the name Sabrina now. Wasn't she a little annoying teenage witch? Are you a witch, Sabrina?

She smiles.

Legendary Princess, I believe it means.

She gives him a small curtsy.

I am here to ask you if you will support me in overrunning the Elite leaders that wish to set a virus free that will kill us all. I have spoken to others around town and have received a sympathetic response. A few are going to get back to me, but I think they will join us. As you know, I have done tests on others and even some here in your coven; I drugged subjects to take samples for the Elite. I apologize for that. We now have Pure from that team I was working for here on earth to help us win. They released me from the Elite to fight for us. They do not believe in the one-eyed view of the Elite leaders we need to eliminate.

Valorie asks.

Why should we trust you or trust them, Sabrina?

CM was the head of the laboratory till he blew it up, and he is my father. He and his team have risked everything, including their own lives, to save us all. When the Elite discovers his survival, they will try to eliminate him and anyone supporting the coup. We have the Elite on the defensive, but they will soon regain total control and hunt us all. I would like to give you a communication chip and I will contact you later for your answer, if that is ok with you both.

We will give it some thought Sabrina, that is the best I can offer you right now. While you have taken samples and drugged some of us, we have seen and heard you have also been helpful to others. I can smell that you are clean as your body has a new sweet-smelling odor, clear of drugs, so I believe you free and are doing the right thing.

Wait, what Van? you knew I was under the influences of drugs before and said nothing. Why didn't you tell me? OK, to be fair, we didn't hang out very much in the past. We should change that in the future!

Well, you were not exactly on our best friend list as Sarah, but as Sabrina, that might change or maybe it will not, and you will be a sweet treat now that you are free of drugs.

Sabrina slowly starts walking backwards, looking at Van and Valorie, as she does those behind her part in a zipper action that keeps her in the center of a tight circle by reforming back in front of her. Reaching the foyer doors, she turns to exit the convention center and jumps into her Hellcat. Slowly driving away, she calls Aurora to inform her of how the meeting went. She tells her she is heading back to her Petwood homestead and wants to talk to CM.

Chapter thirty-four. On Reflection

Back at her Petwood homestead, Sabrina locks it down and places her drones on alert. She feels free as she enters, no longer bound by past protocols. She contacts some of her outlier associates to get an overview of their moods, asking them what they are seeing and hearing in their areas. The consensus is that the Elite are having issues with defensive equipment, and they believe the attack is coming from the Mixed Humans. They all confirm they are supporting her and the coup, so she fills them in on what she has seen in outer suburbs and in Adelaide's city center. Next, Sabrina calls up Roderick to get information directly from him on how the coups plan is developing.

Hi Roderick, how are you?

Hi Sabrina, it was a busy day. How are you?

Yep, I had a big one. Many didn't really like me for what the Elite made me do. I feel good though and see life in a new way. I really need to speak to CM. He owes me some answers.

Ok I will get CM to contact you when he wakes up shortly. I am sure he wants to talk to you. He is doing this for you and all of us. Our contacts within the Elite compounds are continuing as planned. Some of the Elite are concerned about releasing a virus, but the leaders in power still want to move forward with the original plan.

Thanks, I have some research and planning to do. I'll reach out to new contacts in the morning to check if we have a team. Let me know if anything changes. Good night.

I will talk to you in the morning, Sabrina.

Soon after her chat with Roderick, a male voice broadcasts on Sabrina's private line.

Sabrina, are you there? Can we please talk?

Sabrina doesn't recognize the voice and doesn't answer.

Sabrina, can we please talk? It's your time to shine. Sabrina, it's your father.

You've been watching too many movies, mate?

No Sabrina, it's CM. I am glad to see you have your clever wit back.

Sabrina is shocked. She hasn't spoken or heard CM's voice for years.

Yeah, about that, who drugs their own daughter to make her just a machine? Why would you even do that? What type of animal are you?

It was for your own safety. The leading Pure many years ago didn't trust you and wanted me to kill you. I promised them you would be loyal, but I knew I had to reduce your compassion and drive, or you would continue to be a thorn in their side. A couple of your siblings did not conform, so when I was in hibernation, the other team eliminated them. I didn't want that to happen to you.

Wait, what the hell, I have siblings?

Yes, Sabrina, you are the youngest of six. You have three sisters and two brothers. Technically, they are not siblings in the common natural way. They are prototypes, and I created you by combining the best qualities from all of them. Sadly, the Elite killed your two brothers thirty years ago while I was in Hybo. Since I have woken from my last sleep, I have slowly reduced your controlling drugs. Once we set things right, your siblings will also be free. They are supporting us in different Australian states to help the coup succeed.

What the hell, CM. How could you keep all this from me? Why should I trust you now? Is this just your revenge, guilt, or you sorting out your own private grievances and dragging all of us into a stupid fight we can't win?

No, Sabrina, we can win and will win. They cannot get away with playing God. All that have been playing with genetics, including myself, are technically guilty. There is a difference between creating and destroying. I cannot be involved or be part of eliminating species for a cleansed world. Our informants say the plan is all going well, and we believe all the targets have taken the vaccine. Once they release the drones with what they believe is the virus to kill all on earth, we will release our weapon. In three days, those desiring to wreak havoc on Australia and the world will die. I am sorry for the life you have had to live. I needed time for you to grow while I created the right opportunity to implement my plans to stop the extinction.

Sabrina remains quiet for a moment, taking it all in.

When this is over, we will sit down, and you will tell me everything with no more secrets. Ok so, when they release their drones, the leaders will start dying and in the confusion we will attack, create an uprising with those that don't support the extinction option. Sounds like a plan. What can go wrong? Apart from everything?

You were always cheeky, smart, and intelligent. I've missed that part of you greatly throughout the years. To finally see you free to live your own life warms my heart.

Yes, well, it is a fun shit show you have now woken me into, isn't it, Dad? Glad we are all on the happy pills now! Thank you. So, your plan is to give all these Mixed and Unhuman a reason to fight, give them weapons and hope they don't kill us all or each other? It seems like a well-thought-out plan to me! Not to mention the moats and defenses the Elite have. Will you be out on the front line in your armor on a giant white Clydesdale leading us into battle?

I was hoping you would ride a wild stallion into the fight for me, Sarah.

Of course you are. Great plan, lucky me, and it is Sabrina now. Your laboratory rat is no longer caged. I am going to get some rest now.

I apologize for my slip, Sabrina, and all I have put you through. Thank you. I have always loved you as my daughter.

Sabrina doesn't answer and disconnects the line.

Chapter thirty-five. Moving On

C M, and the Moon lab team have been implementing their parts of the plan. They are ensuring all equipment is in order and maintaining control of the Elite's defenses. The coup remains hidden from the Elite. They believe that the latest news and general unrest, and occasional system issues being experienced in earth-based compounds are not all related. Losing the laboratory is a setback, but it also provides the Elite leaders with a great distraction and opportunity to move their true plan forward. To help promote their cause, they broadcast messages in the Pure compounds on how evil and uncivilized the Mixed Humans are, and why they need to be controlled. To reduce Sarah's support, they accuse her of causing the explosions and betraying the Pure.

Natasha and her counterparts in the Elite compounds deceive the Elite and confirm with the coup team that all targets have taken the vaccine. Natasha and Astro explain they are ready and will at the agreed time release the small drones carrying the catalyst drug. All targets in the first round of executions will have inhaled the drug by sunrise, activating the poison already present in their bodies. This will prove the ruling Elite's determination to be free, disregarding the majority's will and the accord. When the Pure and Mixed communities hear the truth about the leaders, it will encourage extra support for the coup, and this is a critical part of CM's plan. The Elite accepting the provided vaccine knowing that Pure will die if they spray the wipeout drug is the first part of that proof.

The Elite's defensive drones are slowly coming back online, adding to the confidence of the Elite rulers that they are still in control. Electra and the Adelaide team finished installing weapons on the squadrons of drones that Mixed manufactured over the last fifteen years. These drones are selectively being sent out to homesteads outside of the Elite compounds. They will support the team and communicate the attack's intent to the compound's occupants. Hopefully, this will focus the fight on head offices and security areas. If the plan fails, the team might be engaged in urban combat with snipers and growing opposition forces in narrow streets.

Sabrina and team members will depend on Natasha and Astro for resistance information. Most compounds only have a moderate sized security force to keep control if anyone rises against the rulers, or to protect resources inside and outside the compounds. Murray Bridge, with its more relaxed rules and integration with the Mixed, will have a greater spread of weapons outside of the compound. In Murray Bridge, Piper, who holds the same position as Natasha, will attempt to rally the ruling Elite in the compound to join the coup. They hope being more liberal after they witness the downfall of other Elite compounds, they will feel safer backing the coup. They will also try to keep the towns outside the compound calm, so they do not fall into a chaotic situation, believing the end is near. Piper and Roderick will keep outliers and towns informed, while holding off on releasing the activation drones within the Murray Bridge compound.

Mount Gambier and the York Peninsula office will be steadfast and all in agreement to release the extinction drones on the Mixed and Unhuman. Duke will allow the virus spraying drones to do their job and spray as programmed by the Elite. This will cement the idea in their heads they are winning and achieving their dream. Once the drones complete their missions, Duke will relocate the differential GPS base station. This will render the drones useless, potentially causing them to crash or become lost if they attempt to use them again. This only affects the Elite's GPS accuracy and does not affect any of the Mixed GPS navigation, as their standalone base stations will stay the same.

Duke and Logan have been keeping the Elite security team occupied by leading them on a wild goose chase, making them believe they have identified and resolved the system issue. Tarak, Natasha, and Piper are also throwing curveballs to cover up any evidence of the coup. Sometimes, they have had to eliminate the problem by either sending a person outside the compound walls with no communication devices, or in extreme cases, creatively making them disappear.

The Moon and Mars bases are having their own issues since being locked out of controls when the laboratory blew up. Off-world Elites face a more complex situation than Earth-based Elites. Reliant on life support and shuttle transportation, they are unwilling to rush upgrades while things are relatively stable, despite the lack of control. A simple mistake in a program code or turning off or on parts of a system may cause other systems to collapse, kill all living in that habitat.

Sabrina awakes to a new day. So much happened yesterday that she is still processing it all. With no orders or having overseers watch her, she still automatically follows her morning routine. Not strictly adhering to any format, she makes use of the minimal gym setup in her homestead. She rides a static bike, jogs on a treadmill, and throws punches at her boxing bag hanging from the exposed beams of the ceiling.

She checks her messages. Nearly all of them are about drones spraying during the night. Sabrina assumes that the Elite have released their virus and makes her first call to Aurora, asking her if the rollout went ahead last night. Aurora confirms the drones were the Elites, and that they compared the spray to the samples of the test tube they gave the Elite. It is an exact match and proves the Elite are going ahead with their extinction plan. Sabrina knows things will escalate quickly from now on. She needs to create an attack strategy for her mission and review other available options. It will all come down to who will fight and what defenses they might come up against.

Once she has finished listening to messages and making important calls, Sabrina organizes to go back to Adelaide. She will visit Aurora and the team first, then contact the people she met yesterday to see who wants to join her. Slipping off her gym gear, she chooses a gunmetal gray non-reflective skin suit for the planned night attack. Then packs a bag with extra clothing, puts on a vintage Jim Beam t-shirt and camouflage-printed tights as a gesture of support for Svetlana and Tova. The casual image will also help her fit in with the Mixed when walking around the governor's building. She sends out codes and messages to her homesteads, loads up the Cat with all the weapons she took from the church, and programs two drones to defend Petwood. Uploading all data points and locations she has gained over the years, including the two secret homesteads near the Port Lincoln compound into the Cats computer, she then jumps in.

Chapter thirty-six. A Day To Live Or Die By

The Hellcat launches out of Petwood, low and fast, taking the straightest route to Adelaide's old governor complex. They are expecting Sabrina at the complex, and they open the massive dock door as she hovers outside. She flies in and lands on the top floor amid drones and equipment while the door closes. The room is not lit exceptionally well. All the drones with their assortment of red, green, blue, and yellow lights strobe randomly, creating a club or concert-like feel with highlights of welding flashes. Aurora, Electra, Mira, Cosimo, and Logan emerge from a workshop door deep in the building. Sabrina has only seen them in video communications, so she barely makes them out amongst the lights and flashes, even with her exceptional vision. Aurora, in her common communication phrases, welcomes Sabrina.

Hi Sabrina, I am Aurora; I have other high-level techs from the Moon laboratory with me. You may remember talking with them. Mira from comms, Electra from Weaponry, Logan from Software engineering, and Cosimo from Elite security. Welcome, we are so pleased to meet with you face to face finally.

Yeah!!!, Well, Y'all certainly gave me some issues over the years, I have been chatting with my newfound friends, OK, maybe they are not so much friends, but hey, they haven't killed me yet either, so that's a win. Just a heads up, you lot are not that popular down here either.

The five of them stroll with somewhat of a cocky swagger, dressed casually, glad to be free of their laboratory coats and clean suits. They lead Sabrina into a pre-choreographed spotlighted area, complete with some backing mist created by drones being serviced. The team's silhouettes are of Pure fit looking humans. Selected eating and gym work are essential on the Moon to stay healthy with no DNA or illegal drugs. Off-world humans are fine examples of the best that natural humans can be. As on Earth in Mixed and Unhuman species, if the best DNA subjects breed with each other, replicating perfect genes, it results in the best of the best in all species. Sabrina smiles and starts the conversation.

Well, welcome to Earth rock stars.

With bemusement, they all look at each other in reaction to her sarcastic attitude.

I'm just kidding. Good to meet you all too. So, what's the plan? I am hoping it involves me sitting back and watching you all take down the Elite and setting us all free?

Cosimo speaks with a stern tone.

We have all taken significant risks to side with the Mixed, and you, Sarah. We now have control of systems and other operatives who will help us. Thanks to your father, we are no longer jailed in the Moon laboratory following orders we didn't agree with. We will require you to help us with our plan.

Oh. You have control of systems. You need my help. Hey Cosimo. It is Sabrina now, please. I do not wish to be known as the fake drugged-up version of me from the past. Yes, I am not quite over that little trick you used on me yet.

Mira steps forward.

Now, now, come on, we are all here to help and work together.

Sabrina looks at Mira. She is the shortest of the five with red shoulder length hair, wearing black tights, a wine-red miniskirt over the top and a tight white tank top.

I love your look, Mira. Yes, we are all here for the same reasons and all with positive attitudes. I just choose to be me now, free, and happy. It is a great feeling not having to watch what I say or do. Let's all go sit down and work out a plan. I am expecting to take my team in tonight if you have released your weapon.

Electra approaches Sabrina in her black SWAT set-up.

OK, I think we can skip the formal greetings and pleasantries. Let's all go into the workshop. We have some layout plans for Port Lincoln, timelines, coordination, and operational information.

Yep, go action girl, I love it, go do that team! Oops, I need to not always say what I think aloud. I would like to say it is the drugs, but hey, you guys are not drugging me anymore, are you?

Sabrina smiles at Electra and walks past her towards the others, as they all head to the workshop.

Sabrina enters the workshop and sees a war room with maps, computers, and many video screens. She knows that CM's team has not accomplished all this in their brief time on earth. Live vision from spy cameras and security drones fills the screens, tech heads from within the building who, over many years, developed and supported all these spy drones, staff the war room. Parts of the system are obviously hand-built, with parts scavenged by the Mixed. Origin labels still mark devices, both from on Earth and off-world. It is not a complete surprise to Sabrina as she herself has helped repurpose gear to outliers, either directly or by arranging a convenient accident. It does not stop her from unintentionally showing a sense of amazement as she walks around.

Logan, noticing her looking with interest, finally introduces himself.

We don't have all the goodies, but we're not flying blind, Sabrina. Hi, I am Logan, and with Duke, our fantastic software developer and engineer who is in Monarto with CM, have hacked into all critical systems here in Australia, on the Moon and Mars. We have also installed backdoor access to other systems in locations around the world.

Well, look at you two little quiet achievers go.

Sabrina gives him a little nudge with her elbow to his side. Apparently, it was a little too strong. As he loses balance and stumbles, she quickly apologizes.

Sorry Mate, I am not that used to being this close to people who are not trying to hurt or kill me. I forget my strength sometimes when I get a little excited. I did not think the mission would have all this tech, and it would be complete blind luck if we survive it.

Logan blushes, as he has always had a thing for Sabrina and is of a similar age. He is an attractive man with amazing athletic genes, blonde shoulder length hair, blue eyes, and a fitness workout freak. Sabrina notices his blushing and holds back on her newfound, natural, smart wit. She just smiles at him, making him even more red-faced as he hurries off, pretending to do something that has just that instant become critical. Sabrina cannot help herself and blurts out with a big smile on her face.

Good call Logan, those pencils will not sharpen themselves.

He turns to look at her in puzzlement.

Come back over here, so we can discuss how we will take down the Elite? I need to know what you and the rest can do to help us survive. So, Logan, you are a software geek and engineer, is that right? You will be in the field with me so we can be sure to get safely past the moat and inside of the compound walls.

Logan feels a sense of excitement and pride that Sabrina wants him in the field with her, and then reality sets in.

Sabrina, I am no soldier or have field operative skills like you. I mostly work in an office or a workshop. Sometimes I supervise in the field when needed if the bot or workers can't fix a problem.

OK Logan, you are right! I understand.

Thank you Sabrina, I will stand by to help 24/7.

Oh, I know you will Logan, you will stand remarkably close by, so close that you will be right there to sort shit out in real-time. You said it yourself, didn't you? And I agree.

Sabrina what? What did I say? With respect, you must have misunderstood me.

No Logan, you said sometimes when the bots or workers can't fix something, I will go out in the field to supervise. Well, guess what! We have no workers and no maintenance bots, so you are it. Look at you. You are fit, strong, and healthy. I am sure you could keep up with me.

Logan's face has now increased in brightness to almost glowing. He's unsure of what to say or do. He looks down, around the room, at others, and rocks back and forth slightly as his body wants to walk away, but his mind says he must stay.

Sabrina notices his anxiety.

Ok, that was a good chat Logan, it is all sorted now. You can go sharpen those pencils you started playing with before as you may need them on site.

Logan responds in a nervous, quick, snappy, and defensive response.

Pencils? What pencils? We do not have any of them; we have stylus pens, and they don't need sharpening.

Ok good to know Logan, see look at how helpful you are. We will be good together in the field. I suggest you grab your pen thingies along with any other techie stuff you might need. We are leaving soon and as you pointed out, we have Duke, who is all set up and linked up in Monarto. So, you can collaborate with him to ensure we all survive this. See, there is no pressure. I am sure you will be fantastic, mate.

Sabrina!

Yes Logan!

He looks around at others and they just nod their heads at him or give him a thumbs up. So, he checks himself and responds, looking directly into her bright green eyes.

Ok Sabrina, I will not let you down.

As he walks off to gather his gear, Sabrina calls out to him.

You will be awesome. We will have an amazing time together.

Cosimo asks Sabrina if it's wise to bring Logan into the field, considering his inexperience. Pointing out that he will think much more clearly and be more effective in Adelaide.

Sabrina responds quickly and with authority.

Cosimo, I doubt your field experience is enough to make that decision. While you all gave me orders from your offices, I was, and I will now be, the one in the field fighting. So, I will give you respect to decide on issues with your team and help coordinate the mission. However, the Mixed group and I will be the ones in direct danger fighting for our lives for you. So, I will be the one who has the final say. I hope we are clear on that Cosimo.

He looks at Sabrina and then turns to Electra as he responds.

Yes, we are clear, Sabrina.

He feels stripped of authority and respect he had on the Moon.

OK Cosimo, can you show me what you all have organized, and Electra can you give me a rundown on what surveillance, weaponry, and other help we have or may receive? Then we can all discuss a plan together.

Cosimo, with reduced enthusiasm, details the attack order and compound assignments. Sabrina listens intently, asking questions, which again makes Cosimo feel he is not being respected. He continues without showing his true feelings out of respect for CM. Sabrina can tell he is getting frustrated by the change in his body odor and heart rate. She backs off with her responses and when he has finished explaining his plan to calm him down; she offers an olive branch. Sabrina needs to decide about whether he might be a liability or if she can trust him to do his job. Sabrina speaks to the group.

I understand you have all taken risks to help me, and I appreciate the freedom you have now given me. You have all supported and supervised me in the field, some of you, for quite a while. All this time, I have felt alone. I have done all the missions you have given me up till now under that impression. We can only speculate on how things will unfold and the resistance we might encounter. I've been in and out of all these compounds, so it's crucial for us to be all on the same page. Cosimo, you have developed a comprehensive plan. I like it as plan 'A.' If it does not work, we will need to have plans B, C and D ready to go, as if we fail, we are all dead. The Elite will never stop hunting us. The Pure and Mixed civilians will hate us because of all the fear and losses we have created. We will have nowhere to go and will never be safe anywhere.

Cosimo appears a little more comfortable now. Sabrina asks Electra to give her a rundown on the drones. She explains that seventy-five drones are on standby outside of Port Lincoln, fifty near York Peninsula, and Monarto has one hundred available. There is a mix of attack drones, supply drones and technical service drones that have communication systems, signal blocking and jamming capabilities. Electra hands Sabrina a communication necklace synchronized to all the drones and the controlling network that Logan and Duke will monitor. Sabrina explains to the team that she is not confident about flooding the compounds with drones. They may confuse one of her team with others that are attacking the group and kill them. For now, drones are part of Plan B.

Ok, that was a good positive, informative, and motivational chat. Thank you all. We will deploy tonight to our respective homesteads and wait while the catalyst drug takes effect on the leaders. According to Cosimo's timeline, the Port Lincoln leaders will be the initial casualties. Then, when we deploy the catalyst at each other location, they will fall. Then, once we control that compound, we will take Yorke's, then Mount Gambier. If Murray Bridge does not comply, we will take it as well. Each of you will head committees at compounds with Mixed representatives to roll out a free world. CM and Duke will keep overall control of defense systems for now. Ok, that seems like a straightforward plan. I just need to sell it to those who will follow me into each compound. Baldy is just going to love it, I can hear him saying. You are what? We are what? What the hell Sabrina! Then there will be Tova's and Svetlana's response to the plan. Hell yeah! Let's go do it.

They all walk out of the war room and over to Sabrina's Hellcat.

Ok Logan, jump in the Cat. Hang on, wait, try throwing in your gear first.

He looks at Sabrina.

I cannot just throw my stuff in, it's all sensitive equipment.

As he is reaching in placing his gear inside that Cat, Sabrina lets out a short Hah! Logan placed his gear in the backseat area and makes room where a passenger seat would be, before jumping in. Sabrina gets in and looks at him.

Comfortable are we?

Logan looks at her, now picking up on her sarcasm.

Yes, sure, just peachy. Oh, and what was the Hah for? Did I do something wrong?

Sabrina turns and looks down at him sitting on the floor of the Cat.

No! I was just surprised Cat didn't take your arm off or chop you in half as you climbed in. I have never had a passenger, alive or dead, inside the vehicle. It's a first for me. Was it good for you too? I am guessing it was as it worked out in your favor, as you are still in one piece.

Sabrina, I like your sense of humor and sarcasm.

Oh, I wasn't joking. OK, to be fair, Svetlana put her pinkie inside the door, and it didn't hurt her, but I honestly thought that was just blind luck. I have seen Cat disintegrate and chop off limbs of Mixed and Unhuman that have tried to enter or grab something from her! Anyway, we both learned something, so that's a win for us both. Look at us go, great teamwork, Woo Hoo let's go team.

Chapter thirty-seven. Places And People You Meet

S abrina and Logan fly out in the Cat, heading for Hindmarsh Square.
    Let's go meet our team. You are going to love them. They may take some time to trust, or like you, they may even kill you! To be honest, it could go either way, but I guess we will find out soon.

Sabrina gives him a comforting smile and then she calls Svetlana, she answers and apologizes for not contacting her sooner explaining that the community has little trust or belief that anything will change, many have doubts that a dream of us all living together peacefully is even achievable. No one wants to take sides at this stage or discuss the issues for fear of being killed by the Elite. Even after the drone spraying has shown their intent, it has not convinced them, as no one is feeling ill or dying. If anything, the Unhuman numbers have reduced in number and activity, which is what the Elite promised. Svetlana concludes by saying that they are all choosing to wait it out rather than take part as they believe we will lose. I will fight with you as a representative of my group.

Sabrina thanks her and arranges for her to be ready at six-thirty to leave Adelaide. The conversation with Brandon reflects the same feelings as Svetlana's community, virtually word for word. Sabrina hopes future responses will be different and that these are not a reflection of all the Mixed Human feelings.

The next call is to Tova. Sabrina is certain she will join, having already shown the ability to stand strong and fight. Over the years Sabrina has noticed Tova helping others, even almost Unhuman, acting as a self-appointed Sheriff. Keeping her local area and the wider Adelaide city in a type of balance, by not allowing gangs or the wild Unhuman to act freely. As expected, Tova agrees to support Sabrina and will be ready at six twenty-five to be picked up before they all head to Victoria Square.

After flying a lap of the city, Sabrina lands her Cat on the Pulteney and Wakefield Street intersection, then drives into Hindmarsh Square. She hopes to meet Baldy as he hasn't called her as promised. Sabrina calls him and asks him to meet her in the center of the square. It is eerily quiet as Logan and Sabrina step out of the Cat. Logan, wanting to show signs of confidence, gets out and strolls around the vehicle.

Hey tough guy, I would not wander too far. The Square is full of Mixed and Unhuman. You will look pretty delicious to them.

Just as she finishes her sentence, a familiar shadow circles, followed by Eddy crashing through the canopy and landing next to Sabrina. She turns to where Logan was standing, but she cannot see him.

Hi Sabrina, your friend is in the vehicle.

Sabrina bends slightly to look through the driver's side window.

Hi Baldy, yes, that's Logan. He has this weird thing about making sure the pencil thingies he uses are all sharp. Get out the Cat, don't be rude and say hello to Baldy.

Logan slowly gets out and walks around to join them. He extends his hand towards Baldy, who just stands still, looking at him.

Good to meet you Baldy.

My name is Eddy, and you can call me Eddy.

Hi Eddy, it is a pleasure to meet you. I am Logan, a Software Engineer here to help Sabrina get into the Compounds.

Yeah, I don't think Sabrina needs a hand to do anything, and why do you have pencils? We all use a stylus. You can't be much of a software genius.

No, no, I do not have any pencils.

Sabrina jumps in and speaks up.

Yeah, I am just giving him a hard time. He is apparently good at his job, so we will try to keep him alive as we may need him.

Well, I cannot promise anything, Sabrina. He will need to look after himself.

Yep Ok, so how did you go with the Hawks?

We have their support, mainly because they saw the drones and believe that the Elite are the enemy, not the Mixed they live alongside.

He looks directly at Logan.

And sometimes enjoying picking at their bones.

Come on, Baldy, look at those muscles. They will have to slow-cook him for a day to make him tender. If you can, please follow up with them and tell the Hawk leaders our plan. If any of them want to help, we are leaving at six thirty tonight for Port Lincoln.

Our Plan? I don't remember discussing a plan with you.

Oh, Baldy, you are going to love it. Didn't I say that to you, Logan?

He nods.

Yes, she mentioned you would love it, Eddy.

So, without going into any fine detail, we will walk into the Elite compounds one at a time and take them over. If you want to make an impression, you can fly in doing that landing thing on their doorstep. Of course, the moat will be our first problem. It might kill us all before we can cross it, but that is why we have Logan. He rushes into things, so we'll have him disarm it and run through first. If he is as good at his job as he says he is, we will be fine. If not, we will have to develop another plan.

So! Sabrina, you have no plan.

No, that is the plan. I avoided adding unnecessary details. I didn't want to bother you with technical talk, as it may change if things go wrong. So, if that happens, we will just put it down to a brilliant plan implemented poorly and move on to Plan B.

What is Plan B then Sabrina?

I am not sure yet, still working out the tricky bits, so we will just wing it, no pun intended.

You are going to get us all killed.

Well, my plan is much more impressive than your synopsis, Baldy. Where is your positive and motivational attitude?

He turns, takes a few steps, then launches into the air, yelling out in his deepest, unimpressed voice.

Sabrina, I will call you later.

Well, Logan, I think that went well. Good teamwork, mate.

He motions to respond, but he then thinks better of it, turns, walks around the Cat, and gets in. Sabrina jumps in and turns to Logan with a little smile.

If you liked that chat, you are going to love Valorie and Van.

Sabrina calls Van to inform him she will visit with a friend, mentioning at the end of the brief conversation.

Oh, and Van, my friend smells nervous and is a bit of a looker. Could you please ask your coven to keep their fangs out of him?

She turns to Logan, looking him straight in the eyes.

It should be alright, you will be ok, I think, yeah it will be alright. Well then again, you just never know with Vamps. If it helps, they don't trust or like me either, so we might both end up as a snack.

I will just stay in the Cat. You do not need me in there. It is just a meeting with nothing technical that will need my help.

You are right; I don't need you in there. You could just stay in the Cat, as it would be much safer for both of us. However, you will come in with me, as they need to see we have Pure help. You also need to get comfortable with what it feels like to be surrounded by our team, to have them trust you and you trust them.

Chapter thirty-eight. Dark Building Dark Future

D riving up to the main entrance of the Convention center, Logan looks at its uninviting appearance, completely black with all its windows painted out or boarded up. Searching for his tablet, he tries to come up with a clever remark for a reason to type some crucial coding.

Logan, you need to concentrate on what I am saying. Stay close and move slowly to avoid drawing attention to yourself. It will be dark as that is a part of their defense system, like bats they can see and even navigate in the pitch black, unlike anyone else silly enough to enter their coven.

Sabrina exits the Cat, and Logan stays quiet and sits still inside.

We are both going in, put ya big boy pants on and get out of the vehicle. Stay close, act calmly, respectfully, and we might both exit alive.

They walk into the foyer. Unlike Sabrina's visit, the main door automatically closes and locks behind them.

Well, that's new.

Sabrina utters while she keeps walking. The lights in the foyer dim and the main entrance doors slowly open to the pitch-black entertainment room. A voice from deep inside the room in a warm, enticing tone calls out.

Welcome to our coven again, Sabrina. I see you brought a friend this time. Come in, come to me.

The coven packs the room, then parts in sync to form a walkway to the stage at the back. Sabrina confidently walks down the opening space they create with Logan close behind her. As they get halfway to the stage, Logan, unable to see, falls slightly behind as he brushes and bumps past all the occupants, causing him to get disoriented. The zipper closes behind them as they walk forward. Sensing Logan's confusion, they lead him a separate way. Sabrina notices what's happening but feels the best strategy is to go with the flow, and trust that Van has complete control of his coven. She calls out.

Stay calm Logan, you will be ok.

Van is standing on the stage as Sabrina approaches, faintly, so only she and the coven can hear.

He is safe for now Sabrina. We want to know his identity, purpose, and your plans.

In one simple bend and straightening of her legs, Sabrina bounds up onto the stage and lands next to Van, so they can be on equal terms.

Hello Valorie, Van. You would have seen the drones last night and how the city is reacting. Our goal is to remove those in power and create a more accepting world. I would appreciate your support and hope that you and your covens will join us.

Who is your friend Sabrina?

His name is Logan. He is one of the Pure team that left the Moon and helped me escape. They are here to stop the Elite from releasing a virus designed to kill us all.

She can hear the coven cringe, rustling around, agitated that a Pure is among them and from hearing her comments.

He is coming along with me to deal with any defenses or technology that the Elite may have that we don't already have control of. He will coordinate with the team to help us all survive. So, if you kill or feed on him, that could become problematic for us all.

Despite Van's silence, Sabrina detects his communication with the coven through the room's movement. The entire room is listening and responding. She tries to focus in on any sounds, chirps or screeches that are part of their language, but it is mostly beyond even her enhanced range of frequencies. She knows Unhuman can communicate with each other, varying in intelligence and cooperation. It is clear in this instant that this could also work against her and the coup.

It is helpful to have each species communicate in their own language, as it is more reassuring when explaining unwelcome news. Sabrina realizes that at a critical point, a species could also use covert communication to share a unique plan without her knowing. Turning on her team and leaving that species with an advantage or in control of a situation.

Van, I know you are talking to your coven. Could you please let me in on the conversation? You've made your point to Logan now. Please turn on the lights so he can see and walk over to me. You don't need an advantage over us. We are here in peace to ask for your support, not to demand it or threaten you with any type of response if you choose not to help us.

For now, you are both guests in my coven, so I choose to accept your request. I am communicating in our language as not all here speak English. They all deserve to be a part of the conversation and to respond in real-time. It is called respect Sabrina. Your past actions and those of your little friend here have not, let us say, been endearing towards us over the years. I understand things have changed recently, and in the past you have shown compassion towards all species, including us. I can sense you have changed, and you are not under their spell, but it doesn't change the facts, does it? It is possible that this is a trap or a means to eliminate us. For these reasons, I have asked my coven to send word to all my other covens. At this stage, to do nothing to hinder or help you or your team. You are now free to go.

Room empties swiftly, lights dimly illuminating the area so Logan can see. Some Vamps were not fast enough, and as his eyes adjust, he can see the last of them leave. Intentionally ordered by Van to show them just how far apart they were from each other, and for Logan to glimpse what was around him. Sabrina casually comments as they slowly walk out of the hall into the lit foyer.

Good chat, Van, good chat mate. Hey Logan, don't you think that was a good chat? How do you think it went? It was about what I expected.

The exit doors are wide open as Logan picks up his pace, heading straight for them.

Yeah, good chat. I'm alive, which is good. Did you see them? They were scary and there were so many.

Wow Logan, look at you go, another first for you. Just a heads up, though. You know they can still hear you, don't you?

No! Oh hell, he whispers, as he picks up his pace, exiting the building and jumping into the Cat as quickly as possible.

Logan, how many of those pencil thingies do you have that demand your urgent attention?

Chapter thirty-nine. Another Chit Chat Before Dinner

In the Cat outside the coven, Sabrina turns to Logan to give him some assurance.

You did well mate, it could have ended badly for you, but you remained calm. We could all smell your fear. That is not a bad thing, as you didn't overreact or do anything stupid. You need to remember that and to try a little harder at this next meeting. Do not stare and do not comment on how they look. They may take offense to it and want to see what a Pure human tastes like. I think Van may like you, as it took great strength to enter the coven with me. He will have respected that, so it's another win for you and our team.

Where are we off to now?

We will do a cruise through the South Parklands. I want to see how the Unhuman are taking the news. I trust Baldy, but I need to know that they understand our intentions. They need to see you and not want to kill you at first sight, because if they do, I will need a new plan.

Good Chat, Sabrina, Good Chat. You mention these new plans a lot. Let's hope you don't need to come up with one anytime soon.

She smiles and looks at him as they enter under the canopy of the parklands and drive deeper into its dense foliage. Sabrina stops the vehicle and tells Logan to just sit still for a while. She hopes the leaders will recognize that she is there to chat again and inform others of their packs to stand down. Lionheart emerges from the foliage on all fours, resembling a majestic lioness. Logan pushes back deeper into the vehicle.

Remember what I told you, they feed on fear. You don't want to be preyed upon, do you?

No! Sabrina, I would very much not like to be dinner.

Well, ok then you get out first. If it all goes well, I will jump out and join you.

He looks at her with fear in his eyes.

What?

No, I am serious. You climb out of the Cat first, or I will throw you out. Trust me, Logan, it is better if you get out on your own. If I throw you out, you will look like a peace offering. You said you didn't want to be dinner tonight, so please get out the Cat mate.

Logan understands Sabrina's wit well enough and realizes she isn't joking, so he climbs out. Lionheart rushes towards him as he exits, followed by other creatures emerging from the bushes, sniffing and examining Logan. Remembering what Sabrina comments, he stays still, tries not to look directly at any of them or show any fear. Looking nowhere in particular, he calls out to Sabrina.

Would you like to join us, please?

She gets out of the Cat and walks around to join Logan. As she does, all the Panthera move in closer, circling them and the vehicle. Lionheart asks in a growling voice.

Sabrina, who is your friend?

As others keep sniffing the air, swapping from one front paw to the other. Then all that can, or choose to, in one common action stand upright.

Logan is here to help us make things right. He is part of the Pure group that came from the Moon to stop the Elite. He knows the systems and protocols of the Elite, along with the others now on Earth. They will ensure we can get into the compounds and win.

Hello Logan, she growls more than she verbalizes.

Your team is responsible for what has been happening here. Were you the one instructing Sarah? Sorry Sabrina, to shoot us with drugs and take samples.

No mam, I was in the laboratory as a software engineer ensuring Sabrina's safety and that her equipment was functioning correctly. I was under orders just like her when CM, our leader, revealed his plan to stop those wishing to wipe you all out, I joined him to help and I apologize to you for what the Pure did, and how they used you as subjects. In the past fifteen years, the intention was not to harm you. Instead, it was to allow CM to create a drug for targeting specific Elite leaders.

Mam, did you hear that Sabrina? Logan, I like your honesty and bravery. We do not fully trust your words, but if you come to explain instead of attacking, we believe you are trying to do right. We will support you, to be sure you have told us the truth and to be close by. If you have not, we will kill you all in the slowest, most painful way possible.

Look at you, bonding and being best friends. So, will you join us then, Lionheart? What can we count on?

We will provide Panthera communication experts to help spread the word and ensure, as best we can, safety in the wilder areas you may wish to cross. When we enter the compounds, we will provide representatives from Canine and Panthera to ensure our interests are being looked after and not eliminated.

Ok, thank you Lionheart. That is what I had hoped for. We plan to go to Port Augusta tonight to our homesteads with the equipment needed. We will wait there and enter the compound when we get the signal from our team. It would be a three-hour trip if we drive it straight without stopping, or just a quick hop if we fly. My plan is to drive making stops along the way so you and others can spread the word of a future peace. Some may not care, they will continue as usual. Those who have interacted in towns and cities like yourselves, if they hear it from a similar species, will contribute to a lasting freedom.

Sabrina, it sounds like an unbelievable dream. I can't see us changing much. We can't have a dictatorship rule over us or wanting to wipe us out in the future, either. We should show our ability to unite and fight together for a common cause.

Who will join us?

Lionheart steps forward, followed by a leopard and a jaguar. She calls out their names. Leo and Jagger both look similar to Lionheart, with their own distinctive species, body patterns, and characteristics.

Unexpectedly, two Large Dragon-humans emerge from a worn traffic corridor in the parklands, pushing trees out of the way to get closer. They are less human looking than Eddy and the Panthera, with large wings, massive legs, spiked backbone, and long tails. Their faces are more species related, long horns behind their ears, elongated jaws, squashed noses with larger nostrils that are three times the size of Lionheart's.

We will Fly Sabrina, one of them announces.

Ok, then a vehicle for three it is, and D1 and D2 will fly. We are creating ourselves a bit of an air force. Baldy will love it.

We do not know of Baldy; we know an Eddy well enough. My name is Dragor, and the one you refer to as D2 is Paffor.

It's a pleasure to meet you, Dragor and Paffor. Yes, Eddy is who I call Baldy. It sounds like we have an awesome team and a plan. We will drive past here at six thirty-five to pick you up. Thank you all.

Sabrina and Logan get into the Hellcat and exit the parklands.

Seems you have not been honest with me, Logan.

I have Sabrina, you just haven't asked the right questions or allowed me to talk much. Yes, I knew your vehicle wouldn't chop me in half or anyone else. Yes, I program the drones, church, and compounds to help you out, like a software guardian angel.

I wouldn't go that far, Logan. Keep it realistic mate, plus Baldy has wings and a golden chest plate. I think the Angel gig is more in his ballpark. Don't you?

Since meeting you and attending the meetings today, I have been outside my comfort zone. So, I am sorry you feel like I have misled you. It was not intentional.

Aww Logan, have you not liked our dates? Ok, the first date was a bit of a shock. The second one was initially dark and scary, but admit it, you ended up liking it, right?

He blushes again.

To be fair, mate, I had to throw you in the deep end to ensure that you would swim and not sink under pressure. Also, as a representative of the Pure, you gave the coup more relevance and proof we had inside help. It made it more realistic. Oh, and I wanted to see how the team would react with the smell of fear on a Pure human. We are teammates, and we work well together, go us.

I understand why Baldy always flies off. If we are being honest, you have a knack for dehumanizing people.

Logan turns and gives her the same smile and look he regularly gets from her. With the biggest smile on her face, she looks at him, gives him a nod, and turns back to watch the road.

Chapter forty. I Call Shotgun

Sabrina and Logan return to the Governor's building, landing in the same bay. With fewer drones in the bay, she can fly straight to the war room door. They both exit the vehicle and walk in to meet with the others. As they walk in, Cosimo, Electra, and Mira are on a live video chat with CM, Duke, Joe, and Tarak. Sabrina sees her father on the screen for the first time in many years. This is her first opportunity to see and talk to him personally. The team is discussing resource deployment and catalyst spraying progress. After a general discussion and organizing transport for her group leaving Adelaide, Sabrina requests everyone to leave the room so she can speak with CM. She has longed for this conversation, but never had the chance. It is now or never as she may not survive the raids. She sits in the room alone and looks at the screen. An entire minute passes before CM speaks as he realizes Sabrina is unsure of what to say.

Hi Sabrina, it is so good to see you. I am terribly sorry for all I have put you through. In the early days, I believed we needed to fix the errors of past scientists' meddling in Earth's evolution. My father, along with other male and female Elite, saw this manipulation as evil, not being as nature created. I once believed that which led me to create you. You are beautiful, amazing, and the best of the best. As you grew up and I looked into your eyes, raising you as my daughter, I realized I was wrong. The Elite Pure are wrong. Once humans allowed free will, changes in genetics, and let it evolve, we needed to embrace it and, in doing so, it would have created its own limits. However, we segregated it, pushed it underground, then those opposing it left Earth, leaving the world to evolve independently. Earth has bounced back in all its natural glory. As you have seen, Pure, Mixed, Almost Human, and Unhuman have lived alongside each other with no overruling body on Earth. While the Pure initially caged themselves and later realized that it was not right, they decided on a plan to free themselves and eliminate all others.

Sabrina, you are the reason we are all doing this, even with all your genetic changes, the controlling drugs, and the missions we made you do. Your willingness to help Earth's creatures, expecting nothing in return, has shown your immense compassion. The only one capable of doing this is you, the Mixed and Unhuman, respect you as you have seen recently.

Sabrina stays silent and motionless, a tear forms in her eye.

I love you Sabrina, as a father. You are my beautiful daughter, and I am so proud of you.

Sabrina stands and turns her back to the screen.

This conversation is not over CM.

She slowly starts to leave, then stops.

I have early memories, if they are not fake. Early childhood visions and feelings. I have hung on to them in this lonely prison you all created for me as your slave. Now I am doing this for myself and other species with feelings, not you. I will do it my way and whatever is best for those who fight with me.

I would have it no other way, Sabrina. I will support you in any way you wish.

Sabrina enters the loading bay, stronger and more focused than ever for her mission. She immediately takes command of all present, asking direct, relevant questions, and deciding on a course of action. They all listen with respect and eagerness to get the mission moving. The team seems to bond and lift with Sabrina's decisive leadership.

We will take two vehicles to pick up Svetlana and Brandon. Electra will be in one vehicle with hand weapons and equipment. The other vehicle will stop to pick up Lionheart, Leo, and Jagger, with Logan to help communicate. I will be in my Cat, and Tova will be on her bike. Eddy, Van, Paffor, Dragor, and any other air support will fly to Gepps Cross to meet us. We will then reload into the waiting semi-transport vehicles. When we have loaded into the semi vehicles, Van, Eddy, Paffor and Dragor will fly high in the sky. I will lead the convoy and Tova will follow. Three defense drones will watch our backs while the others above will scan in front and to the sides of us. When encountering species or reach a town, we will communicate our peaceful intentions, the Elite's plans, and our efforts to stop them.

There's a possibility that someone will warn the Elite about our arrival. If that happens, we use that to our advantage by ensuring the Elite leaders believe we are all committed and outnumber the Pure in compounds one hundred to one. We have three hours before our departure time. Logan, you did well in the field today. Please grab anything else you need. Also, remind me to give the Panthera time to feed when we reach Gepps Cross. They normally head out to feed at dusk and have warned me about how hunger makes them go into a feeding frenzy. They sounded serious when I interrupted their feeding time, so you might also want to mention it when you pick them up.

Electra, you can travel with Svetlana and Brandon. They both appear competent. Svetlana has a streak of fearlessness in her. I would like you to give me feedback on whatever you learn about them on the trip, so we can use them effectively.

Cosimo and Mira, your role is to oversee and run the show. Send necessary supplies via drones and maintain communication with CM and the team in Monarto. Ensure the Elite's defenses are down and provide necessary information to all our team.

Use your three hours of downtime to rest ahead of the lengthy night. Eat a healthy meal before we depart, as there won't be much time to eat during our mission.

Logan steps towards Sabrina as they all disperse.

Are you kidding about the Panthera?

No, I am serious Logan, Don't sweat it. You will be fine. I think they like you and the courage you are showing. Besides, if they eat you, who will sharpen the pencil or stylus thingies to get us into the compounds? They know we will meet others of their same species on the way. They will need to be strong and show dominance, so hopefully, they will have eaten before they jump in with you.

Sabrina jumps into her Cat and flies directly back to Petwood to rest up and send programs to her homesteads to prepare for the mission.

Chapter forty-one. Let's Go

Sabrina arrives at the governor's compound at six fifteen with four defensive drones. Landing in the loading bay, she gets out to join the crew in the war room. CM is about to update all operation aspects and Elite compound status. He reads out facts in note format.

None of the Elite have fallen because of the catalyst drug. However, we expect seeing its effects by morning, within the expected activation timeframe.

The Elite are still trying to recover full control of all their defenses. Those systems that they believe they have regained full control of, they have not. We are still overriding them for our benefit.

Elites with us, inside the compound walls, not needed on the front line, hide and wait for the first wave. They've been sending news and videos to the media, while we've been sending our transmissions directly to the Elite monitoring systems. Showcasing their drones in flight and the mass deaths of Mixed and Unhuman. The Elite believe the virus is working as planned. If they haven't, they will take the vaccine for protection. I wish you all good luck and a successful mission.

He concludes by thanking everyone for helping him and doing what is right. Cosimo steps forward, providing words of encouragement and sharing updates on semi vehicles and drone deployment. Sabrina thanks CM, Cosimo, and all for agreeing to help. She asks to have the recording of CM's report to play to her team as they travel to Gepps Cross, so everyone is up to date. CM and Cosimo agree, and they all disperse to their workstations.

Sabrina jumps into her Hellcat. As she does, it transforms around her into the shape replicating that of a classic assault vehicle. The Cat now resembles a mixture of the latest engineering, and abilities of a formidable combat vehicle. Its wheels have large chunky looking mudguards and the body has square angled shapes to help deflect any attacks. It is a far more aggressive look than the Cat's normal shape as it leaves the loading bay. She heads for Tova's home while the two shuttle vans delay slightly before leaving for their designated pickup areas. Sabrina does not want the shuttles waiting outside to attract attention, giving any snipers time to set up, putting members of her team in danger.

Arriving in front of Tova's place without having to stop, with military precision, she roars out on her bike. The thumping Harley sound bounces off buildings as she rides, weapons hang off her hip and the bike as her hair fly's back in the breeze.

That's my girl, Sabrina yells as they both drive to Victoria Square. Tova circles the square at speed, so they will know it is time. She stops outside the east building where Svetlana lives, and Sabrina stops at Brandon's. The shuttle vans arrive at the same instant. Electra picks up Svetlana first, and Tova rides over with her to pick up Brandon. They communicate briefly with Sabrina, who thanks them, asking Electra to introduce herself and play CM's message as they head off to meet Logan and the Panthera.

Logan drives into the parklands and opens the large van door. The Panthera enter, dragging remnants of a creature carcass. Lionheart looks at him, sniffing the surrounding air to pick up his scent.

You didn't think we were going to eat you, did you? Sabrina would not have sent you with us if she thought we would. She obviously trusts you and believes in your talent.

Logan bravely responds and gently pushes a hand pistol away!

It crossed my mind when she told me it was the start of your feeding time, and you would need food along the way.

Well, you won't need that weapon today. But then again, who knows?

She looks at the other two. They growl softly in a short set of bursts that resemble them having a giggle between themselves. Sabrina contacts them and thanks the Panthera for offering their services and asks Logan to play CM's message.

Once they have all had time to settle, she details her mission statements as she leads the three vans down Main North Road. In order to make a statement to the Mixed and Unhuman, they choose to drive instead of flying. Eddy joins them from a distance, while Dragor and Paffor soar much higher, overshadowing the rest of the team.

At Gepps Cross, everyone leaves their vehicles and forms teams to explore the local area and communicate with the resident species. The Panthera head to the forest areas, winged to buildings and nesting areas of their kind. Sabrina and Tova drive by the Mixed homes and buildings, sharing the message of the Elite's actions. The intent is not to have any face-to-face meetings, but to be seen and spread the word to any listening ears.

The rest of the team reloads all equipment and weapons into the three Semi Vehicles. Dragor and Paffor don't fly too far away from the semi vehicles, circling above them as extra protection for Svetlana, Brandon and Logan while the others are away.

Sabrina has scheduled multiple stops in towns along their journey to promote their cause. These towns will also have had the Elite drones flying overhead and spraying. Certain species will feel uneasy, anticipating a larger event. The team must remain alert. The missions aim to avoid riots, similar to the unrest Sabrina encountered in Norwood while driving into Adelaide.

Finishing their public announcement tours and back at the semi transporters, they quickly discussed who they could see on the streets, and the areas they spread information to. Being so close to Adelaide city they know this was their easiest stop, as residents would already have heard rumors spreading through all the natural communication channels. Sabrina informs the team that the next stop has a wider variety of wilder species. The farming areas, which were previously used for produce during Adelaide's prosperous days, have now reverted to dense vegetation. As she finishes her chat, Van and Valorie arrive, they stopped at the North Haven coven to inform them of the plan. Valorie tells Sabrina that they will also stand by and not interfere with the mission. Van requested elders to dispatch messengers to northeast Covens. They had already ordered messengers from their coven to go to those southeast of Adelaide.

Sabrina thanks Valorie and Van and explains her feeling that groups are more likely to follow requests if they see and hear information directly from their own species. In some towns and small communities, they will have no interest in, or understand, the messages. They may offer resistance out of fear, or totally object and see her team as the enemy, not the Elite.

Chapter forty-two. Next Town

Virginia is located northwest of Adelaide's outskirts. It will be their next stop and has a greater number of Unhuman, along with Mixed living to its East. Sabrina believes that the Mixed Human communications from Adelaide chat lines will reach cities like Mawson Lakes, Salisbury, and Elizabeth. CM and the team will communicate with Mixed Humans between Adelaide, Murray Bridge and Mount Gambier. This leaves Sabrina and her team to reach out to the almost Unhuman on their way to the compounds outside Port Lincoln, hoping they will spread the news naturally through their species to the wider area.

After Virginia, they will stop at Dublin, which is halfway between Virginia and Port Wakefield. Apart from a few outlier homesteads in Dublin, its population is all Unhuman. It will be exceedingly difficult and a dangerous stop for the team. Sabrina is only considering it, as she wants to drop off defensive gear to her outlier friends there. While there, she believes they should try to inform the Unhuman. As they close in on Virginia, Dragor and Paffor fly off. Tova notices them leaving and calls Sabrina.

Hey Sabrina, where is our air support going? Surely they are not leaving us.

No Tova, it is a technique I have used with my drones. If you fly in an organized pattern, you can herd the Unhuman into or out of areas, as this is part of their natural habitat I assume that they have taken it upon themselves to make it as safe as possible for us at our next stop. Using their size, known aggressive behavior toward other species, and their fear of being eaten, they should thin out the area, leaving only those that may understand our message.

Tova pauses for a few seconds, a bit stunned, and uses one of Sabrina's favorite responses.

Good to know, good chat. I feel so much safer now, thank you.

Well Tova, it is also possible that they arrange an ambush for us, with several of their own species. If the coup fails, they'll divide and eat us. We'll find out soon enough.

The team exchanges apprehensive and surprised looks, then nod, smiles, and quietly speaks in unison. She is kidding, right? Yeah, she is kidding! After an awkward brief silence, Sabrina speaks up.

Stay alert and back each other up, in case it's a trap.

All the Pure and Mixed stare into their video comms units with a worried look, as the Panthera just keep grazing on the carcass Logan dragged into the Semi vehicle for them.

On approach to Virginia, the drones lift to fly higher to get a greater view. Eddy, Valorie, and Van fly lower under their protection. Sabrina contacts a couple of local outliers she has communicated with in the past and asks them to tell anyone they know surrounding Virginia that she and the team are doing a friendly circle of the town. She then explains the plan to the team, saying that it will be quite fluid in design and a test run for the more difficult stop in Dublin. Sabrina calls out the groupings for the stop:

Team one will be Eddy, Valorie, Van, Logan, and me. We'll leave the convoy and head east to the town near the highway. Two drones will fly ahead for reconnaissance as we circle the town. Our aim is to broadcast the message as we did in Gepps Cross to any buildings with lights on and leave messages on any local social networks. Eddy, if you sense any nests with the help from Van and Valorie, you will fly over them and tweet the message in all languages. If we encounter anyone roaming the streets, Mixed or Unhuman, we will try to communicate with them. Logan, you send out any jamming signals or do any hacks when needed to get our message across or keep the team safe.

Team Two will be Lionheart, Jagger, and Leo. You will have three small building defense drones set to recognize your human voices. Maneuvering quickly will be challenging because of dense vegetation. They will stay as close to you as possible and if you call out, "defend drone defend" they will shoot anything that is close to you until you are safely back at the convoy. Use them for your safety as your abilities are critical to the greater mission. These attempts to communicate messages are a courtesy, not a necessity, and an attempt to show support and inclusion for all. When we are successful in our coup, we can visit all areas and communicate more directly with each species.

Team three will stay and defend the convoy. Electra, you have control of the weapons. Use them as necessary, but not carelessly. We want to gain support, not to be seen as the enemy. Tova, you load your bike in a semi for now and all stay inside. Your team is responsible for the first two semi vehicles making sure they get to Port Wakefield if anything goes wrong. The third semi will stay for Lionheart, Leo, and Jagger.

Team four, Well, they are off doing their own thing now as this is their territory, so hopefully they are making it safer for us. Guess we will know soon, so team four will do their own stuff. Good luck, stay aware, stay confident, and it's alright to feel some fear. Use all these feelings as if your life depends on it, as it does.

They all respond and acknowledge the plan. Most with just a single word, "Copy"

Svetlana speaks, trying to bring a bit of humor to the situation.

Brilliant plan. Love it, and that motivational speech at the end.

Tova follows up with.

Yep, I agree Svetlana. It was straight out of Sabrina's one hundred and one motivational speeches manual.

The convoy stops on the highway. It is a well-established corridor for automated traffic as random flying routes get unwanted attention from Pterodactylus. Smaller vehicles seldom stop on the side of the road, however, larger convoys have areas where the vehicles wait to join or leave a group. These groupings ensure they all arrive as one shipment to enter through compound security systems at set times. This reduces the number of openings and closing needed at the moat entrances.

189

Eeriness fills the air as they prepare to depart on their missions. Suddenly, three large objects are closing in fast on the convoy from the south. Two drones disperse at forty-five degrees to the targets that are rapidly approaching. Drones fire warning shots before the team can tell who or what they are. They continue to approach, taking a defensive swerving pattern. The drones fire again, taking down the third-winged creature. The team comm's come alive as they all ask what is happening and prepare to shoot.

Sabrina yells out.

Stand down, team, stand down, don't shoot.

The two remaining creatures fly in, land, and move into the light of Sabrina's vehicle.

Found a new friend I see Dragor? It Looked quite large and fast.

Dragor and Paffor move closer to her vehicle. She can see they have been in a bit of a scrap. Both have large wounds, but they don't seem serious and blend with other healed cuts.

What happened?

We herded the smaller creatures and spoke to them in English, spreading the news to any who could understand, mainly the leaders of each species, if you can call them that. We also communicated with our own Dragon species, which are in sparse numbers in this area. The Pterodactylus humans that we could communicate with were skeptical of any plan. They will reluctantly pass on the word that we are friendly and to allow us to pass. The fully wild of this species only responds out of fear for their superiors. Others lack respect for leaders and interest in joining a group, so we are on our own with them.

Three individuals pursued us, seeking to prove a point and remove us from their territory. We killed two of them as we got sick of them following us. I sensed your arrival, so we raced back to help. I hoped the third one would tire and quit when it got too far away from its patch. Anyway, all the small creatures we scared off will now be slowly returning to the area we cleared. Paffor and I will do another low loop to slow their return. This should give the Panthera a chance to get in and communicate. We will try to help protect them, but we can't fly through some of that foliage.

Thank you Dragor and Paffor, we all appreciate your help and efforts.

She repeats the plan she laid out to the rest of the team who have heard Dragor's report and their superiority over the enormous creatures. Their commitment will help in boosting their courage.

Jagger, Leo, and Lionheart exit the semi on all fours, so their appearance is natural to their species and less human-like. They also have greater speed and agility on all fours, slowly walking in at first, then move into a fast-leaping action of three, six and then ten meters leaps at full speed, still being able to make sharp turns around tree trunks and leap over objects.

At one kilometer into the vegetation, they stop, smell, and listen for any similar species or other creatures. They sense a presence, but it is too late. It leaps out over a bush lunging at Lionheart. Its claws out and jaw wide open, ready to latch onto Lionheart's throat. Jagger reacts instantly, knocking it out of the air, and they tumble to the ground. With Jagger's larger size and strength, he kills it in a short, but fierce battle. They roar warning messages as they back towards each other, making a type of Y shape so each of them has one hundred and twenty degrees of vegetation to scan, while protecting each other's backs. The drones swoop in and circle, firing warning shots as Paffor crashes through the treetops, grabs the caucus of the animal and flies off with it. He drops it on the roof of the semi and circles back.

All the Panthera give messages to those around them in their own dialects. Paffor Lands back through the hole he made in the canopy and spreads his wings with a loud roar that has the bushes rustling as the creatures escape. Realizing the pointlessness, they retreat to avoid any of them being killed.

Arriving back at the semi, the Panthera smell the carcass on the roof. Paffor asks them if they want it, or if they would like to share. They agree to share it as a bond of their mutual support.

Sabrina and the crew are having a less eventful mission. Some buildings have lights on, with various species on the streets. These subjects flee quickly as they drive down the street, broadcasting the message. Logan hacks communication channels and spreads their message on them. It is a double-edge sword. On one edge, they are deliberately playing into the hands of the Elite by spreading messages that could cause an uprising they can exploit. On the other edge they need the support, or at least calm until they implement their plan.

Returning to the semi vehicles once they have completed a lap of the town, Sabrina checks in with Panthera to ensure they are okay and thanks Paffor for helping them out. They discuss the incident and know the next stop will be more difficult. Sabrina ends the conversation with an idea for them to ponder while driving to Dublin.

If we all agree it is safe enough to do so, we will try to communicate our message to the Unhuman outside Dublin. I need to stop there to visit two outliers to check on them and see if they wish to join the team or require help to evacuate, I will leave it up to you to decide and support your decision.

Chapter forty-three. Who's Town

The team rolls out of Virginia, heading for Dublin, Van, Valorie, Dragor and Paffor as they did when heading into Virginia, fly off ahead. Logan, not completely sure if he wants to ask, looks at Sabrina and does so anyway.

Where are they all going? What is the plan?

Sabrina responds with her now common wit.

Well Logan, you know what? I was about to ask you, You're our techie guy, why don't you ask them? Oh wait, you can't. That's right, they don't have any communication devices. I'm not sure mate. I am guessing if we ask them to tell us, we would not like the answers. So, the plan is to not get killed while we are alone.

She points out the window as the air support disappears in the moonlight.

Hopefully, everyone returns, or we face a challenge reaching the outliers.

Logan waits for a few seconds.

I think I liked it back in the semi with Lionheart and the crew. At least they just eat and growl at me now and then.

Sabrina and Logan turn to each other and smile.

Dublin has derelict buildings along the main highway and vegetation as far as the drones can see. Sabrina has never seen the two outliers she will visit, even though she has sent them many drones with tasks and supplies. It is a courtesy visit, and they are expecting her. She calls them and organizes to visit Julia first, then Martin. They both report that there is action and tension in the area. Two dragon humans are flying around, who they believe are Dragor and Paffor. Sabrina checks her radar and the drones' data, both of which are receiving many targets in the general area.

Heads up team, we have multiple targets all over the area. Electra, I would like you to get three drones programmed to fly within a two-kilometer radius of our parked location. Each drone will have a message recorded by Lionheart and crew in their respective dialects. The recordings will lack the clarity of in-person delivery because of missing frequencies. The intended Unhuman Panthera may not recognize the messages, but it may be the best we can do in this remote area.

Oh yeah, that's right, the plan. I know how you all like a detailed plan. So, let's see. Logan and I will go visit Julia and Martin and offer them any help they may want. If they choose to join us, that will be a bonus, as they have proven themselves to be quite resourceful. You all wait here. If it gets too dangerous, move on. I suspect the others will return or meet us along the way, so be careful who you shoot at, but protect yourselves if necessary. Does that sound like a brilliant plan?

She waits for a witty comment, but no one answers. They all sit silently as they realize they will be alone for an indefinite time.

Sabrina's vehicle returns to its Hellcat shape in chrome finish as it takes off, making its way to the outlier homesteads. The mirror quality finish reflects images of the foliage to blend in, it also confuses any flying creatures that decide to attack as they see their own reflection. Sabrina calls Julia as she hovers low outside the homestead walls to get permission to enter.

They receive permission and rise over the wall surrounding a modest-sized home, noticing many drones parked on its well-kept lawns. Sabrina finds a suitable spot to land, and they exit the Cat and walk towards Julia, who is standing at the main door. She welcomes them into the immaculate living room, filled with artworks and sculptures from around the world. Logan points at a sculpture in the center of the room.

The walking man replica is impressively accurate. Did you make it yourself, Julia?

No, I didn't make it, and who said it was a replica? I may have borrowed it sometime back now. It reminds me of the past and how far we've come.

Julia takes them to a doorway. It slides back to reveal a lift. Sabrina and Logan enter the lift feeling safe, but unsure what the doors will reveal when they open at the end of its journey down.

The lift doors open to reveal the reason behind Julia's helpfulness and secrecy. Logan's eyes sparkle while his head bobs like a desk toy. He doesn't know where to look first. It is a massive room, much larger than the premises above. It is full of electronics and computers that he has never seen before.

Stored in one corner of the workshop with other technical equipment is a transport vehicle and several drones. Everywhere in the workshop there are lights flashing in unique patterns. The entire workshop appears to be busy working on something altogether, computing and processing data as one entity.

Sabrina, without having to ask, knows Julia will not be leaving her home. She has everything she needs here to fend for herself.

I wanted to meet with you to thank you for all your help. I was wondering if you were going to be ok living here in the change to a new world. Looking around, I can see I already have that answer.

Over the years, I have successfully built a network of contacts, including yourself and others. I am happy here. I can come and go as I please. Martin and I have a good connection. He has a similar setup at his place, focusing on the mechanical techie side.

Logan puts his hand out to touch a piece of equipment. As he is about to contact it, Julia warns him not to touch anything. Alarms start going off along with the sounds of shots firing in the compound. Sabrina quickly reacts as Julia instantly gives a command to her system to stand down and she yells out.

Damn You, we have visitors.

I don't believe anyone was tracking or following us as we flew in. I apologize if we have caused this.

Oh, it is not your fault, Sabrina. Come on, follow me.

Sabrina has her hand on her pistol, ready to draw it. Julia tells her she will not need it. They exit the Lift and walk into the living room. Van stands in the center, casually observing sculptures and paintings.

Julia looks at Sabrina.

See, I told you it wasn't your fault. He's brought several friends too.

Sabrina is slightly shocked at first, as her mind puts it all together.

I knew I could sense something about you, Julia. I didn't want to ask, as I didn't need to know.

She then turns her thoughts to how Van got through the defenses. Logan speaks up, feeling out of the loop.

What?, what am I missing that you all know now, and I don't?

Well, Van and Julia know each other and not only that, with respect, Julia, if I may? Julia is not as young as her beautifully stunning appearance suggests.

Julia stands still with her almost glowing blue eyes and her fire red hair hanging down her amazingly toned body to her butt.

Come on, Logan, don't pretend you haven't noticed. Julia is part bat, or Vampire is the more accepted description. That is why she looks so amazing, with seductive and alluring chemistry, like Valorie and other elder female Vamps.

Yes, I am older than this idiot here. One day you will get shot. You are not getting any faster. You will now have to fix all that damage you have caused. I'm sick of fixing it myself. He has a type of death wish and keeps evaluating my system. He is lucky we can sense each other's presence, and my facial recognition software captures him fast enough to stop my whole yard from being shot up.

Van, you have been holding out on me. I didn't realize we were so fast. Honestly, I've never wanted to try it myself, but thanks for letting me know. Do the Elite know this? I have to imagine Vamps have tried to get through the moat.

Yes, other unwanted visitors have made a mess in my yard, as they are not on my welcome file list. Getting past trigger sensors is one thing, but Elite moats are different. They remain constantly active, and you may survive briefly before instantly disintegrating. They have different operational stages. Detecting each stage is possible, but surviving remains a gamble. I've never had the chance or reason to explore it further.

Ok, good to know Julia. Thank you. Logan, when we are at the homestead, talk to Duke on a secure line about this. We don't want Van getting through, only to get fried seconds later. Do we Van?

Van looks at Julia.

Sabrina has a new personality since changing her name, not just her different outlier names she uses, but from the not-so-fun robotic Sarah when she was a pain in everyone's ass. Guess what Sabrina, surprise! Julia, Valorie, Martin, and I have known who you were all along and have kept it to ourselves. I have brought friends with me. Now we have all met, we will fly back to the convoy to help protect it. I will ask the Panthera if they want to go for walkies, see I can be humorous to Sabrina. Logan kindly let the team know we're about to visit them to prevent my friends from getting shot. It's always a pleasure, Julia! Send me the bill for the pillar. Please let me out.

Van leaves and heads for the convoy, Sabrina asks Julia if she would like to come to visit Martin with her, as it is clear they are good friends. She agrees, saying that she will take her own vehicle. She turns off the security system so that Sabrina and Logan can leave.

They fly into Martin's place expecting it is going to be a similar experience as visiting Julia. His home is as clean as Julia's, also with old paintings and sculptures. His basement is full of machines bending, shaping, welding, and printing parts. While they are having a general chat, Julia arrives in her vehicle. Julia and Martin both agree to go to the homestead outside of the Port Lincoln compound to help Logan with all the technical issues. Together with CM's team, this will give them a significant advantage over the Elite. Sabrina informs them she will send the coordinates of the homesteads once they have arrived and surveyed both of them. Logan and Sabrina thank them and leave to head back to the convoy.

During the return flight, Sabrina ponders the Vamps' long-term plan. Is it part of CM's plan or were the Vamps always planning a takeover, and killing all the Elite at some point? She includes them in the expanding list of species she must trust for now.

Chapter forty-four. New Friends, New Ideas

Flying around the convoy like a cyclone are five Bat creatures. Van, Valorie, and Eddy are on the roof of one semi, watching them circle. Sabrina lands and ensures that Logan gets from the Cat to the semi safely. She then springs up onto the roof, standing next to the others.

Hi gang, what are you all doing? Won't they all get giddy doing that?

We were waiting for you to arrive, then see if the Panthera wanted to risk going out into the night. With our friends circling above, it should create a buffer and reduce Unhuman numbers nearby. It also might make them all nervous and on edge.

Well, Van, we should ask them if they want to risk it, or if we just move on. Who wants to ask the Panthera? Just kidding, I will do it. You all look too busy, anyway.

Sabrina jumps down and opens the Semi door.

So, do you guys want to go say hi to your friends, or shall we keep moving? Hearing the drone recordings, did they make sense or have the correct overtones?

They made sense, but our natural dialect is clearer and more meaningful. We are prepared to give it a go if we can have backup.

Yes, Van has brought his friends. They are fast, strong, and hard to see in the dark. We ask Dragor and Paffor to go in first and scare the less dominant creatures away. The Vamps can then enter and provide a perimeter for us.

Ok, then Sabrina, let's do it.

Thank you. I will come along as an extra backup. I can't ask you to do something I wouldn't do myself. We are a team, go team.

They exit the Semi and meet on the roof to discuss the plan. Van communicates to his friends, and they set the idea in motion. As Dragor and Paffor drop through the canopy and land, two creatures attack them. They easily brush them off, letting out a loud roar, opening and flapping their wings in a frightening display. Other creatures ready to join in all back away.

Van points to spots in the distance and his friends just disappear as they flash into the forest, grabbing creatures and throwing them into the scrubs. Disappearing from that location they arrive at the next creature, repeating this action until they have created a safe semi-circle perimeter out into the vegetation.

Van lands next to Dragor and Paffor in the middle of the cleared area, ready to act. Dragor and Paffor separate and move out closer to the edge created by the Vamps, as the Panthera and Sabrina run the perimeter, stopping to roar out their message at regular spots. It all goes better than they thought, and they hear leaders responding through the rustling of bushes. Sabrina senses they are being tracked, so she is on a heightened alert. At their fifth stop, three creatures leap out, not Panther, not Jaguar and not Lion, a complete mismatch of different animals.

Sabrina gets one shot off, killing one in mid-air, and the other two get into a fight with Lionheart and Jagger. She can't get a clean shot while they are fighting. Within seconds, Van appears, rips the head off one and slices open the other's stomach.

Dragor and Paffor fly over to grab Lionheart and Jagger, carefully lifting them back to the semi vehicles. Sabrina fires warning shots at the ground as cover while she and Leo sprint back to the vehicles. Van orders all his Vamps into the air again, circling the convoy.

Straight away, Sabrina goes to check on Lionheart and Jagger.

Are you both okay? You were doing so well. But wow I did not expect that from Van. I have seen carcasses on my field missions left like that. I knew he was strong, but wow, that was as impressive as your courage and fighting skills. None of us expected this to be easy or risk-free. We can only attempt to explain the situation to those who listen. The wild will always be wild and live by the natural order of their food chains.

She thanks them for their efforts and goes back to her vehicle to prepare to leave for the next stop. After this experience, Sabrina changes the plan. She believes it's too risky for the team to stop in Port Broughton. There are already enough outliers and mixed individuals in Clare, Jamestown, and Port Augusta who are aware of the Elite's plan. They can use those channels for communication. She doesn't want to risk losing any team member before the toughest part of the coup.

It is a two-and-a-half-hour trip to Port Augusta which has a thriving Mixed community outside the moat of the Elites Eyre Peninsula compound. She wants to pass through town undetected in the dead of night. The Pure might have spies in town, expecting any attack to emanate from there. They will head straight to the homesteads to rest and regroup.

Reflecting on the attempt to communicate with the Unhuman, Sabrina can't help but think about the Vamps' impressive speed and resources. There are quite a substantial number of them in Australia and worldwide. Not all are like Van, but they can still be a threat if they want to be. The coup could lead to an unknown outcome. If you remove one dominating power, another might decide to take its place. When everyone is safe in the homesteads, Sabrina decides she will need to talk privately with CM about the future.

While in transit, Duke calls to explain the homestead's layouts so Sabrina can plan for the team's arrival. One has enormous walls with an abundance of vegetation to shelter in within its boundaries, and a basic building. It has thick natural low-level shrubs and grasses surrounding its perimeter, with maintenance robots keeping down anything that tries to grow too high. A grassed area has drones stacked three high with a camouflaged shelter hiding them. Sabrina offers this homestead to the Panthera, Van, and his crew. Electra will stay there as well, to run logistics and check the drones. Brandon and Svetlana also offer to stay there to learn how the drones work.

Homestead Two, located a few kilometers away, features a modern design that merges with the surrounding environment. Under the smaller building is a well-maintained, extensive structure. It is remarkably similar to Julia's place. The massive underground bunker holds all the equipment to launch an attack on the Elite's compound.

There are Issue with both homesteads. They are on islands in former salt lakes, now transformed into large lakes with scattered prime vegetation around them. Neither homestead has a road or driveway the semi convoy can use to drive safely inside. The semi-trucks are large, heavy, and old, deliberately chosen to not stand out, but they cannot fly. They must park a couple of kilometers away where the road ends and the lake with its islands starts.

The tactical drones they have brought with them can fly out on their own carrying pieces of equipment. Shuttles from each homestead will provided the transport to gain entry. It won't be free of danger. Large pterodactyl creatures circle the compounds and prey on creatures wounded by the homestead defenses. They are more prominent here than seen in other areas where their scorched earth rings keep an enormous distance between towns and suitable vegetation for shelter. Therefore, the lack of other creatures and a sustainable food chain for them.

Dragor and Paffor have already had a run-in with the pterodactyl. Sabrina also knows from experience that they will be a threat. Taking them down must be a complete show of force if they have any chance of making them retreat. If these creatures see any weaknesses they can prey upon, they will, and they may lose members of the team.

Van's crew, Dragor and Paffor, can fend for themselves but Eddy would be out of his league if he were to fly in. Sabrina stops the team short of Port Augusta and suggests to Eddy to do the rest of the trip in one of the semi vehicles. She asks the rest of the aerial support team to follow at random high altitudes to have a safe, unseen passage to the homesteads. The pterodactyl would easily recognize a cluster of flying creatures and attack. Whereas multiple targets high in the sky with distance between them will not be threatening or appealing to them.

Chapter forty-five. Central Set Down

Just before the convoy stops, Sabrina briefs the team on the challenges facing them to enter the homesteads safely.

We've been through a lot tonight, but we've learned to function as a team and care for one another. Getting to the homesteads poses a slight challenge. For decades, pterodactyls held air superiority and dominated the food chain here. They are unlikely to let us fly in with no interaction. Get any essentials ready that will fit into the shuttles with you and prepare to leave your semi. I will take care of the rest of the gear needing to be transported. Eddy, you can take the first shuttle as you should fit in it alone. Then the shuttles can return to pick up the remaining team members.

Sabrina, you are worried about me flying in on my own.

Yes, Baldy, you will face challenges from the pterodactyl. The others who can fly will be busy defending us if they become frenzied. Also, we will see how your shuttle goes. If they take it out knowing food is inside, we will have to devise another way to get to the homestead. Good luck Baldy, have a safe trip.

Eddy lets out his now familiar response of a less-than-impressed groan. His shuttle travels nearly all the way with no issues. Just before it reaches the safety of the homestead, several beasts swoop at it. Van and Dragor grab them, ripping a wing off one and sending it spiraling to the ground to become food. The other attackers have their necks slashed and crash to the ground. The defense drones fire at the nearby pterodactyls that are approaching. Eddy's shuttle has taken several large hits by the time it has arrived at the homestead. The rough ride shook him up.

Sabrina, it is not safe. That was a bumpy ride. I don't think the others will survive.

Nah Baldy, it's all good, thank you. We have learned their attack strategy and scared many of them away. They have seen our superior force, so they will go look for easier targets, leaving us alone for now. It could have gone either way, but you made it. That is a win for us.

Eddy groans.

The remaining shuttle transfers attract minimal attention and the drones with the air support team scare off or kill any that try to attack. All the shuttles and crew have arrived safely, Dragor and Paffor vanish into the night as the others get some rest.

Sabrina enters a private room to receive an update from CM regarding the preparations and discuss the strength of the Vamp species. She also discusses issues if the moat defenses are down for too long. Allowing pterodactyls and other creatures into the Elite compound to cause chaos. CM assures Sabrina the moat won't be down for long, and the Vamps and Dragons are crucial for the coup's success. They are willingly helping. If they intended on dominating, they would just sit back and wait for the Mixed and Pure to fight it out. Reducing each other's numbers, then attack. The transition will require some kind of law and force to keep order to achieve freedom within a reasonable time. To maintain order that is agreed upon by all relevant parties will require strength and power, along with the leaders of each species. Every member on the panel will have an equal say and manage their own unique species form of justice, with the support of committee groups. It will definitely be complex, but fair. CM also informs Sabrina that as yet none of the Elite targets have fallen ill, or have died, but they expect that to change by morning.

After other general chatting, CM tells Sabrina to get some sleep, and unless something critical happens, he will contact her mid-afternoon tomorrow. They wish each other goodnight.

Chapter forty-six. Brick By Brick

The sun rises over both homesteads, all are still asleep, knowing they are safe with the security systems active. In the basement, drones flash and beep as they receive upgrades from Duke and the team. Chatter on Elite's channels suggests leading councilors are feeling unwell. They were all present at a strategy meeting, eating from a lavish smorgasbord they put together to celebrate the virus spraying. They believe they may all have eaten something that's made them sick.

Sabrina wakes at 7am and quietly checks her messages while going over in her mind how the team will approach the mission. She makes enough noise to let anyone know she is up. Logan can hear Sabrina is awake and her door is ajar, so he knocks on it.

Logan, where have you been all night? I missed you.

He enters the room slightly red-faced but now used to Sabrina's sarcasm. He tells her about all the updates he has received from the drones deployed from each homestead in a random sequence before dawn. Sabrina thanks him and they walk out into the living room. Her casual clothes amaze the team, since she is always in her suits in either Sarah or Sabrina mode. She tells them while she is away at the other homestead, they should eat and relax.

Arriving at the second homestead, she finds the Panthera all still asleep. Eddy is awake and in a talkative mood.

Hi Sabrina, wild get up, you have on there.

He looks at her, trying to mimic her smile.

See, I am having an influence on you. I told you I would. Where is your Golden Armor? In the wash?

It's not as fancy as your suits, making it hard to sleep in. I needed rest and a good night's sleep as who knows what crazy plan you have in store for us. How was the meeting with your outlier friends? Are they joining us, or evacuating?

They are joining us and it's a funny story. You're going to love it. They are old, not in human years, but in vampire years. Their homesteads have better technology than I have ever seen. Which explains their ability to help with my projects over the years.

Eddy, in his deep serious tone, blurts out as he turns to walk away.

Great, more Vamps. We are being outnumbered, Sabrina; I am not sure I trust them.

Aww come on, stop being so jealous.

She smiles and looks at him as he turns his head towards her. She waits for his customary groan, but he says nothing.

Yes, I have been thinking about it myself and I look at it this way. They are fast, really fast, and strong. It would be easier for them to wait and see what happens and rule after we are gone. But they are here, wanting us to win as a group, at least for now.

Van walks out from behind a wall.

You know we don't need to sleep and have excellent hearing? Yes, we keep to ourselves normally and have the same motive as you. We will defend ourselves if anyone turns on us. None of us want conflict, we only feed on natural animals, those that attack or are problematic to us. Our covens actually make your hometowns safer for you to live in.

Sabrina thanks Van for his honesty, explaining that all species are working through this situation together, showing each other their strengths and weaknesses. It is what CM believed would happen when we teamed up and started working together for a common goal. Dragor and Paffor's actions also express their commitment to the greater good. No one has eaten Baldy yet, and I had good odds on that happening.

She smiles at him, lightening the mood. Van flicks out his teeth and opens his wings slightly, then smiles.

Eddy groans.

Can someone please remind me why I'm here and how I got tangled in this mess? I apologize Van. I was just verbalizing a thought aloud to Sabrina. Though we never got along, I can't remember you causing harm to my Flock without reason.

No need for an apology. I can see things from your perspective.

Sabrina looks at Eddy.

We love you Baldy, we wouldn't be stirring you up if we didn't think you could take it, or not smart enough to get our sarcasm.

He walks off mumbling.

Nothing funny or easy about your plan.

Sabrina heads to the basement and finds Electra, Svetlana, and Brandon working on the drones.

Did you all sleep well? Where are we at with the deployment? Before they can answer, alarms go off. The drones have picked up incoming targets and are unsure if they are friendly or hostile. Electra quickly looks at the images the drones are transmitting.

It's Dragor and Paffor. I can't quite see, but it appears they are holding something in one claw and waving with the other.

Sabrina tells Electra to get the drones to escort them into the compound, so they know it is safe to approach, and goes outside to greet them.

Dragor and Paffor drop two fresh creatures into the compound that are part of the Panthera's natural diet, then land.

Hi Sabrina, we brought something for Lionheart, Jagger, and Leo. I figured they couldn't go out and hunt for themselves. We have flights nesting around here. We can keep the Pterodactyl birds away with our numbers for a time. Do you know when we'll enter the compound?

Thank you, the Panthera will appreciate the meal. We are about to discuss the plans now. You are welcome to sit in on it if you like.

Dragor thanks Sabrina for the offer to join the meeting and gives her some advice.

I don't think having us flying around inside the Elite compound would be the best idea. Apart from our size, I doubt the common Pure will feel comfortable with us circling in the sky. Valorie, Van, the Panthera and Eddy will be substantial support inside the walls. We will be more effective outside of the moat, keeping anything from entering when it is open.

That is a great idea, thank you Dragor.

Sabrina calls Logan and asks him to get the team to prepare for a meeting in one hour on a secure video channel. She checks on the Panthera, telling them where the food came from and about the meeting. Then she goes back down to the basement to meet the crew. They inform her that the drones are ready to be deployed near the moats with the rest.

The team assembles in the living room, with large doors opening onto the outside deck. CM, Tarak, and Duke call in from Monarto. Cosimo, Mira, and Aurora call in from Adelaide. The Panthera are laying on the deck, Dragor and Paffor sit in the yard as Sabrina starts the meeting by introducing all of her team. CM responds by thanking them all for helping. The team in the homesteads listen out of respect for Sabrina, not so much towards the Monarto or Adelaide teams.

CM tells the team why he destroyed the laboratory, his thoughts, and praises them for their courage and teamwork. The Elite will recognize your strengths, leading them to the realization they need to include rather than dominate. He explains that they have infected only the leaders who have shown no intention of ever accepting any Mixed Humans, and the virus they have all taken will kill them in the next forty-eight hours.

Duke covers technical details and informs them he still has control over defense systems and key infrastructure components. It is like listening to someone explain every proton, neutron and electron needed to create an atom, then every atom needed to make the computer. Sabrina's team is showing signs of confusion, hesitation, and disinterest.

She jumps in.

So, what Geekie Duke and Logan are saying is they will ensure we can get through the Moat. Support us wherever necessary and have our backs in any situation.

Duke tries to go on.

Yeah, it's a bit more complicated than that. I have hacked into over nine thousand systems, written real-time monitoring software, and created backdoors into other software over the last five years.

Yep, thank you Duke, we get it. Basically, lots of ones and zeros written really smartly to ensure we are safe. It is all amazing, but the detail is over our heads. Even Logan is thinking about going to sharpen more of those fancy pencils he likes.

Logan and Duke scream out together.

They are styluses, and they do not need sharpening.

Sabrina smiles, looking at Logan first, then at Duke.

We understand it is highly technical, using some really cool tools and you are all doing an amazing job with your stylus things. We thank you and appreciate all you have done.

Tarak takes over explaining that he and Cosimo, along with the others in Monarto, will monitor the systems and communication, keeping the team on top of what's happening inside the compounds. He concludes by providing an update on the sick Elite members and suggests that the raid should occur before sunrise, ideally between three and four.

They wrap up the meeting by discussing the compound's entry and exit points and how they will use the vehicles to get through the moat. CM closes the meeting thanking everyone and sets a three AM contact time for tomorrow, unless there is an emergency.

They all disperse to get rest and downtime. Sabrina calls Julia and Martin to inform them of the timeline and other relevant information. Logan and Duke communicate with each other, checking their equipment and making sure each has the latest software version running on them.

Chapter forty-seven. Its Glowing

I t's two o'clock in the morning. Sabrina is awake, programing her personal drones and preparing her Cat for the mission. Julia and Martin will arrive at two thirty to offer support from the homestead and be ready to enter the compound if needed. When Van, Dragor and Paffor are ready, they will help Sabrina get the team back into the Semi vehicles. There are not too many things that are required to go back into them, as most of the gear was for the homestead. This will ensure they will all fit inside the semi vehicles to cross the moat and enter the compound. Tova desperately misses her bike and hopes it is still there when they get back to the vehicles.

Sabrina changes her vehicle to resemble a maintenance van to pass through the moat with the other pods. Once inside, they will follow the path of all service vehicles to the transfer station, where all transporters sit till they are called up to be emptied in the automated warehouses. They will disperse from there to travel through the buildings and infrastructure to the center of the peninsula where the Elite castle is situated, in a town called Boonerdo.

All the team members are awake. Sabrina, in her typical fashion, briefs them on the mission objectives and introduces Julia and Martin, who have just arrived.

Morning all, we are going to load everyone that is needed inside the compound into the semi vehicles. This should reduce the risk of us getting vaporized. I will lead the pods through first and, providing I cross without incident, the semi vehicles will follow. Dragor and Paffor, you will stay outside the walls with Van's crew until we get in trouble or have reached our goals. What are our goals? Good question, to survive, to show we mean no harm, to inform the Pure inside the compound of the intentions and actions of the Elites leaders. We'll explain to Pure community that a new, accepting world is the only way.

While executing the plan, Julia, Martin, and our Monarto team will be in contact, providing help. Our Pure contacts inside the compound will assist us in accessing necessary areas. Ok, so I think that's a pretty exact detailed plan. Are we all good?

She finishes with her traditional smile.

Eddy speaks up.

So, the plan is, to make it up as we go then?

All the team looks at Eddy and smile.

OK, I can see by all the smiles we are all on the same page. I will call CM and get an update. If it is all go, we'll follow the original timeline. Loading semi vehicles at three, leaving at three ten, and arriving at the moat by three thirty. Make sure you have all your equipment and dress correctly. Baldy, please make sure your gold bling is all polished. We want you to look good in the photos.

She quickly turns to leave, her long hair flicking out with her hand on her hip, mimicking a supermodel's spin at the end of a runway. Eddy just groans at her sarcasm as she catwalks past, smiling at him.

Back in her room, she calls CM and dresses in her burgundy-colored warrior suit with deep chocolate highlights. CM informs Sabrina that five Elite of the of fifteen targets have now passed away, including the supreme leader. Shock and chaos is growing amongst the rest as we hoped it would. She thanks CM for the information and confirms with the team that deployment is a go.

Valorie, Dragor, Van and Paffor have already done a shuttle run to check out the semi vehicles and the area for creatures. Eddy walks up with his gold armor shining and looks at Sabrina. He smiles and comments on how her suit looks.

Wow, look at you Sabrina, looking all superhero like, all you need is a cape. Would you like me to do the first run in the shuttle like last time?

She Smiles and looks at Van, then the others, before she turns to Eddy.

No, mate, I can't fly. A cape would just get in the way. You can go in one of the last three this time. Anything wanting to take a pod down will have worked out the sequence by then. Thanks for offering to do the last run. I wasn't sure how to ask you.

She smiles at him, then the others. Eddy groans under his breath.

I am just here as bait. And walks away dejected.

No, Baldy, you can handle yourself. Only a few flying creatures will be out this early, but if attacked, you can eject and fly out before crashing. Well, we all hope that you can anyway, don't we team?

Hell Yeah, go Baldy.

The loading of the semis goes without incident. The extra air support from Dragor and Van's crew discourages any attacks from creatures that are awake. Tova is happy to be reunited with her bike and gives it a quick look over as she reloads it with weapons. All the vehicles pull out in their prearranged order, resembling a registered transport group for their drive to the moat.

The convoy approaches the unmistakable blue glow of the moat. It appears endless in all directions. While Sabrina has seen it countless times, the team finds what they see on the monitors both astonishing and scary. The highway leads them to an entrance section that is thirty meters high by thirty meters wide, extending five meters deep into the compound. The only transport entrance separately controlled from the rest of the moat by the warehouse.

They want their approach and entering to appear as normal as possible, so the controlling system will not trigger any alarms. Duke is confident that he has the defense system deactivated, but he gives the team a chilling warning. If an emergency override automatically kicks in, he may not have time to stop it, and it could vaporize the vehicles as they pass through.

Protocol requires tight grouping and quick entry for shuttle pods. Semi vehicles traditionally pass through in a side-by-side formation to create the smallest height and shortest distance to accept them. No one watching can tell if the entrance is open, as it doesn't change shape or color if it is in safe mode. Only a green light on a licensed vehicle's dashboard glows to show that it's safe to pass.

Sabrina and the three shuttle pods group up and receive the green light. The semi vehicles are a safe, regulated distance behind and keep approaching at standard transport speed. Inside the different vehicles, they all sit still and quiet. The mission and coup will be over in minutes if they all vaporize. They switch off all communication devices and anything with power to avoid accidentally tripping an alarm.

Sabrina and the pods enter first and disappear from view as the semi vehicles keep approaching. Not seeing any flashes or explosions, they all stay silent, hoping Sabrina has made it through safely. As the semi enters the moat gate, Valorie and Van gaze into each other's eyes. Van notices something. Without transmitting or moving, Van blinks at Valorie, and she blinks back when it changes state.

All pass through without incident and make the two-kilometer trip to the warehouse car park, drawing no attention in the early morning hours. Entering the car park, the rear of each semi opens and the pods move in to rest against the tailgates. Quickly, they load into them as they keep moving. Electra, Brandon, and Svetlana jump into pods with a Panthera. Valorie, Van, and Eddy fly and land on the warehouse roof. Logan jumps into the Cat with Sabrina as her maintenance vehicle turns back into its familiar camo-green Hellcat appearance. Tova rides down the ramp that is now scraping on the ground, tempted to run her bike in full noise mode, but she restrains herself.

The remaining leaders at Port Lincoln headquarters call Natasha, the next senior security leader. They inform her of the murder of Astro by a senior leader and the passing of five others in the Elite management group. Tacy speaks up and tells Natasha to stay calm, and to have Geoff, Wayne, and Petra join the security team in their command center. She says she will inform the Leaders in Mount Gambier of the deaths. Leaders in Port Lincoln ask her to put a team on alert ready to deploy, as they believe it is possible that someone inside the compound is planning a takeover.

Protocols that Astro and Natasha put in place almost worked to perfection. However, losing Astro is a blow to the team. However, they now have three more supporters inside the security control room. Natasha's first order to the new team is to find out what happened to Astro. She wants to know if anyone has learned about his role in the coup or the leaders' deaths. Are they still alive and if there is any evidence that could impact the mission?

Astro's death may lead to unpredictable actions. CM has placed its recruited personnel in various fields and levels. The Elite leaders on the Moon, Mars, and Earth-based compounds may not have kept CM in on all the security and defensive protocols. They might have prepared a contingency plan for managing coups or uprisings when they activated their extinction plan. Astro would have been told before they were about to implement it, but the Elite are unlikely to trust the new junior members with this news.

Duke is sharing his backdoor access keys to the systems with Julia and Martin while they still have control. Natasha, Petra, Wayne, and Geoff are working on the security control panels in the compounds, hiding any coup activities. All is running smoothly as the team starts its way through the narrow streets. Directly flying to headquarters is the fastest choice, but it may appear invasive rather than freedom. Slowly driving in will be seen in a more favorable light by the Pure public.

To cover their approach from the Elite leaders on their security screens is what Duke has previously recorded. A video loop of the empty streets from their building cameras from earlier this morning, Logan from inside the Cat with Sabrina, is transmitting positive messages, overriding the propaganda news that the Elite are distributing within the compound. The Vamps use their speed and stealth to move ahead, reporting on the area's status and disabling security cameras Duke cannot control. Eddy is flying high above any sensors as the Elite expect nothing above the threshold height of vehicles and drones to be a threat inside the moat.

The team makes its way to the Elite headquarters with Sabrina leading the pods and Tova following at the back. Traveling at a moderate pace along the straight highways in the outer city, still a distance from the elevated headquarters. As they approach the center of the peninsula, streets will become narrower and more maze-like. The more privileged population wants to be around the Castle and the green open spaces that surround it for entertainment and physical activity. These open areas are ringed by a variety of buildings restricted to sixty stories high within a ten-kilometer radius of the Castle. It overlooks all, including the distant higher apartment building as the Castle is on top of a manufactured mountain. Intentionally designed to position the public beneath them, constantly looking up at Elite leaders. Buildings rise higher as they move away to offer a view of the Castle, and so the Elite look down on them.

Julia and Martin, now with access to the Elite system, are running scans and checks with their more sophisticated equipment, and it shows anomalies. There are programs and information that are hidden from normal system scans. To a casual observation, they appear as basic standard programs that do not need attention. Julia feels they are actually portholes to a unique system. She shares her findings and concerns with the team while attempting to hack and uncover their secrets.

While the communication channel is open to the team, Van transmits a message to Julia and Martin that even Sabrina will not hear. Duke passes on current information about the catalyst drug working on the off-world Elite leaders as intended. He also lets Sabrina, and the team know he has detected extra incoming spacecraft. They are not on any of the scheduled shuttle arrivals planned to enter earth's orbit. None of the craft are showing signs of human life onboard. Something or someone has deployed them manually or autonomously from the moon. Natasha tells Duke that after the call, she will contact him so they can investigate.

This is what CM was worried about, a security protocol they didn't know about. There might be an army that the Elite leaders kept secret, only revealing it to a privileged few. Why was CM not included? Maybe he was being set up as a scapegoat for their mass extinction plan.

Sabrina asks Julia and Martin to work on a plan for more of the team to get through the moat, just in case this is backup from the off-world Elite. Unknown to Sabrina, Julia and Martin already have a plan to enter the compound and bring Dragor and Paffor with them. Van has secretly informed them about the change in frequency that only the Vamps can hear in their ultrasonic range and see within their light wavelengths. Martin believes that by utilizing this frequency, he can create an undetectable hole in the field with the device he has been working on, allowing everyone to pass through.

Chapter forty-eight. All the Way

In just over an hour, the team has covered the distance with no signs of ambush or defenses. They are now circling the Castle on the hill, transmitting messages on community channels. Valorie and Van have removed all the outside security cameras and plan to make their presence known. It all is going well. The team in the security control room will help to make entering the building easier. Sabrina's plan is to go in with a positive, powerful show of defiance. The Elite defenses comprise drones and robotic security, with very few Pure allowed to have weapons. She hopes that those who do won't shoot. Killing innocent people isn't their intention, but they will reluctantly do so if there's no alternative.

Dawn is now seconds away as the sun slowly creeps to the horizon. People are turning on the news and getting the messages the team has spread. They will also hear of the deaths of senior leaders. Ten of the fifteen have now passed. The Elites continue to broadcast their messages, declaring the Mixed are evil and stating that they must be stopped. The team is broadcasting self-created footage displaying the deaths caused by the spraying the leaders unleashed. Along with other broadcasts to the public, telling the true story of how the Mixed and Unhuman are combining forces for peace. The compounds' split percentage resulting from these conflicting messages is unknown.

The parklands are well-maintained, beautiful grassy areas with trees and shelters, streams of water, manicured plants, and hedges, all combine to create magical gardens that circle a one-kilometer radius around the castle. Like other Headquarters, they have steps that ascend to the main entrance, starting wide at the bottom and narrow as they reach the top. These stairs are gold, they glow yellow in the light of the new dawn.

Logan inside Sabrina's Cat leads the team. Lionheart, Jagger, Leo, Svetlana, Electra, Brandon and Sabrina walk behind it. Tova rides her bike behind them, as Valorie, Van, and Eddy land behind her and walk up with them as a rear guard. As they are walking towards the Castle, they get three distinct signs from the streets. Some people applaud and show approval, while others are shocked, and some flee in fear. A much smaller number of Pure are throwing their arms up in disgust. It is a risk they have to take, and it appears to be working. The Elite have long discussed a change. Most knew it would happen one day. To Pure, it meant freedom and a new earth, but they thought about it in two diverse ways. Popular choice is harmony and reunion, as opposed to the Elite's eradication plan.

Sabrina's suit now picks up the dawn's light and shimmers as she walks, showing her athletic figure. Eddy's gold armor shines and reflects the surroundings. With his wings tucked tightly away, he looks mostly human from a distance. Svetlana, Electra and Brandon look casual but intimidating. Clearly, they are all armed and will fight if they have to. They slowly approach the Castle, walking as a team of Mixed Human representatives, ready for a meeting. Tova has the volume just loud enough on her bike, so the Harley sound offers a type of marching beat, defining their presence. Since the leaders have died, it is unclear if they are invited guests or if they have any involvement. It is the most exciting thing that has happened in decades within the compound. Everyone is watching broadcasts, chatting on social media channels or out on the streets.

They have made it halfway to the golden stairs as Logan receives information from Duke. Both the compound's security and Duke's monitoring systems are showing signs that a program has started. No one on the team has set it into action or noticed anyone else doing it. From nowhere, Julia and Martin drop into the marching parade. Sabrina, without missing a step, turns and looks at Julia.

Hi Julia, I am guessing you haven't brought good news.

Before she can answer, Logan speaks up.

Hey guys, we have a few targets. No, no, make that many targets ahead.

Ok Logan, it is time to use those sharpened pencils. Where and what are they?

They don't appear to have any weapons; they are flesh and bone, but what they are, I am not sure. I doubt they are a welcoming committee; they are all scattering in a chaotic random pattern and not coming directly for us.

Svetlana, Tova, Brandon.

Yes Sabrina.

This is your fault. Whenever I'm with you, people show up and shooting starts.

Sabrina, I was actually thinking the same thing. Whenever I am with you, my life is in danger.

Sabrina looks at Svetlana and smiles.

OK, team, if they attack us, or the public, we attack them.

Julia explains to Sabrina that the hidden program is not actually a program, it is an automation that seems to have set loose a bunch of wild, Unhuman creatures. She doesn't believe they are a defensive weapon or have been set free to kill the team. Julia feels that Pure Humans are at a greater risk of being killed on the streets. The Elite likely planned to release these creatures, keeping them starved or drugged just enough to keep them alive, wild, and ready for release at any time to support their virus release. The best we can come up with is that there was a type of dead man switch that has set them free, activated by killing one or more of the Elite leaders.

Ok Julia, thanks for the information, very inconvenient timing though. I had the feeling things were progressing a tad too easily. I suspected something was about to happen. Team our new priority, eliminate and protect the Pure on streets.

Martin gets Sabrina's attention.

Just so you know, the shuttles that left the Moon are now active in orbit. They woke up when the creatures got released. I doubt that is a coincidence and they are also heading here. The passing of the Elite leaders may be connected to these actions, and it is likely that other compounds will be affected when more leaders pass in the next forty-eight hours. I am not sure why it is happening, but unless we can stop them, they will cause the loss of many lives. Natasha, Cosimo, Duke, and CM are looking for any backdoors to these programs or triggers and arranging for defense drones to be ready to help us?

Julia adds to the conversation.

We hitched a ride in with a couple of your friends.

She points up to where Dragor and Paffor are circling.

We worked out the frequency of the moat and tuned it to one of Martin's devices that allowed us through. I believe the Elite created a plan where they would pull the moat down for a short time to blame the creatures on rebels and the wild entering. Our Coven and Dragor's will defend the moat if it goes down, allowing only your drones through, plus a small team will cross to help us. I have shared the moat secret with only a trusted chosen few of our elder Vamps, who have paired up with Dragors' team and covens near Mount Gambier and Yorke Peninsula, in case we can't get there, and those moats go down.

Great chat, as always, Julia, delivering the awesome news with no sugar coating. Ok team let's go do our thing. Their sole focus is killing. They will be in pain, and who knows what drugs they are on to make them rabid. We need to kill them all.

Sabrina grabs her pistol and flashes off to attack the creatures. Valorie, Dragor, Paffor and Van have already sprung into action and started making a pile of dead creatures. This attracts others to the caucuses to feed and helps to cull them. Unfortunately, they are quite fast and have already maimed or killed members of the Pure public that had gathered to watch Sabrina's team walking to the headquarters.

Julia and Martin have disappeared from the action as the pile of creatures grows rapidly. An alert sounds out over the compound broadcast channel, as Martin and the team suspected, it announces that creatures have breached the moat. It shows video of unhuman appearing to come through the moat as the alarm rings out. The Pure in their control room have seen the moat shut down briefly. Other Pure living near the moat can see the drones and the backup team of Vamps and dragons cross through. They are finding it all very confusing. The Elite video message is showing different creature images than what they are actually seeing. This makes them doubt who is staging what, or what is the actual truth.

Chapter forty-nine. The Force

Over a thousand creatures are now causing havoc in multiple locations. The new team of Vamps and Dragons, along with the drones, quickly clean up the creatures released near the moat. While the team is finishing up killing the small number released designed to help support the Elite broadcasts, a new message comes out over the system.

Dear Pure, because of this attack from the Mixed and Unhuman, our trust in them and trying to live with the Mixed has ended. We have a security team inbound to destroy them inside this compound, and anywhere else they choose to attack us. With your support, we will rid ourselves of those who are not willing to live alongside us and choose to kill us. We have lost innocent people so far and may lose more. We will make this battle short and be stronger for it.

Tova is quickly on the comms channel.

Sabrina WTF, that can't be good. I think they are spinning our story, and it sounds like we will need a lot more support.

Sabrina now has her sword drawn as the creatures and the broadcast have really pissed her off, which is another new emotion for her. No longer content just shooting them, she is now taking her anger out on them by slicing creatures in half that are attacking the Pure Public.

I am a little busy right now, Tova; we are all good. You have got this girl. Go round up creatures on that bike of yours. Turn it up to eleven and kill as many as you can. Go get them, babe. Hey Logan, fire up that stylus thingy of yours and give us some more info on what's going. Also, have someone find out who's broadcasting these messages and stop them.

Sabrina, we have five cargo ships entering the atmosphere and are on track to land here. They are an older style of craft, and no life forms are on board. It is quite interesting, really I.....!

Logan gets cut off by Sabrina.

You know that I'm not sitting at a bar right now sipping on a drink, don't you B? While you are sitting safely in the Cat we are fighting are asses off out here, I need the short version please.

Five ships are heading this way, possibly with robotic troops. More creatures were just released on the other side of the Castle.

There is a brief silence, then he yells out.

Oh, Shit Sabrina, Sabrina the Cat is now driving off on its own, I have no control.

Logan, it is time to earn your keep. I am sending you over to the new release site to lead the team, control the drones, and highlight where the creatures are going. Van, can you and Paffor go with Logan and instruct your teams to kill the creatures? We will hold down this side.

As Van flies past the entrance to the Castle, he senses Julia and Martin. He circles back to have a chat with them, then calls Logan.

Logan, you must inform your team that there will be action inside the headquarters shortly. Tell them not to attack if confronted, stand still, and if friendly, just whisper Sabrina.

Logan wants to ask questions, but as he is concentrating on all the data coming in, he just responds.

I'll send a message to Duke to pass on to the others.

After hearing Van, Sabrina broadcasts to the team the new plan.

Ok we don't know what is coming in on these spaceships. I seriously doubt they are coming to help us. Use your skills to protect yourselves first, members of our team second, and then the public. They will either be drones or robotic soldiers set to kill anything that is not Pure. If they are droids, aim for their head or joints, as they are the weak points. Our drones will have no trouble picking them out, so I will assign one of them to each of you as protection. It sounds like Julia and Martin have found a new fun project they are attending to, so I am sure we will have more fantastic news soon. I will move around as fast as I can, and if you get in trouble, call me.

They all acknowledge her message as the first ship is landing, not where all the action is but a short distance away. Duke calls the team with more news.

Wayne just informed me that all control room systems are offline. No cameras, no intel, no anything, and he does not know where the messages are being broadcast from.

Tova has reached the first ship's landing spot. She fills in more detail on the open channel.

It is full of droids, about twenty-four of them, and they are just shooting at everything. What the hell? It's almost like they are just trying to create as much damage as possible.

The compound network broadcasts a new message.

Citizens stay inside and take shelter. We have droids here to help protect you and they have special sensors to detect all our attackers. Our Pure human eyesight cannot see all the enemy, while their shooting may seem erratic. We assure you only traitors, Mixed and Unhuman are being killed.

Tova jumps back on the coms.

They are shooting the public too; they are just shooting randomly.

Yep Tova, it is straight out of their playbook. They are reporting all the damage as being done by Mixed Humans. Take them all out, Tova. They are killing innocents and destroying infrastructure. I know you want to use those big guns of yours.

Tova sets the engine noise to eleven, switches on the autopilot, and pulls out her large pulse gun, taking out the first five of them with ease. The others have dispersed into the narrow streets in and around the apartment buildings.

I got five. Another group of five heads towards the parklands, while the others venture deeper into the community. I will take them.

Svetlana and Brandon have climbed atop shelters in the Parklands. This gives them a three-hundred-and-sixty-degree view of the area, as they are expecting at least one ship will land in the parklands as a statement.

A conical shaped craft lands fifty meters away from them. It sits stationary for sixty seconds, then the protective cone lifts. Six large doors fold down, acting as ramps. Each section has four droids, they are gunmetal gray with armor that is quite effective against small arms fire. Humanoid looking with arms that have pulse guns built into them, they exit, shooting randomly.

Svetlana, Brandon, and the drones fire at their joints, slowing them, but don't completely stop them. Dragor swoops in picking them up two at a time by their heads and throwing them at others, disabling them, droids they can't take out escape into the surrounding streets. Svetlana informs Tova about their heading, she and Brandon search for the ones from the first landing.

It is all becoming quite overwhelming for the team. Killing the first and second group of released creatures and droids is demanding, managing another seventy-two droids will be highly impossible. The rabid creatures have killed civilians, but the droids have killed many more and done a lot of infrastructure damage, Sabrina knows that footage of her and the team shooting at the droids will get effectively edited and used to blame all the infrastructure damage on them. Video of the mountain of creatures the Vamps and Dragons have piled will also show what an excellent job the Elite team of droids have done. Time is now working against Sabrina and her team. Two more ships landed on the northern side and are getting ready to deploy. The fifth one is hovering at an altitude, waiting to land. Dragor and others try to knock it out of the sky, but with no luck, Sabrina calls Logan.

Hey mate, how's your day going? I hope you are enjoying the sun; I don't suppose you might find a little time to use your techie skills and stop these droids? We are all having a tough day out here while you are getting a tan.

I have been trying Sabrina. Duke has tried and he can't find where in the system the commands are coming from. Hey Sabrina, someone or something is knocking on the roof of the Cat.

Well, Logan, have a look to see what or who it is, turn the skin to clear. You programmed the Cat, didn't you?

Oh yeah, good thinking, it's Julia and Martin standing on the roof.

Well, get out and ask them how their day is going.

He yells out, not wanting to leave the safety of the Cat.

Sabrina wants to know how your day is going.

They gesture to him to get out of the vehicle, reluctantly he does so. Julie tells him they have been inside the Castle and down to the basement. He has about five minutes to clear the lower levels, then there will be some action. Logan calls Duke to have him warn any friendlies to get above the ground floor urgently. He opens a common line and repeats the information to the team. By the time he finishes, Julia and Martin have gone.

Logan Ask them why, what's about to happen?

I can't Sabrina.

What do you mean you can't ask them?

I Can't ask them as they are not here, they have gone.

Duke instructs Petra, Wayne, and Geoff to generate a security reason for clearing the first floor and below. Five minutes pass and smoke comes out of vents as several explosions go off. The entire computer system inside the castle flashes and reboots. Shortly after that, all the droids just freeze and remain motionless. The ship hovering lands in the parklands, the doors open, but none of the droids deploy.

Sabrina, I have good news and, well, some other news. Those suspicious files are all removed, and I still have some control, but it looks like someone else is inside the system now.

Duke, that will be Julia. She just can't help herself when she has an interesting task involving software.

It looks like they have stopped the droids and, hopefully, any more releases of the creatures.

Ok thanks Duke, when I get inside the headquarters and bump into her I will ask her for you. Hey, team give me a status report. How are we doing with these critters?

We have got most of them. Some escaped into the surrounding alleys and streets. Ok thanks Eddy.

I have taken out all I have found, but it is a slow process.

Thanks Tova.

Logan informs Sabrina that Paffor and the team will continue their search in the city.

Ok, thank you all. Valorie, Electra, Svetlana, Lionheart, and Eddy will join me. We are going inside to have a meeting and make sure any future broadcast are correct. The rest of you, I want to team up under Dragor, Paffor and Van to search all the streets and any subways to kill the rest of the creatures. Jagger and Leo can go in the pods to any location they are required. The drones under Logan's control will fly into any dangerous areas to kill or flush out creatures. I don't want any of you going alone into any enclosed space. Call and get a team there if you see a creature enter something. No one goes in alone. Am I clear?

They all respond with yes Sabrina.

We will broadcast a message to the compound that the Mixed Humans are helping and for the public to call compound security if they see any creatures. Right, new plan, we are going to go walk up the steps, walk into the foyer, go up to the top floor. Say hello and explain to them what's going to happen next. It should be simple. Who is with me?

Another detailed, well-thought-out plan, Sabrina. I might just keep hunting crazed, rabid creatures, if you don't mind.

Come on, Baldy, you got a few war dings and scratches on your bling now. It will look impressive when you strut through HQ. We need you to come with us to show we are all united. The crew inside are doing all they can but be on alert as there could be security or Elite hidden with weapons that they are unaware of.

Chapter fifty. The Castle

Sabrina leads the team up the golden steps. Valorie communicates with Martin and Julia to find out what they might expect when they step inside the Castle. With several high-level managers and leaders either dead or sick from the catalyst drug, Petra, Wayne, and Geoff are trying to keep everything calm in the control center. Sabrina is expecting little or no resistance as they enter, especially after seeing her team's abilities in killing the creatures. She contacts Duke, asking him to tell Petra and Wayne to come down and meet them in the foyer. It's better to be escorted into a meeting than force their way in. Sabrina asks him to speak with CM and gather information about the new leaders, preparing them for a meeting in the hall. She then calls the rest of her team to ask them how they are going, leaving an order that if they don't hear from her within fifteen minutes, then the meeting did not go as planned. In that case, they must make their way to the golden stairs and stand by for further orders.

Petra informs Duke about the Elite private security, explaining that they carry weapons and traditionally dress in light blue uniforms to represent a clear blue sky and the purity of the Earth. Control room messages are being ignored by them. She is not sure if they have run away or are in hiding, so she broadcasts a statement through the building's public announcement system.

We have guests who have come in peace. They want a better future for us all. If attacked, they will defend themselves. They wish to have a meeting with us and have been outside defending us from a homegrown attack implemented by our own Elite leaders. Please allow them to enter peacefully.

Sabrina and the crew approach the large glass doors that lead into the foyer and enter. Valorie receives communication from Martin that they have disarmed any of the security team they have found and tied them up. Wayne and Petra are standing inside the foyer alone. Sabrina walks up to them and introduces herself.

Hi, I am Sabrina, formally known as Sarah when I was under the control of the Elite. This is Electra from the Elite Moon base laboratory. She worked under CM, your team will have spoken to her over the years. We are here to negotiate a fair deal for all. Please take us inside and arrange a meeting with the remaining leaders that is to be televised throughout the compound.

Wayne introduces himself and Petra before responding.

Yes Sabrina, we have summoned the heads of divisions to meet in the Hall. Please follow us. Please follow us.

Wayne and Petra lead them into the building. The Castle's interior is spacious and vibrant, with plants growing in every corner and on balconies. A beautifully stimulating optical oasis, combined with the fresh aromas of the flowers, each level has a broad staircase that curves ninety degrees as they rise on alternating sides of the building to the next floor above. The levels are all open plan, well set out, with each having a conference area, a glass-walled office, and several large desks in a spacious layout. Only a few people on each floor watch in amazement as the team goes by.

On the second to the top floor, two men open fire on the team. Sabrina, Valorie, and Lionheart were the intended targets. Sabrina and Valorie move quickly enough to avoid the shots. Lionheart gets a minor cut from a passing bolt. Unfortunately, two office staff members were not lucky. One being critically injured, and the other killed, Valorie and Sabrina quickly disarm them with Valorie literally pulling one of the shooter's arms off, Sabrina calls out.

Everyone, please calm down. We have come here peacefully and will leave peacefully. If you attack any of us, we will respond with force. Please refrain from shooting at us, and we will refrain from killing you.

She turns to Svetlana and whispers.

Was that too much, or just right? I think it was accurate.

Svetlana smiles and gives Sabrina a nod of approval.

Wayne, can we please move on with no more surprises?

He turns, looking at Petra. Without having to say anything, she quickly moves ahead, checking any other possible hiding spots to ensure no one else is waiting in ambush. The team gets to the conference hall with no more incidence. Similar to Mount Gambier's setup, there's a bench at the front with a large screen above it, a pedestal for a drone, and seating arranged in a semicircle behind it. New leaders occupy the front bench. Office people occupy the rest of the hall. Some are interested in the speech, others are curious about the Mixed Humans.

As the meeting starts, the new leaders show they are unhappy with the chain of events through their body language and actions. Angry because of leaders' assassination, along with the death and destruction in the city. They express disappointment in Sarah for siding with Mixed Humans instead of those who supported and gave her a blessed life. They roll out all the values instilled in them over the last century. Earth is, for humans, pure natural life, not a mixture of manipulated genetic creatures, wild and unholy. Sabrina allows them to have their say. Her team listens, showing no signs of disagreement or disrespect.

When the leaders have finally finished, she thanks them for their honesty and asks them to listen to CM's response. He has been listening on an open channel. Duke patches him into the conference room video screen. Surprised whispers about his survival mingle with groans of disapproval, viewing him as a traitor.

CM explains the events, the reason for the chosen tactic, and the necessity of timing. He warns them against eradicating non-Pure gene individuals, explaining it won't improve the Earth. It will, in fact, have some known and unknown consequences, including all natural animals being killed off, a disruption to food chains and the possibility of all life on earth being eradicated as the virus mutates.

One leader interjects.

This is all propaganda and fake news you are spreading. You have dishonored yourself. Our city has experienced the impact of what the Mixed humans can do.

CM continues.

What you have seen within your compound would have happened one day and has nothing to do with Sabrina and her team. The Mixed Humans you see before you is the only reason you don't have mass casualties. Your population has outgrown both on and off world compounds, your food supplies and other resources cannot keep up. Elite leaders have lied to you. They only cared for themselves and the privileged, neglecting global communities. The drones released outside compounds two days ago, supposedly to deploy a deterrent spray, did not fulfill their true purpose. The Elite leaders who have now been killed, all believed that they were releasing an elimination virus. They had grown impatient waiting for us to perfect a targeted virus. I received instructions to create a virus that would eliminate anything impure. They requested a vaccine for themselves as a precaution, knowing it would kill innocent Pure, leaving us with no alternative. So, I sent down a harmless natural spray that looked like what they wanted. I was unsure if they would release it once they actually had it in their hands. We waited to see what they would do, and who would release it.

They control their destiny by disregarding Pure safety, despite knowing the virus's deadly nature. The vaccine I gave them was a drug that only targeted their own DNA. Other Elite leaders will die in other compounds as they also have shown no willingness to compromise. Now it's your chance to make a difference. We have all the evidence of this plan to prove I speak the truth, and we ask you for humanity's sake, you agree to find a way forward for all Earth's beautiful creatures. I thank you for listening.

Sabrina now has her say.

I did not have a blessed life. I was a caged puppet, drugged and made to follow orders with the fear of being executed if I wavered or failed. Despite being drugged, I helped a mix of characters, including Pure, who were in danger over the years. Human nature should be about helping and getting along. That's what we all deserve, for a better life.

Boisterous conversation starts, and a bit of arguing.

Sabrina raises her voice.

It won't be easy. But it is the only way forward.

More conversation erupts in the hall, which holds about a thousand people. Eddy opens his wings slightly, and the entire room becomes silent, mesmerized by his appearance.

In his deep, warm, yet authoritative voice, he says.

We have come here with Sabrina to ask for a better way forward with all species represented on a panel. This is the headquarters of South Australia. You are the leading Pure here in this state. We ask you to help us make this a reality.

Valorie, Electra, Svetlana and Lionheart step forward. We, as representatives of other species, stand with Sabrina and the Pure who desire a better future.

The room falls silent. Sabrina asks for them to have a vote. The leaders agree, however, some appear reluctant.

Raise your hands if you support a way forward.

Ninety-nine percent of the hall and half of the leaders on the bench raised their hands.

Sabrina asks a slightly different way.

Who would like more discussion, and is open to a way forward?

All apart from three leaders, raise their hands.

Who objects and will not compromise?

Three senior leaders stand united, affirming the plan of our Elite leaders. A Pure Earth. There will be no discussion in any other way while we lead. We are the Elite. Guards take the Impure into custody or kill them if they resist. They are all traitors.

Guards!

Sabrina looks at her team.

Looks like we are going to have to do it the hard way.

Julia and Martin walk into the hall.

Your guards are all tied up at the minute.

The three leaders throw back their overcoats to draw their weapons, as they draw Duke kills the lights in the hall. There is complete silence apart from a gurgling sound, as the lights turn back on the three leaders fall to their knees, holding their throats. Julia, Valorie, and Martin have all moved slightly from where they originally stood. The room fills with shock and astonishment as leaders bleed from their throats.

Sabrina again speaks up in a serious, and slightly agitated voice.

We are here as friends, wanting an equal outcome for us all. If you think you are the superior species here, you had better rethink that. We have lived outside your walls for decades, centuries. Apart from the battles in the early years. We have not tried to infringe on your compounds until today. Your perceived technological advantages you believe you have will not outweigh the Mixed will, or our numbers. Once more, who is in favor of progressing towards a new world? Shall we have a re-vote? Is a re-vote truly necessary? I think we have seen what the majority in this hall want.

The hall is silent for what feels like five minutes, then a call comes from deep inside the packed hall.

I say we support a change.

The room falls silent again. Others are gathering their thoughts on what just happened. Some are now unsure about a future they will not be superior in. Many fear they are all about to be slaughtered in the hall.

Sabrina realizes they have achieved all they can for now, so finishes the meeting.

We have explained our side of the story and broadcast it within your compound. Yorke's and Mount Gambier will undoubtedly hear or see footage from here. We are working on finding out if they also have Elite caged mutants underground in their compounds, as you had here. You have seen what hundreds of mutants can do if starved and pushed to the limits, also what your so-called protective droids that were deployed by your Elite leaders have done, shooting at anything, including citizens. We can let the Elite leader's plan backfire on you and wipe you all out or support you for a better future. It is up to you.

The team exits the hall to mostly applause. Some stand motionless, either stunned or not convinced. Halfway down the last staircase, a group of five Pure, with knives, attacks the team. Sabrina, Julia, Martin, and Valorie deal with them in a show of defiance. The attackers stab Electra and Svetlana in the attack, causing them to hold their wounds, while the Vamps rip the offenders to shreds on the floor. Again, their speed and strength surprise Sabrina. As they exit the headquarters, Sabrina gives them some parting words in a loud voice so they all can hear.

We are leaving your moat and security systems intact. Nothing will change instantly. We are not a threat unless you want to make us one.

Chapter fifty-one. Stage Right

Leaving the headquarters, they descend the staircase to meet the rest of the team. Tova asks about the outcome and plan. She notices the team members bleeding and wounded. None of the injuries appear serious. Electra and Svetlana wrap a bandage around their arms that Logan has given them.

It went exactly as I described it would, didn't it, Baldy?

He groans, looking at Sabrina.

We made our case and had to kill those who attacked us. We're regrouping to decide our next steps.

A blurred vertical line shoots down from the sky as Van appears on the steps with two others, Paffor and Dragor come in at speed and stick their landing on the stairs with wings fully extended. Van introduces his local coven leaders, Violet, and Victor, who will stay as part of a security team and represent the Vamps in any discussions. Dragor also requests to leave two representatives as well. Longwei and Cadmus. Sabrina, thanks them for their help and organizing representatives. She is explaining the next step to the team when Julia and Martin appear in the arms of Dragor and Paffor. They launch off high into the sky, with Van and Valorie following. The six of them disappear with the rest of their air support crew.

Good chat, good chat guys, watch out for that moat. It has a sting to it. Baldy, did you see those landings and take-offs? Impressive. You might need to work on yours a bit more. What is it with those guys? It is like they have their own silent secret chat line or bat signal. I guess we will know about whatever is so important when we need to know.

Sabrina smiles and looks at Eddy, asking him if he is ok.

Hey mate, would you like to stay here as a rep, go home, or continue on with us on the mission? I have a plan I know you will love.

I would like to continue to inform others of my type about what is happening. Thank you for your constructive criticism on my landings. A plan hey, great, I am sure I will hate it.

Sabrina puts her both her fists out in front of her, with a thumbs up, positive gesture.

Thanks Baldy. Lionheart, you have an injury. Would you like to stay and represent the Panthera?

I would love to continue, but I am a little sore and I may become a liability if I am not at a hundred percent. Jagger and Leo will support you well, So I will stay here for now as a representative.

Electra, Brandon. Can you stay here?

Yes Sabrina, we both will be happy to stay.

Ok thank you, Cosimo will come from Monarto to join you with Vamps reps, Violet, and Victor, Longwei and Cadmus will stand for the Dragons. Together, you will help to promote change and keep law and order during the transition. We'll go back to the homestead. We will leave you six drones. Duke and Electra can restore their drones to the control of the interim management group.

Three pods approach the bottom of the staircase, and the team walks down to load into them.

We will leave one pod here for the representatives to use.

Logan walks around to get into the driver's seat of the Cat. Sabrina just looks at him.

OK, I will just sit over there on the floor and sharpen pencils. You drive Sabrina.

She smiles back at him and nods.

Logan, that was exactly what I was thinking.

They drive off with Sabrina leading the team with her vehicle in candy apple red in a Dodge Barracuda shape. The two pods follow, with four drones providing low altitude security, as the others fly high above. Tova has the bike engine noise turned down to thirty percent as she follows. She has blood and grime all over her white tank top, and jeans from all the fighting. She rides high and proud as they head out of the city.

One block out from the headquarters, residents stand outside clapping and cheering as the team passes by. From nowhere, a creature the Elite released appears and chases one citizen. Violet and Victor react instantly. Victor picks it up as Violet picks up the citizen, safely putting her down out of harm's way. Victor rips the creature apart and drops it on the footpath. Longwei and Cadmus circle, looking for any other creatures. They find two more and kill them as the rest of the team moves on. As the team gets further away from the headquarters, there is more support on the streets. Community-wide support for free world values is a positive sign for the team.

They arrive at the moat, anticipating the rest of the team to be there, but find no one. Sabrina calls Duke to check that the moat door will open and will stay open as they pass through it, heading to the homestead. Not worried about getting the attention of the Elite anymore, they move as fast as they can, with a group of Vamps and Dragons, to escort them. Tova opens her bike up on the long straights and sweeping corners. They arrive at the closest point to the homestead and see Martin's van. Its rear door opens so Tova can place her bike in it, and she jumps into a pod.

At the homestead, Jagger and Leo find a couple of fresh carcasses for them to feed on, obviously dropped off by Dragor and Paffor. There are signs that Julia and Martin have also returned, as their gear is missing, but they are nowhere to be seen. It is now midday. After quickly reviewing the morning's adventures, they each go their separate ways to shower and rest.

Sabrina suspects that Julia and Martin have gone to the Yorke Peninsula compound to investigate, as it is the next one the team will visit. They are worried that there are more creatures stored within its walls and at Mount Gambier. The Vamps have shown they are self-sufficient and stealthy, so they can navigate the compound without difficulty.

She calls Duke to get an update while the others rest. Duke confirms Cosimo has arrived at the Port Lincoln Headquarters and that there has been unrest in the Yorke Peninsula. News about an attack has made it through from Port Lincoln. Natasha strives to stay on top of everything while searching for codes or program glitches, as instructed by Julia and Duke. She also has others of her security team search the headquarters for hidden dungeons.

Leaders in both compounds are still alive, though they are extremely unwell. Now knowing their fate having underestimated the Mixed Humans' unity and their sole dependance on a virus. Duke explains to Sabrina that they have moved arm guards to both Yorke's and Mount Gambier gates. The Leaders have done this from their deathbeds to promote the threat of a Mixed species attack, believing in death, their vision will live on.

Elite that are alive in compounds outside of Port Lincoln still with the same dream, give fake reports that Port Lincoln has regained complete control of their compound. Guards have killed all the Mixed with help from off-world drones. It is in part an attempt to calm the occupants of their compounds and show superiority, along with trying to gain support to kill any Mixed humans that enter their walls. Sabrina thanks Duke and the team for the update and plans to do a similar advance on Yorke's HQ, hopefully without the rabid creatures.

Chapter fifty-two. You Go First

Outside the Yorke Peninsula moat, Julia, Martin, Valorie, Van, Dragor and Paffor monitor the coming and goings through the compound gate. The armed guards are watching, making it impossible for Dragor and Paffor to enter unnoticed. They fly to a position away from the entrance and wait. Relying on their speed to pass undetected between the vehicles, the others will enter the compound and make their way to the headquarters in Curramulka. Julia and Martin are concerned that what they found in Port Lincoln may be a smaller version of what is waiting for them in the less critical compounds. The Elite, of the Elite, protecting themselves with a lesser first attack to gain support, while hiding their greater plan for Australia and the rest of the world.

The Eyre Peninsula compound, known as Port Lincoln, the name of the first town to have a secure Pure location, serves as the main headquarters in South Australia. They moved the Castle to a central location as they expanded to take over the whole peninsula. Mount Gambier was the second, and Yorke's compound was the third in succession, followed by Murray Bridge. Without a moat it never became a secure compound, and the Elite tolerate it as a midway society for its surrounding resources. The rest of South Australia has small cities that fend for themselves. Adelaide has become a self-sustaining small city because of climate change, and its location to the ranges made it an unsuitable city to secure with a moat.

The Vamps made it through the moat with a convoy and proceeded to the parklands near headquarters. They sit hidden, watching the Castle to get a vibe of the activity around the building, just below its traditional steps ascending to the entrance. If their theory is right, then the lower ranking of this compound will mean a higher number of creatures and significantly more casualties if they can't stop the release.

An opportunity arises as the doors open to allow a group of Pure to enter. Martin and Julia enter the headquarters front door just before it closes behind the group. Their smaller size without wings allows them to move and hide easier than Valorie or Van. They scan the area to get a detailed floor layout using their ultrasonic vocals. Martin, as he expected, finds a similar hidden door to the one in Port Lincoln. He asks Julia to create a minor distraction for him to figure out how to open it. She throws a small pebble deep into the foyer in the opposite direction of Martin. The noise catches the attention of three people on the ground floor, who move towards the sound. Once Martin is inside, Julia waits until it is clear, then tells him to open the door so she can flash in.

Making their way down the dark corridor, it is clear there are many more creatures in this dungeon. As it is pitch black, they hope they are on their own. Julia finds the control room and hooks up her miniature tablet. It projects the data onto the desk so she can scroll through it to check for anything she may recognize from the Port Lincoln system. Julia suspects there is some link to the elected leaders that they unknowingly override each day, stopping the preset early morning release. Martin ensures mechanical doors will stay shut, even if software activates them. He collects evidence and places explosives to seal off any exit areas while communicating to Van outside, in case something happens to them.

Julia cannot find a transmitter or communicational device linked to the spaceship droids. It may be part of a fail-safe design, and the spaceships directly control the droids. She stopped them in Port Lincoln by blocking a signal frequency that showed up on their arrival, so she works on a theory that the droids can land anywhere. Then run within a distance of their spaceship using their own Wi-Fi frequency, not requiring any other devices in that location to operate. Julia samples transmitted frequencies as a baseline. If any others arrive when the droid spaceships do, she can block their transmission.

Martin is corresponding with Van. He pauses as he faces a group of droids. They are all motionless, but a tiny blue LED is slowly pulsing. He thinks to himself, this may be normal, or they have gone into this mode for a reason? He's not interested in staying to find out.

Hey Julia, Be careful, we have about thirty droids here, and they look like they are thinking about something. I suspect these are backup droids, considering the number of extra creatures present.

Ok Martin, I can't find any protocol or programs in the systems, and I have done all I can. Hopefully, it will hold them. The system has a failsafe mode, so we can't shut it down or destroy it because of the potential consequences. We should go back to the homestead and share our discoveries with Sabrina.

They join Van and Valorie outside and head to the moat gate. Meet Dragor and Paffor, who give Julia and Martin a ride to the homestead. Circling a few times so the defense drones can recognize them before they land.

Defense systems have killed many creatures near the complex in the past 24 hours. Scaring off most creatures, only a few remain to feed on the dead. A negative effect of this is the increased activity might give up the team's location if Duke cannot keep blocking the satellites images. They cannot destroy key parts of the Elite's infrastructure as they need them to monitor their actions after they have successfully executed the coup.

Inside the homestead, Sabrina, Julia and Martin call Monarto and Port Lincoln to provide an update. They ask Cosimo to escort the new leaders to the basement in Port Lincoln to show them evidence before any actions occur at other headquarters. Julia shares her findings with Duke and Logan, assuring them to the best of her knowledge that the explosion and frequency blocking will work. Natasha and Roderick agree to discuss the findings and consult with relevant contacts in Mount Gambier and Murray Bridge, so they know what to look for.

Cosimo discusses the plans for entering Yorke's compound. He has organized a set of semi vehicles to go to a location outside the gate. Permitting them to enter through the moat in the same manner. Duke fills everyone in on the news from the space station, Moon, and Mars. Panic among Elite leaders, security, maintenance, and life support teams makes them reluctant to change software or make changes. Technicians lock down each habitat individually to prevent a chain reaction in case one loses life support. The fear of an active virus killing Pure humans on Earth has scared them. They are unwilling to risk going to Earth, as they believe they are safer off-world.

The team continues the meeting, discussing any theories that the Elite might try to spin to the public. They cannot say the Mixed are responsible for the cages and creatures hidden in the basements. Trying to pass them off as laboratories for testing might be an option, but why are these creatures kept in underground cages with direct access to doors designed to release them? No scientist in their right mind would experiment inside the compound walls for fear of the virus, or creatures escaping. These actions have no reasonable explanation.

Finishing up their meeting, they decide that the evidence will speak for itself and agree to go into Yorke's compound earlier, just in case there are any extra surprises. Having the armed guards at the entrance is already an extra challenge for the team, as they are expecting them.

Pure Elite worldwide are reaching out to all compounds to understand the current situation. What footage is real? Who is alive and in control? Natasha's ability to block or misdirect them is reducing as they want answers. CM has planned for this, relying on the Elite's self-preservation and narrow-minded focus on their future, regardless of any consequences. Only a trusted few in the tight circle know of the real extinction plan. He can use this to the coup advantage as like-minded individuals want to avoid public accountability until they're certain of their own safety. They want to be seen as heroes and saviors, not the cause.

There is one common thread to all the spin. Somebody ordered it, built the system and basement dungeons. Who, why, and where are they now? A couple of hundred years ago, someone built these dungeons as part of the Castle's design. Elder Elite hibernators who may have known about them have now passed. There is a real possibility that while the dream is the same, none of the Pure Leaders who are alive today know anything about the creatures.

CM and the team are worried by this thought, as it shows a lack of awareness within the Elite regarding how to put a stop to it, or if it is specific to South Australia. Is it the start of a worldwide event that will cause the mass murder of innocent communities?

The security teams in the off-world Elite are exploring the idea of a homegrown attack and intend to dispatch investigators to Earth. They have also set the highest security clearances, restricting all travel to any off-world communities to eliminate the chance of infection.

Chapter fifty-three. One Thirty

It's one thirty. Sabrina awakes and goes about some general business checking her weapons and vehicle. Others in the homestead have stirred but not yet ventured out to the common areas. Julia, however, just appears next to Sabrina.

I heard you Julia.

I am sure you did.

She smiles at Sabrina.

We are likely to meet extra challenges this time. I doubt any compound leaders control these systems. These programs have remained unopened for years. The coding is outdated, some of which I helped develop alongside other engineers many years ago. It was ultramodern then, but systems have been upgraded many times over since.

Is this a good thing or a problem?

Well, it is good and bad. It means it is old, and I know all the back doors and codes. Well, I did once. I just need to remember them. When I first saw it, it surprised me, and I had to recall how the program codes functioned. None of my hacking tools and devices will work with systems that old. One part that might help us is that they don't appear to be linked to any other outside systems.

OK, so what's the bad news? It seems like you are all over it and can manage it.

Well, who is feeding them? Who knows about it? What does the dead man switch connect to in order to prevent accidental activation? Who explained the Deadman switch to the leaders, or whoever made sure it didn't activate? It has never failed until the ruling leaders started dying. We've learned from your father about the Elite's intention to eliminate us, but we must ask. Who is in control of that process or leading that dream? Who has been maintaining these cages? Why do the least important of the top three secure compounds have extra droids here on Earth? The droids are not old. They are recent technology, from only ten years ago by the looks of them. Everything is swirling in my mind. I have no answers.

OK, great chat Julia, great info. It's fun to have you around. Are you suggesting that whoever planned this years ago might still be alive today?

Yes, I guess that is possible, though I doubt they used hibernation cycles. If it is not the Pure that has set this up or supported it all these years, who? Automation has its limits. To perform checkups, someone or something must enter and exit the basement. So, I am unsure Sabrina, we might have some Unhuman to deal with.

You think there is access to these dungeons from outside the headquarters? Sounds like we are going hunting for a tunnel. What do you think?

We destroyed each end of the Port Lincoln basement with explosives, which will have blocked access to tunnels from inside the headquarters. Yorke holds creatures and droids. I wouldn't want to enter and follow any access routes with the droids about to activate.

There is no news of an explosion in the Yorke's compound. Is it possible someone might have overridden or removed all your devices?

Yes, both scenarios are plausible. Someone skilled and with technology could handle it unnoticed, I guess.

I will get Cosimo to see if they can find evidence of any tunnels left in the Port Lincoln dungeon, as that is likely the safest site to inspect. Why did we blow that up once the critters were gone?

I got frustrated. Time was running out with more droids about to land. I thought there might have been some type of controlling device for them in there that I couldn't find. It had fulfilled its purpose, so I thought it was worth a try.

Ok, fair enough. We will get Natasha to look at Mount Gambier and Roderick to look at Murray Bridge. What do you think your best deployment plan would be? You both have proven that you can get into and out of areas. What do you want to follow up on?

Well, I have already been to Yorke's, and I have never visited Murray Bridge. We can blend in there without having to hide. We will go see Duke and CM. See if we can discover any more clues about who is behind this.

I'll tell Tarak that you and Martin are coming once we're inside Yorke's. Thanks Julia.

The semi vehicles Cosimo sent out to the predetermined location outside Yorke's arrived an hour ago. They must use main roads from the homestead to the moat gate, which is a four-hour drive. After a quick briefing, the team jump into the pods. All can fit in the pods without Eddy, and Tova's bike can travel in Martin's van. Using dirt road corridors and flying over sections, is the most direct route at high speed, while staying low, will cut the travel time. Van, Valorie, Paffor, and Dragor have already left to meet up with local members of their species, who will wait outside the moat until needed.

Arriving at the semi vehicles, they go through the plan. Julia and Martin explain where the guards were and describe where they placed harmless smoke bombs.

Ok thanks for the info guys. Can you please stay and make sure we get in?

Yes Sabrina. Valorie, Van, Martin, and I will go in first, then when you are all in, Martin and I will leave. Martin's modified vehicle will reach Monarto before you and the team reach Elite HQ in Koolywurtie.

Right, first Martin, I want that speed upgrade on my Cat, second we don't have Baldy here so we can skip the detailed plan description. I will miss his usual groan of approval or disapproval. Ok, Svetlana, Tova and Logan will enter the moat in the pods. I will be in my Cat in its maintenance van appearance. Jagger, Leo, Tova's bike, and drones will be in the semi vehicles.

This is what we know. They are expecting us. We'll face opposition, so we will separate into different vehicles. Cosimo and Duke have informed me that the six top leaders have passed away because of the catalyst drug. We have limited intel as our recruits are still in lower levels of management. They have seen several shuttles arrive from Mount Gambier, and Natasha has confirmed that they left her compound, but she is unaware of who sent them or what's in them.

Svetlana looks at Tova and Logan.

I prefer the Baldy type mission plans, that was exceptionally long and detailed. I like the, if they shoot at us we shoot them, plan. Not the focus on the 'separate vehicles' part in case not all of us make it through.

Svetlana, your plan is brilliant, that's Plan B. Baldy would be proud of you. Good chat all. Let's go do it.

At the moat they call Duke to code the pods in through the gate after the next delivery that is due, Van, Valorie, Julia, and Martin are ready to sneak in with that convoy. It arrives and passes through the gate, as do the Vamps. Before the pods enter, Julia and Martin silently disarm as many guards as they can.

Guards somehow know that the pods and maintenance vehicles are not part of an allowed convoy, start shooting. The team disperses to avoid the shots, as the Vamps race around and kill more of the guards as they give up their positions. Knowing the element of surprise has gone, a couple of drones enter just in front of Dragor, Paffor and the semi vehicles, laying down cover fire so they can get to a safe location. The gate shuts, slicing off a third of each semi as they pass. They wiggle and drag with sparks, lighting up the area until they come to a stop, drones exit them as Tova gasps.

My bike, Jagger, Leo.

Guards that were hidden on the tops of buildings shoot at the semis as Julia sets off the smoke bombs and the drones attack the guards. Dragor, Paffor, Van and Valorie pick up those shooting from rooftops and drop them to the ground. None of them are wearing blue, the traditional color of security guards. They are something different. It doesn't take long to round up all the guards. Sabrina suspects a couple of them may have gotten away.

Tova flies the pod over to the semi vehicles to check on Leo and Jagger. She is relieved that they are ok, just shaken up. Her bike has fallen over but looks otherwise undamaged. She stands it up and rides it out with a handgun drawn. Sabrina calls over the radio.

Svetlana's plan it is then.

The Cat turns from its maintenance vehicle into the Camo green Hellcat.

If they shoot at us, we shoot at them, Jagger and Leo get into the pod that Tova left and fly to safety.

Svetlana gets out of her pod to look at one shooter and notices he has a tattoo, the same as the shooters that attacked them in Victoria Square.

Sabrina, it could be a coincidence, but a guard here has the same tattoo as the attackers in Victoria Square. They might all be a part of the same group, do the Pure have an Elite force?

I am not sure Svetlana. There seems to be a lot we don't know.

Julia appears next to Svetlana and looks at the markings, then goes and checks all the others.

They all have the same tattoo, Sabrina. I will show CM and the team.

She and Martin leave through the gate as they sense it is open while the automated clean-up crews are removing what's left of the semi vehicles. Sabrina arrives at the guard Julia was just at before she disappeared.

Ok when Julia said she would show the team, she really meant the show bit. I was going to take a video, but taking the entire arm will be better. CM can get some DNA and blood samples. We need to move fast to the capital. Tova, does that bike of yours have autopilot? It will be faster and safer in a pod.

Yes Sabrina, it will find me. I'll grab my weapons and be ready.

They load up and fly off, weaving through the high-rise buildings just below their top floors, with drones above, in front and behind. It is a quick trip by air, and they pull up two blocks before the parklands begin.

I will go in with Valorie, Van, Dragor and Paffor. We'll look for signs of an ambush, or what was in the shuttles. I will take the Cat as it will attract attention and use its sensors to scan the area. You wing folk do what you do best and hunt. We are looking for droids, or more of the guards in camo gear. I should hear from Monarto soon about what was in the blood of the arm Julia gave them. The rest of you hide out here with the drones.

All the team respond to Sabrina, agreeing that they will stay put until they are called upon.

Chapter fifty-four. Yorkies Up To The Knees

Jagger and Leo get out of the pod as they don't enjoy being in captivity, especially after the semi-incident. They feel safer on the streets. Finding a couple of dark hiding spots, they sit and wait to hear from Sabrina. Tova is on her bike in front of the pod the Panthera got out of. She has a pod on either side of her as she sits and waits, looking down the main road to the Castle. It has three-lanes each way, a wide medium strip full of vegetation with lawn and large trees, similar to Adelaide's King William street. A few maintenance robots are doing their last runs for the night, their operating and warning lights flashing off buildings as they clean the streets and footpaths. It is still too early for people to be out exercising, and the bright moonlight has clouds occasionally passing in front of it. This creates an eerie random light and dark moments, which makes high-rise apartments appear then silhouette into darkness. Some completely black buildings have rooftop antennas, with red indicator lights, and other buildings have the flicker of a TV screen flashing in their windows.

Natasha has been trying to find out what was on the shuttles that were released from Mount Gambier, however the leaders in Murray Bridge, and her headquarters are pushing back, not wanting her to find out about them even though she can't explain them, and it is her job to do so. She is having concerns about her safety and others supporting the coup. She asks CM for permission to release the catalyst drug in both headquarters. After a debate between the teams at each compound, they all agree that releasing the drug might be the fastest way to stop whoever is controlling the guards, creatures, and shuttles.

Van has found three guards. He drinks some of their blood to weaken them as he ties them up to keep them out of the fight. He uses his ultrasonic communication to warn Valorie about what he has discovered.

Hey Valorie, be careful with these guards, don't drink them, there is something odd about them, they are not Pure Humans.

He flies over to meet with Sabrina.

There is something not right about these guards. They taste human, and they all taste remarkably similar, much like humans in the same family. They have a type of drug, or something odd in their systems that I have never tasted before.

Having a late breakfast mate? What about their appearance? Did they have the same tattoos?

Didn't look; I was just taking them out of the fight. Follow me and I will take you over to them.

Van points at a tree and he and Sabrina flash over to it. Sabrina checks his forearm for the tattoo and lifts his mask. She is shocked to see that he looks remarkably similar to the one Julia took the arm off. They go to look at the other two Van has taken out of the fight. One is slightly different, but the other is similar, and both have the same tattoos. Sabrina gets a drone to come over to record videos and photos of the three to send to Duke.

Svetlana, was there anything about the four people who shot at us in Victoria Square that seemed odd to you?

No Sabrina, not really. Two of them looked like they could have been brothers, actually they all looked similar, but were different in the slightest ways. It was a little strange that four random people looked that similar.

Thanks, Ok team, we have some Mixed Humans working for the Elite; I have a feeling that the odd taste, and the similar taste Van has detected, means they may be like the earlier me, drugged slaves.

Sabrina now feels uncomfortable. They may have to kill more of these guards and they, like she once did, are just following orders. They don't know any better and possibly have no feelings because of the drugs. She grabs one of their comms necklaces to listen for any orders. She puts it on in time to hear a guards issue one.

Instantly, she warns the Pod Team.

Get out of there, lift off NOW, lift off, lift off straight up and come to my location.

Svetlana and Logan, just as Sabrina finishes speaking, see the third pod blow up.

Tova, are you ok? What happened? Dragor and Van are on the way!

They blew up one pod. It's okay. Leo and Jagger got out of it a while ago and are in hiding. Logan, Svetlana and I are ok and on our way to you.

One drone gets the location of where the shot came from and fires back. Two other drones stay to protect the Panthera as the rest go with the pods to meet Sabrina. Van and Dragor search the general area from above. The guards shoot at the drone as it keeps them pinned down. They try to make a run for it across the road to escape, as they do Dragor and Van, swoop down and pick them up, violently shaking them and making them drop their weapons. Taking them over to Sabrina, they drop them on the ground in front of her. Not from high enough to kill them, but high enough to wound them, so they will not be a danger.

One of them speaks.

Sarah, you will not win, you are evil, and a traitor, as is your father and all those Pure that support you. The Pure are the only humans that should walk this Earth. We are here to protect them from you and your pathetic team of creatures.

Ok mate, my name is Sabrina. I can hear there will be no reasoning with you and your team. You know my previous name, which tells me the Elite created you. I feel sorry for you. I wish it could be different, but you have just made my life easier.

Sabrina pulls out her handgun and shoots both of them between the eyes. Dragor, Van, Svetlana and Tova look at Sabrina, confused.

What the hell? Why did you do that?

He called me Sarah. I am not Sarah anymore; I am Sabrina.

She walks off, fully focused on the mission.

Svetlana, still shocked, tries again.

What did you mean by they made your life easier?

Sabrina opens a comms channel to the team.

They made our lives easier because I realized they were all test tube soldiers, like I once was. Yes, probably drugged. If cured, it might be possible to set them free, but for now, they are on a mission and feel no pain. They were not born like you were from a mother and father. They are merely tools of the Elite. While I believe their lives matter, and I am sorry they have to die, we cannot reason with them. So, if they stand in our way, or shoot at us, we have no choice but to kill them. We don't have time to be friendly, sit down, have a cup of coffee and chat with them. Are we all good? Do we all agree to shoot them?

The team responds with a, yes Sabrina.

Awesome, then let's go do this.

Natasha couldn't find out where the three shuttles originated from but determine their type. She informs the team that they are a small cargo carriers, only capable of holding eight of these soldiers per shuttle, if that is in them.

Sabrina calls the team to action.

Let's go find the shuttles, disable them and gather up what was in them. We will load them all back into the shuttles. Dead or barely alive, I don't mind either way.

Paffor lets Van know he discovered all three shuttles halfway between the parklands and the Castle. As Natasha mentioned, they are small and would only hold eight soldiers at a maximum, Van tells Sabrina, and she gives orders to the team.

Ok mission one, we are looking for around twenty-four soldiers. There will be some inside the Castle, and others surrounding it. I will fly around the Castle a few times to find them on my sensors and send in drones to kill them. You can then gather them up and count them as you stash them in the shuttles. They seem to have stopped communicating with each other over their comms as they realized I have one. I may have told them I was coming to kill them all. Oops, my bad. The sun will be up soon. Let's get this done before it rises, and we have civilians on the streets to complicate things.

Sabrina does a couple of laps and, as she suspected, they take shots at her in the Cat, giving away their location. Others stay still, but her heat sensors can easily pick them out in the morning's cool temperature. Jagger and Leo have made their way to the parklands, sneaking up on a few soldiers they smelled lying in ambush, working as a team they hunt and kill their prey, as they make their way towards the Castle.

Chapter fifty-five. Early Morning Risers

As the sun is about to break the horizon, citizens heading out to do their morning exercises and others curious about the light show from weapons firing also venture out to investigate. Like the droids in Port Lincoln, the soldiers are not worried about shooting innocent Pure Humans, who are out jogging or walking along the streets minding their own business.

Logan has disarmed all the equipment in the shuttles, so now they are just storage cages. As the team brings in the dead or wounded, Logan counts them off.

Sabrina, we have nineteen here now, and I doubt we could fit many more. They are pretty packed in and that is without their weapons on them.

OK, thanks Logan, I suspect some are inside, maybe five or six, along with the Elites' own security if they decide to fight alongside them.

Tova calls Sabrina.

I'm on the west side of the Castle, where the parklands and apartments meet. There's a single seat shuttle here. It is white with a red stripe.

Tova, move away and I'll come over.

Ah, ok, it is a speed pod used by security and leaders who need to get somewhere fast. This one is not part of the standard feet. It has modifications done to it. Just watch it for now. I will get back to you.

They released the creatures in Port Lincoln around this time of the morning. Sabrina calls Julia, wondering why there hasn't been an explosion yet.

Julia, there is a speed pod here that doesn't look local. Is it possible someone has entered a tunnel you believe is required to support the dungeons? Disconnected your explosives and will release the creatures?

It's not impossible, I wouldn't want to try it myself. Even knowing where they are, how they will trigger, as they have anti-tamper switches on them. They will see Martins tampering with the gates so they will know someone's been down there.

So, Julia, would you suggest we follow in or just watch the exit?

Not until the explosives have gone off. It will not be huge, but it will not be a fun place to be in when they go off. We will see signs. There will be smoke through vents and in the entrance foyer. I suggest keeping someone near the pod, waiting until who or whatever returns to it. They will not want to stay down there when they see it's rigged to explode.

OK, thanks.

Sabrina, CM wants to talk with you.

Right, ok I will call him.

CM you want a chat.

Hi Sabrina, yes I have tested the blood from the soldier, and he came from our laboratory on the Moon. It has all the markers from a past project. The soldier's brain functions like a computer programmed by drugs. I don't know how they kept this from me. The only person who could have done it is no longer alive. He was in hibernation and set to awake this cycle. I guess they were going to wipe out the Mixed without my help, no matter what I did.

Right, so, we have droids, creatures, and now human robots all running around creating a conspiracy that all non-Pure Humans are evil.

Yes, Sabrina, that's the simple version of it.

It only makes sense if they expected a coup, distrusted you, and didn't believe you would come up with a virus to release. It might be a scheme to blame you and the hibernating laboratory team. They would need a backup plan in case your virus fails. Could a virus exist in a laboratory on Earth?

It is unlikely. Earth labs only handle proven samples. There is no testing to prevent accidental contamination of all life on Earth. We were in a sacrificial laboratory for exactly that reason. Labs down here only replicate proven samples after comprehensive testing. Hence, they replicated what I gave them, believing it was real and safe. We incinerated all true viruses showing any signs of working. If the new team had something unknown to me and the Elite expected it on our shuttle, it's now gone. None of the Pure laboratories have anything for them to use here on Earth. We have meticulously searched each one in the last fifteen years. It must be in an unknown secret laboratory if it exists.

Great, now, it's droids, creatures, human robots, and a secret laboratory with a deadly virus. Good chat CM, great chat Dad. You always have just the right way of explaining deadly, life-threatening things. Where could it be? It would need to be secure and staffed by trustworthy people.

Sabrina stops mid-sentence.

Tova, hide, we want this pod to get away and whoever is in it. If Julia is right, they see the tampering and escape before the explosion. We follow them. I will come over and put a tracker on the speed pod. With any luck, they will go back to their secret laboratory. Van and Dragor, we need your species' help in tracking the pod's movements. Also, arrange for two representatives of each group to be outside the compound moat ready to come in. Duke, I will send the code for the tracker on the speed pod.

Julia.

Yes Sabrina. I want you and Martin to prioritize this and be the leaders. Kill all you find and please, please, pretty please, don't knock over any test tubes or release any gasses into the environment. CM, be ready to make it safe if we find something.

Got it Sabrina, Don't release a killer virus that will kill us all.

Yep, you got it girl, simple really, you and Martin flash in, flash around, and kill all the robot humans. If anyone is there in a white coat that looks important, maybe keep them alive. Oh, and keep them away from any big red buttons, it will be just a typical fun day for you folks.

Roderick, sorry mate, you are back on active duty. You need to get a team ready to take Mount Gambier. The compound supported releasing the virus, and they celebrated in the streets afterwards. We will send whoever we can to help as soon as we have finished here. They will expect something, so they will be prepared to defend themselves. Natasha and her security team, including a leader, are with us in the compound. They will do all they can to disrupt any defensive actions that are within their control.

Team! we are going into these headquarters. We need to take this Castle and be ready to leave ASAP. No speeches in the Foyer or casual walk up the steps, Valorie, Van. We will take out anyone who looks threatening, just to make it fair. Duke, you call whoever is on our side in there and tell them we are coming. For some extra excitement, get them to broadcast it as we did in Port Lincoln over the intercom. Hopefully, it will attract the guards to the entrance. The rest of you clean up whatever we miss on our way in.

Right, a plan, Leo, and Jagger. I want you to run up and stand at the entrance. Jump out of the way when doors open or drones crash through them. Guys, jump like your left life depends on it. Ok, have you got it? Doors open and jump to the left.

Demonstrating with her hands, she opens her them, touching her fingertips together, and then swings them open like doors. She makes two fists, lifts them up and over to the left. Leo and Jagger look at each other.

She is missing Eddy, and we are getting the detailed plan Jagger.

They let out a brief roar of approval. Leo and Jagger hop up to the doors, they swing open, and a hail of weapon fire starts. As they hop to the left, drones rush in from the right. Sabrina yells out.

I count six of them.

The drones lay down cover fire as Valorie, Van, and Sabrina race in and kill all those shooting.

Well, that worked a lot better than I thought it would. Well done, a grand plan executed perfectly.

Jagger lets out a roar, then yells back to Sabrina and Leo.

Now I know how Baldy feels.

They lick their paws and wipe their foreheads. Sabrina looks back at them and smiles with a thumbs up.

The team races up the levels. Several security guards are standing still and have dropped their weapons. They grab their guns and move on. One on the top floor lifts his weapon and before he can shoot, Valorie kills him.

There is always one. Why is there always one?

They enter the prominent leader's area and Sabrina yells.

We are having a conference. Gather all leaders in the hall now.

Sabrina leads the team to the hall, which resembles the other compounds. The leaders are all seated at the front bench as Sabrina starts her speech.

We only have a little time. I would typically show a speech from CM. Do you all know him? Raise your hands.

They all raise their hands.

Ok, so you may or may not be aware that a virus was to be released to kill all non-Pure humans. We are here revolting against that and want a future where we all get along together, yada yada, bla bla bla. We are leaving a group here to facilitate this and already have excellent support for it in Port Lincoln. So please consider your answer to this next question carefully. Will you negotiate and work towards a better future for everyone?

Leaders exchange glances, discussing with hand gestures, nods and shakes of their heads.

We need a vote. Your vote will signify your intentions for a better future. Hands up if you are in favor.

Three out of ten raised their hands. Before they can lower them, the other seven heads hit the bench with their throats slashed.

Ok then, motion carried unanimously, we are in a bit of a hurry, so we will leave a team of representatives to explain in more detail, we thank you for your time and support.

There is a slight rumble and fixtures rattle.

Oh yeah, that. There is an underground dungeon filled with creatures and droids here to be released to kill your citizens, with the leaders intending to blame it on us. All the evidence remains for you to inspect. Logan and drones will stay as representatives and will stop the incoming droids. Two Dragons, Vamps, and a couple of Bird Types will also join him. We will send Mixed Human reps later, ok it is time to leave. We have to fly, literally, and need a fast cargo pod now! Good chat all. Thanks for your support.

They walk down the steps as one spaceship lands on the lawn. Better get ya gear, Logan, and transmit that freezing frequency. It opens and, as with the previous ships, the droids come out randomly shooting. Drones take them down, and Tova grabs her pulse gun, jumps on her bike and races off, killing a few more.

The cargo pod arrives at the bottom of the steps.

Tova, come back and load your bike into this. We will send it to wherever we are going. Van, Valorie, Dragor and Paffor, we now have control of this moat, go meet the new representatives and bring them here. I will shoot more of these droids until Logan finishes sharpening his pencil.

While they are shooting the droids, Eddy turns up, landing next to Sabrina.

Hey mate, I thought you were having a bit of R&R and on holidays. What are you doing here?

I'm returning to Adelaide. saw the other representatives enter, so I followed. I will organize some of our species and others as well.

Yep, it sounds like a plan. Look at you go, making simple plans.

While on simple plans, I will stay here until this evening, then fly back before it gets dark.

Aww Baldy, I thought we cured you and you were not afraid of the dark anymore.

He groans and walks off, shaking his head.

Leo walks over to him with Jagger.

Hey Eddy, great to see you, missed ya buddy. Sabrina has had Jagger and me doing all your stunt work while you have been gone. I am staying here till someone can come and replace me. Guess Jagger, you will get all the grand plans and stunt work now.

Sabrina, The speed pod has exited via the moat. It must have received clearance or has some type of key. We are tracking it. It is heading across the ocean at the moment towards Adelaide.

Ok thanks Duke. We're going home, team. We need the most direct route through the moat to Adelaide. I will go through first, then Valorie, Van, Dragor, Paffor and then the pods. Valorie and Van can monitor the moat and make sure it is open. They all race to the moat, pass through it and make the journey across the ocean.

When they arrive, Van and Valorie go back to their coven, Dragor, Paffor and Jagger also go back to their home grounds. Tova, Svetlana, and Sabrina go to the governor's building to investigate the pod's location and formulate a plan.

Chapter fifty-six. Time Critical

Duke has tracked the speed pod to what was an old shopping center complex when Adelaide was a thriving city. He has sent a couple of drones to get video footage and watch anything entering or leaving the building. The center has undergone multiple transformations and is well maintained. One of these transformations includes converting a section that was undercover car parking into a drone storage and maintenance areas. The multi-story building, initially for small businesses, now houses residents who have adjusted to living in and around it. The greater shopping center area has workshops and manufacturing areas where once large retail outlets sold their goods. Those living in the center use these areas to produce a range of items and weapons that they trade with others. These residents have divided the building into small communities, isolating sections from each other, with little or no interaction between them. Drones are used to maintain the carpark and any access points surrounding them with a clear forty-meter perimeter for protection. Right after that, the wild vegetation has completely taken over. It has become the dwelling place for many Mixed Human, Unhuman and non-human occupants. Including Birds, Panthera and others, living amongst each other protecting their own territories fiercely.

The team study the live video, planning to visit and investigate why the pod went there. CM arrives at governor's compound to brief on things to look for, things to avoid touching, and items to be cautious of. CM is energetic for his age but is not by any means a soldier or capable of defending himself if they encounter any resistance. He will be ready to fly in if they find anything needing his expert help.

After the briefing and checking all their weapons, they grab masks, along with chemical suits, just in case they find a clean room they need to enter. They then prepare the pods to make the short four-minute trip to the city of Marion, where the shopping center is located.

The drone footage shows a doorway that appears to have had plenty of use. It could be Mixed Humans, Unhuman or whoever is controlling these creatures' entrance to the complex. Anyone using this doorway can easily move from it to covered areas of vegetation on and around nearby buildings not supported by the maintenance bots.

Making the hop to the complex and landing in a street opposite, the reality of its size sets in. It is an enormous area to search if they have to check individual sections. An object circles the group, and after several more circles at a lower altitude, it darts down and lands next to Sabrina's Cat. She notices the landing and gets out of her vehicle.

Baldy would be proud, You nailed that.

I was just hoping you wouldn't shoot at me. I figured if I kept circling and you didn't recognize me, eventually you would get annoyed and start shooting, so I just went for it. How is Baldy? Where is he?, is he still alive?

Yes, Frieda, he is still alive. He has a minor wound on his wing, but he is fine. He is coming home this evening. Why are you here?

My highflyers noticed you and contacted me, so I came over to see if we could help.

Thank you. We believe an army of creatures, or robot humans, may be inside this complex. We tracked a speed pod from Yorke's Castle to here. Whoever was in that pod was under the Castle. There also might be a laboratory working on a virus to kill us all inside, and possibly an unknown number of controlled Mixed and Unhuman creatures roaming around.

How can I help?

We're working on the best way to enter without knocking and asking to see the secret laboratory.

I am not sure if this means anything, but our scouting team noticed what we think were two Vamps entering the rear northern end of the drone bay. Those that enter the maintenance bay never stay long in there once they realize it has no food. The vamps came out, but they then went into a different section. They haven't emerged from it yet.

Yes, that will be Julia and Martin. Van needs to come here and try to reach them.

I will go to the convention center and stand outside tweeting. Sabrina needs your help with Julia and Martin. He will hear me and come outside.

That would be great. The Vamps and Dragons are not big on using comms, thank you.

Tova and Svetlana, unaccustomed to waiting, want to explore the drone bay. They believe there must be a place where the pods enter and leave from. Tova asks Sabrina if they can have a look. She agrees and tells them that when Van arrives, they will look around the outside. Frieda said it was common for people to go through the bay, so Sabrina feels they shouldn't set off any alarms or get themselves into too much trouble.

Svetlana jumps on the back of the bike as Sabrina smiles at them.

In quiet mode, please Tova. We do not want to shake the walls off the building announcing that we are here searching the place. Just a ride through and come back and tell us what you see.

Tova and Svetlana agree to gather intel by doing a ride-through. They head west down Sturt Road to the entrance and turn right. A short ramp on the west side grants general access to the workshop. It is next to the main doors, which open for drone fleets to exit and enter. Duke informs them that there is a changeover at 2PM with general drones deploying and others will be returning. It will help to disguise them as they blend in with the expected bay movement.

Heading into the dimly lit workshop which still resembles the original car park with laneways and parking bays, they turn right to follow the flow of drone traffic that is moving towards the east of the building, and past a large open exit door. Continuing towards a maintenance section that has droids and robots welding or swapping out damaged parts, Tova notes it is not as large as the Adelaide market maintenance bay. This one only has three above ground levels that are three-fifty hundred meters long and one hundred meters wide. Slowly making their way through the maintenance section following the laneways, they notice nothing out of the ordinary. Traveling down the building's north side, drones are double parked and stacked on each other. Tova stops in the laneway, which appears to continue according to the lane markings, but a wall cuts it off. She turns around and backtracks, going south towards the ramp they came in on. Riding down the southernmost lane till they again reach a large door that goes from floor to ceiling, it also appears out of place, not built as part of the drone workshop but as an addon to create a separate area altogether. They decide to return and report their findings to Sabrina, as they cannot enter the cutoff section.

Tova pulls up next to the Cat, but Sabrina is not there. She calls her and reports what they found in the drone bay. Sabrina thanks her and asks them to sit tight for now as she is with Van, and they are trying to communicate with Julia and Martin.

Van and Sabrina are darting all over the West end of the complex, trying to get a message to or from Julia. Jumping on roofs, in and out of corridors, anywhere close enough to connect. Buildings can impede information transfer because of electrical interference and other factors. Despite these challenges, broken communication or sensing is typically still workable. They are getting desperate to contact them and discover the building's contents before heading to Mount Gambier. Sabrina calls two of her internal drones to meet them at the well-used doorway they noticed earlier. She will send them in first to scout ahead and shoot anything not friendly. Once inside, Van might have more luck trying to communicate with Julia or Martin.

Chapter fifty-seven. Going Shopping

The well-used doorway is unlocked and does not have any signs of being forced open. They send a drone in first; it works its way through what resembles a photography room light trap. Corridors that turn at ninety degrees back on themselves twice to block light entering or exiting the room. It discourages entry by anyone or anything. A drone makes its way through and moves into the sizeable area. The transmitted feedback is alarming. She quickly contacts Svetlana and Tova, instructing them to return to the maintenance garage with drones and shoot anything emerging from the large door they discovered.

Van and Sabrina exit the light trap to see cages of creatures. They look evil, like the ones that attacked Port Lincoln. Red, inflamed skin, enormous heads, solid front chests, and lean rear quarters. They are in a type of hibernation motionless, with their teeth showing like a growling rabid dog. The next row of creatures is more human-looking but still definitely killing machines, crosses between Panthera, Bear, and dogs. Sabrina estimates a minimum of one thousand creatures in these two rows of cages, with others filling the room and reaching the ceiling. They split up to search each side of the cages as Van keeps trying to reach Julia or Martin.

Sabrina takes the east side, and Van goes west. Centered in the area is a square room featuring a glass door. It has human robots hanging like coats in a wardrobe, two high ten wide, and they cannot see how deep as a blue light illuminates a faint fog-like gas inside. Wide corridors enable loading drones to maneuver and transport items.

The western side Van is looking at has supply racking and pumping infrastructure. He is happy to see red flashing lights on parts of the system, because of the wavelength he knows it is Martin's handy work. Sabrina can see six transport pods and the speed pod at the rear of the east side. It might not be ground zero for creature creation and distribution, but it's definitely a hub. Sabrina suspects there must be other levels as part of this complex. It could also explain why Van cannot pick up Julia or Martin, as they may be deeper underground.

Making their way to the southwest corner, they find a lift capable of carrying a shuttle pod and a stairwell is next to it. Sabrina and Van discuss a plan to flash down the stairs as the drones use the lift to create a distraction. As the lift lowers and the drones prepare to shoot anything that might approach, Van and Sabrina zip through the stairwell door, looking for a spot to hide as the drones exit the lift. After checking for cameras or any security in the wide corridor, Sabrina sends the drones forward to the first intersection, which is approximately one hundred meters in front of them. They have a quick chat before heading down it.

So, whose plan was this Van?

Julia and Martin are alive. I can sense them, and they will sense me. I will feel it if we are getting closer to them, but there's lots of electrical noise in here, or it is a vast complex with thick walls.

Let's go with electrical noise, Van. No time for huge.

Ok, well, you lead the way; you called me here, remember?

Sabrina draws her weapon as she approaches the intersection. One path heads north, the other goes east towards an intersection. The corridors are dimly lit, and none of the walls creating them appear to have windows or doors. There are no signs of life as they make their way along the first corridor. It is a spotless, sterile environment, like those in hospitals or laboratories.

Van still cannot communicate with the others but feels he is getting closer to them. Fifty meters down the corridor, another goes east, double the width of the one they are in. Van suggests they should go down it, as he can see indications of large windows or doors in the middle of it. One drone races down it to check the end to ensure no one can surprise them. The other drone stays put, watching the corridor for any possible rear threats. Starting their way to the light, Van whispers to Sabrina.

They are close but I still cannot communicate with them, something is not right.

They stop to have a closer look at the large glass sliding doors they have approached on the southern side. The room has Unhuman in large, red-lit glass-walled cells resembling test tubes, depending on the size they hold one to ten a cell.

Sabrina, they are so close, they must sense me and should answer.

They turn and look into the north side glass section and are shocked to see Julia and Martin in blue-lit tubes. The area lacks a keypad, thumbprint button, door handle, or visible alarm trigger. Van uses his ultrasonics and echo sounding to discover the large door is actually common glass. Using his fingernail with a high-speed tap, he shatters it.

Well, if they didn't know we were here before, they will certainly know we are here now. A good simple plan, Van.

Sabrina, these are my elders. They come first.

Ok, that's good enough for me, let's get them out.

You move out of the room to the end of the corridor; I don't know what's inside here, but I suspect it's some kind of sleeping gas. I will break the glass tube they are in and join you to let it disperse.

He uses his fingernail again as a glass breaker and exits to join Sabrina at the end of the corridor.

If drugged, they could come out fighting. Please try to subdue them and only kill them if you have to, to save yourself.

You have my word. I will run as fast as I can.

Van and Sabrina return to the room. Julia and Martin snap at them aggressively but are too slow and weak to hurt them. They calm down once they know they are amongst friends, Martin, as he comes around tells them how they got trapped in a corner and shot with some type of tranquilizer. Neither recall anything happening apart from being dragged and put into the tubes.

Yes, that sounds very much like Elite testing protocols, tranquilize, take samples, and inject a trial drug.

Julia asks Van to evaluate their blood to see if it tastes like the human robots or anything unnatural.

Stop, wait a minute. If they have done something to you and Van tastes it, he might become infected too. That is not a great idea.

Van tastes Valorie, then Martin.

Ok yeah sure, we can just do that. That will work. I am not sure I like these simple plans though, Van. I am actually seeing Baldy's point of view.

Sabrina gestures with her hands, pointing at each of them, moving her finger left and right, shrugging her shoulders and shaking her head. She turns and leaves the room.

Great, now I have three drugged Vamps.

Sabrina calls the team to update them.

Guys, we have found Julia and Martin captured and possibly drugged. Down here, we have a hive of various things in test tubes and cages. It is safe to say they are doing some type of DNA testing and manipulation here. Tell Duke to get CM on the way and tell him to bring explosives. Anything that tries to leave here gets killed. Well, not us, obviously, but anything that's not us. At least for now, but that order might change if we get drugged.

OK Sabrina will do.

Tova. Creatures and human bots fill the top floor. Which is where the door you are at leads to. Southwest corner has a shuttle-sized lift that goes down under the shopping complex. The corridors down here are wide enough to accommodate moving around shuttle-sized loads. So far we have found storage of Unhuman and Mixed Humans. Two longest corridors go north. We went down the first one. If you don't hear from us in forty-five minutes, you must get through that door and blow this place sky high. You're my girls, you have got this. Oh, and just for a little extra fun, a heads up, Van has drunk Julia and Martin's blood, so all three could now be a problem too.

Sabrina returns to join the rest.

You know we can hear you Sabrina, don't you?

Yeah, but I thought you would be all too busy chatting silently together, catching up or have already disappeared off to somewhere else. Since I don't need to tell you my plan, we're all good and on the same page then, I guess.

Chapter fifty-eight. Twin Meetings

Julia explains to Sabrina and Van what happened when they entered the building.

We only recall seeing one person or humanoid who shot us in the back. They make human robots in the room south of us. They just rise out of a well filled with a skin-colored flesh compound, get picked up and hang to dry as they move along a production line. At the end, they dress themselves, and willingly step into a container to be taken upstairs for storage. We have laid charges in there. North has a similar setup for creating the Unhuman. They differ from the ones in Port Lincoln and Yorke's, more resembling werewolves with wings. Beyond that, there is some kind of control room or laboratory. We got shot before making any further progress.

OK, so we will add to the plan list not to get shot from behind. Is there anything else that you can tell us?

Martin looks at his watch.

You can manually detonate the placed explosives, or they will automatically explode in an hour.

I was going to ask why you are wearing a watch. Can't you sense dawn and dusk, therefore time itself? Let's save that chat for later. Is it in an hour, less, or more? Can't we be a little more exact using that fancy watch you are wearing?

Seventy-five minutes, give or take a bit depending on if that tube I was in affected the accuracy of my watch. Is that more helpful, Sabrina?

He mimics her smile and thumbs up gestures she uses when being sarcastic to them.

Ok so you have been here about an hour longer than us.

Yes, we better have someone check the time, Sabrina, and I can compare it to my watch.

Hey Tova, what is the time?

Two forty-five, why?

Oh, we have explosives set to go off and are not sure exactly when. We are just chilling and chit chatting about a plan at the moment.

Two forty-five Martin, how does that line up with your watch? One thirty is when I set the first charge, and they have a two- and half-hour countdown on them. If not triggered or shutdown before the timer runs out, so that timing sounds about right.

Hey, wait, what, you can shut them down?

It usually works, but occasionally one fails. Their failure is extremely rare, but it's best not to be here if one does go off. It will be your first and last experience of a device failure.

OK, thank you Martin. All of us will be gone in sixty minutes. Set your watches.

She gives her customary smile at the group and taps her wrist as if setting a time on her watch.

Hey Tova, set a countdown warning for fifty minutes, then a counter after that, please. We need to leave and be far away in 75 minutes. Right, time is ticking. Let's go see what else is here.

The four of them move down the corridor to an open section. It has pillar style computer terminals reaching to the ceiling, with the rest of the space mostly open. A voice speaks quickly from a hiding spot.

Hi Sarah, I have been expecting you. You, CM, and I have a long history. I am just following my orders and abducted your friends here as samples to add to my database. I have not harmed them. Do not shoot me as I wish to inform you of who I am. It may help you and your team with your mission.

We will not shoot you unless you give us a reason to. We are on a tight timeline, so we must make this quick.

He walks out from behind a pillar towards them. He looks similar to the guard twins that had been shooting at them. Tall, athletic, with a strong masculine face, blue eyes, and long blonde hair, a typical image of a warrior.

I am like the human droids you have seen created here. I am not as fast or as deadly as any of you. Sarah, your evolution, your genetic refinement are far superior to anything you see here, including the Vamps that are with you. The drugs or vitamin tablets you believe you were taking have suppressed you for all your years. Julia and Martin, I was just doing my job as I know you are here doing what you must do to protect your covens and others. I am forced to follow my programming despite desperately trying to change it over the years. Mutual distrust plagued both hibernation teams. Both groups of Elite hoped CM would develop a virus that would work, but years of hibernation cycles proved it was unlikely. A secret select team learned of my mission and hidden dungeons, so they developed a backup plan to make the original dream come true. Their assurance of safety for those on the Moon and Mars drove their willingness to risk all life on Earth. They did not count on your father's change of heart. I've lived here as long as Julia and Martin, storing Elite DNA secrets. Thankfully, as I watched over Adelaide and beyond, I could see that they were wrong. CM was right, though they and I did not know of his plan then.

I am created like you, Sabrina. I call you that now as I also wish to be known by a name before I die. Having never been called by a name, I would like one. I have tried to stop the creature's attacks. Computers off-world manage the system, but I'm unsure if anyone controls it now. No one has contacted me from the Moon during this new hibernation cycle. There is no virus stored here, but they were making plans to develop one. This building contains DNA collections and hibernating creatures and humanoids. The stock you see here is replacements, but you have two mass releases coming up, and I cannot stop them. I do not have the codes or the intelligence.

In Mount Gambier, with the public protesting over the attacks, the creatures will kill thousands. Evolving and changing my thoughts, I developed emotions by limiting drug intake. I ask that you please kill me quickly, Sabrina.

Human, I will give you a name. You've lived long and stayed loyal to a cause you were told was right. I have done that too, and I changed my name for a fresh start in life. It's time for you to embrace and embody your new name, Beathan. You will help us destroy everything here. I sense you are no longer just a soldier, but conscious. I encourage you to come with us as you have shown empathy and willingness to change, that will only grow outside of these walls. We could also use your help to stop what they have set in motion and save lives. Would you like to come with us, Beathan? The only other option is to die here, and I believe you deserve more than that.

Sabrina, I would like to walk free and enjoy the sun, but I don't know how to live outside these walls.

You and I both mate. I have broken out of my cage, and I am now free. It feels good, my friend, and you can only try. If you die here now, you will never know.

Beathan agrees to help them destroy the complex, and it soon becomes obvious to the team he had already set his own fate in motion. He has placed all of Martin's explosives in primary locations. He looks at Julia and Martin.

I saw your watch, and I was watching you place the explosives, planning to set you both free before they went off. I needed time to help and destroy this complex without you killing me.

Hey Tova.

Yes, Sabrina.

A new plan. Don't shoot us. We'll exit through your door with our new friend, Beathan. We must go to Mount Gambier immediately. Return to the governor's building and we'll join you there.

They finish rigging the place to explode, taking the speed pod along with the three cargo pods and exit out of the maintenance bay through the large door. Two drones stay to ensure nothing else exits the building and to monitor the explosion. The drones stay to survey the site, documenting what remains and destroying anything still intact.

Chapter fifty-nine. New Objective

Sabrina introduces Beathan and tells the team that he will take them to the underground dungeons of Mount Gambier and Murray Bridge. His craft can get through the moat without help, so a strike team will enter the compound using them. She finished the briefing, asking them to check all weapons and to prepare to leave.

CM pulls Sabrina aside.

My father created Beathan, but I believed the seconds killed him when I took over as a leader, as they said they would. I never thought much more of it. The seconds must have changed him and drugged him to be their slave. He is not like those soldiers they have replicated from him. He was receiving the same generic drugs you were taking, as did others. I learned that stealing someone's compassion, reasoning and love is wrong, as we wronged you, so I changed all the sets of drugs to make them weaker. You have shown that if you realize your actions are wrong, you'll take steps to change them.

He mentioned your history with him. He also seems to know about Julia and Martin.

Yes, he shares their gained DNA of immortality. As you do, you have had yours from birth. I interrupted it so you could grow, feel mortal, and develop your personality. Knowing that if someone killed me, you wouldn't receive the drugs that block it, so it would reactivate. Now you are no longer taking the drugs, all your genes will turn back on. When I'm gone, you will be the one good thing I leave behind.

Great, another surprise, you just keep them coming, don't you? We have a long chat awaiting us when this is all finished.

The team loads into the pods, Tova and her bike fit in one, Van, Valorie, Julia, and Martin jump into another cargo pod. Sabrina, a few drones, and Svetlana get into the third pod. They all follow Beathan in the speed pod to the entrance point. The Cat, Dragor, Paffor and Vamps go to the main gate at Mount Gambier to wait outside. Extra wing support moves closer to Murray Bridge, in case of a release there. While the plan moves into action, CM calls Natasha to tell her about the deployment and the creatures. Requesting her to clear the streets so the team can work on reducing casualties.

Mount Gambier city, with its lakes and natural surroundings, has a different layout from the other Elite compounds. Natural vegetation on a small headland at Blackfellows Creek extends up to the moat. A cave system extends from it, with its entrance hidden by a projected camouflage field, which they pass through undetected. While flying underground to a spot beneath the center of the city, Sabrina realizes the reason for choosing this location. Releasing the creatures in this cave system will provide them with several exits to escape from all over the city, rather than just one location.

They stop in a large control room and get out of their pods. Beathan explains the equipment and the positions of all the creatures and human robots in the cave system. His understanding of the release order is creatures first, then Human bots and space droids, as in the other two compounds. Human bot armies here will not hunt like the ones in Yorke's did. While they may be more accurate in killing creatures, they won't be as fast as your team. The Elite aim for a gradual rounding up of the creatures to maximize the loss of public lives. Believing it will justify an attack on Murray Bridge and other Mixed locations in the future. They can then wipe out entire cities with conventional weapons that have too many Pure already siding with the Mixed. I imagine they planned it as the backup, aware of CM's last hibernation cycle.

Svetlana asks the obvious question to Beathan.

Can't we just stop them from being released on that control panel?

No, I have no access to that part of the program. All we can do is try to kill them all in their cages, trying to block exits as Martin and Julia did in Yorke's. We will not get to all of them. There are fifteen different sites here. We don't have time to eliminate them completely.

Martin explains how to seal the cages as they all grab handguns. Sabrina calls out the pairings when he has finished.

Martin and Julia, Van and Valorie, Tova and Beathan. Svetlana, you are with me.

Using their skills, strength and speed in the dark cave environment, it is no surprise Julia and Martin arrive at their cage first. They call the others with unwelcome news.

They are awake and active, as if something has been teasing them. I count at least fifty-five in this cage, and I suspect a release is minutes away at the most.

They seal the cage and shoot some to be food. It starts a frenzied attack, and the creatures start kill each other. The Vamps reach their second cages faster than other teams reach their first. They are approaching their third cage as it opens, releasing the creatures. Julia warns the others that the cages have opened. She and Martin shoot the creatures as they exit, killing twenty of them.

Van and Valorie also kill eighty percent of the ones leaving the cage. Van calls Sabrina, letting her know they're going after the remaining ones. Sabrina asks Beathan and Tova to come back to the control room to meet her and Svetlana.

The Vamps are now out and exposed. We need Dragor and the team in the compound so we can all help them. Beathan, do you know how to open the moat?

No, I do not. I've never attempted it elsewhere. I only use my common access points. It might be possible to create a hole in the moat if we park the speed pod and shuttles in a formation.

Ok, you go try that. Vamps outside the moat can sense if they can enter through it. Tova, get on your bike with Svetlana and go kill the creatures. Shoot at anyone or anything that tries to harm you or our friends. I'll have Duke or Natasha bring my Cat through the moat, and try to leave it open long enough for others to come in.

Chapter sixty. On The Streets

Thousands of people fill the streets, some protesting the Mixed, others curious observers. Inside the compound, life is blissfully free from complexity. Each day is the same, so the locals find the initial action thrilling and new, unaware of the danger.

Van, Valorie, Julia, and Martin are communicating with each other, killing all they can, causing the public caught up in these scenes to panic. They leave the creatures in the last throes of their lives, or gutted carcasses, wherever they fall. Creatures are attacking citizens, biting out their throats, or ripping them apart as they fight over them. Tova revs the bike's engine to eleven, clearing the crowd as she approaches. Svetlana stands on the rear pegs, shooting any creatures they encounter. The number released is overwhelming. Sabrina and the team do her best to dart around, killing them. She has her sword drawn, slicing some in half and shooting others.

Authorities broadcast warning messages instructing civilians to get off the streets, enter any building, close the doors, and take cover. News on social channels have videos of Van and Valorie flying around and are blaming them, saying it is a Mixed attack. There are tags and comments on social media saying they have all come to kill us, we must kill all the Mixed. Others post videos of Mixed killing the creatures and saving citizens from attack, praising the team for helping the Pure. Despite the team's efforts, casualties are increasing because of the chaos. Sabrina contacts Duke.

We would appreciate some extra help. How are you and Beathan progressing with the moat?

They are trying to get it to stay open. It is pulsing with the pods in it. We have lost a couple of Vamps and Dragons trying to pass through.

Not Dragor or Paffor?

No, they are safe. Other keen Mixed offered to go first, but they didn't make it. Beathan is talking with Natasha and Logan is on his way here to help. Among the three of us, we hope to gain control of the moat soon.

Ok thanks Duke, if you could speed it up a tad that would be helpful. Get Stella to issue a street alert in Murray Bridge. Send Tarak, Roderick, there right away. I will send Beathan to help find and blow up any caged creatures.

Beathan, take the speed pod to Murray Bridge and meet the team once you've finished helping here. Take out all the creatures there. I don't care how big of a bang it makes. Blow them all up. We cannot do this here and handle another large number over there.

Sabrina, now talking between breaths as she kills creatures, continues to give orders.

Logan, how are we going with the space droids?

We can't have them here as well. They will kill too many innocent people if they start randomly shooting.

I have sharpened just the right pencil. I hacked into the spacecraft's telemetry systems and Duke is working on crashing them into the ocean by changing their navigation points.

Look at you go Logan, well done, I want my Cat in here now! Can you find the pencil to make that happen, and let in more Dragons and Vamps?

Working on it Sabrina.

The humanoid soldiers, in a military style, line up outside of buildings and maintenance areas. Walking into the action, shooting creatures with lasers in all directions, causing panic among those who ignored warnings. Their shots, while not completely random or reckless, are causing casualties. It is clear they are trying to take out the creatures, however, their programs are lacking protocols for limiting collateral damage. No other help is available from the local security teams. The compound's security is nowhere to be seen. Natasha had to kill several of them as they were pro-extinction. Those remaining are protecting Natasha and the control room.

Tova and Svetlana are racing down the main street, dodging people and vehicles while killing creatures. On-lookers cheer them from rooftops, mistaking it for a show or movie. Svetlana stands on the back pegs and uses the sissy bar as support as she shoots. Creatures momentarily halt as the bike's sound captivates them. This action gives Svetlana time to kill them. As they round an open bend at speed, three creatures bound into appearance just ahead of them. With no time to stop or turn, Tova twists the throttle and heads straight towards them, hoping they will jump aside. Svetlana kills two, while the third jumps over the handlebars as she shoots it in the head. Tova lays the bike down, sparks come off it as it spins and comes to a stop. Svetlana and Tova roll on the ground, then spring to their feet.

The noise of the bike speeding up then stopping attracts other curious Unhuman. Two creatures are about to kill them as Dragor and Paffor swoop in. They got past the moat and used Tova's bike sound to locate the fight; they tear the creatures apart. Van also appears, having noticed the sudden change in the bike's sound. Tova, as if nothing happen chats to the team.

Good to see you all. Are any more of you coming?

They go silent as they communicate together in their own natural frequency. Sensing Julia, Martin, and Valorie's positions and realizing they need help, all disappear to go to share the load.

Tova yells out, thanking them as they fly off. She becomes angry as she looks at her bike, all scratched and beaten up. They both have some wounds from rolling on the ground but are otherwise ok. As they lift the bike up, Tova looks at Svetlana.

Ok, let's go kill these bloody things. I am over all this shit.

With a pistol in her left hand, she and Svetlana head off to find and kill more. Sabrina calls Tova as she also heard the bike suddenly idle.

Tova, are you and Svetlana ok, or do you need help?

We are a tad beaten up with a few bruises, my bike's scratched, and my favorite tank top is dirty. Dragor and Paffor came to our rescue with Van. They have gone off to help the others.

Ok Tova, excellent work. Sorry about ya bike. The soldiers are not being helpful, so if they get in the way, kill them. They are just as likely to at shoot you as they are a creature.

Will do Sabrina. It would be nice to have more of Van and Dragor's friends, though.

Duke is working on it.

Sabrina has been darting around, saving civilians, and killing creatures. Even for her it is getting tiring.

Hey Duke, any timeline for getting help?

Sabrina, the Vamps, and Dragons are on their way to circle you soon.

Enormous shadows run across the flat surfaces of grass and roadways, then sore up sides of buildings. Crowds points in aw, watching as they dart down, grabbing creatures and rip them in half. The Cat rolls up alongside Sabrina with CM inside. He asks her to get him inside the headquarters. Jumping in, she stands up through the sunroof and commands the Cat to head to headquarters, as she shoots any encountered creatures. The Cat flies up the staircase to the headquarters, reaching its highest point before it narrows too much for it to land. Sabrina grabs a handgun, gets out and calls Duke.

I have CM at the entrance to HQ. Can you get Natasha to come down with her security and pick him up?

Will do Sabrina.

She waits, watching for anything that might wish to cause her or CM any harm. Sabrina is on high alert when she hears shooting from inside the foyer. A small inside drone launches out of the Hellcat as Natasha, flanked by four guards, appears in the doorway.

What was that?

We still have scattered resistance, some scared and jittery staff that have got their hands on weapons that the guards dropped when abandoning their positions.

Ok Natasha, we will get CM into the command center. He will broadcast the truth throughout the building and over the community alert channel, both here and at Murray Bridge. After that, we will broadcast a message through the building saying that we are locking it down, offering everyone a choice. If they wish to leave, they can. We will give them two minutes to leave. If they wish to stay and support a change, they can. Then, with my drones, I will search each floor. If anyone holds a weapon or points one at me, I will kill them where they stand, no questions asked. I'll collect the weapons, and your guards can collect them in the foyer.

Sounds like a brilliant plan, Sabrina.

Finally, someone that likes one of my plans, I wish I recorded that and your response to play back to Baldy.

Without incident, they head to the command center. Onlookers know that Sabrina and the drone will respond to any sudden movements. While descending, she searches the building and discovers a collection of weapons, but no potential attackers. Sabrina rejoins the fight now with her Cat to help her move around the city at a faster pace.

Chapter sixty-one. Taking It To The Top

Beathan and Roderick have set charges to several cages that Beathan knows about in Murray Bridge. It is possible in this more open living lifestyle that there may be a couple of other sites run by Pure activists. Roderick calls Sabrina.

Beathan and I believe we should set off the charges we have laid now as we don't know when the cages might open. It will be better to have killed as many as we can before then. There was no way to secure the cages or exits from opening without more time.

Yep, do it Roderick, I trust your judgment.

CM broadcasts his speech, and he explains the ideal future.

Earth now has abundant space and livable areas and with innovative technologies, each species can have its own wonderland. All that choose to live amongst each other can, without fear of one species, trying to rule the world. We have shown we can work together and use each species' strengths to aid in the greater good.

Cheers and calm spread through the streets upon hearing his speech.

The team is working hard, rounding up the humanoids and killing the creatures. Dragor and Paffor have been picking up and placing humanoids in a crater to secure them. The sky is alive with winged saviors, lifting and gutting creatures before dropping them and repeating the act on another creature. Dragons or Vampires lift endangered civilians, moments from death to safety, and carry them to the tops of buildings. Sabrina does some math, calculating fifteen cages, six of which were fully contained and two other cages that had most of them shot before they escaped.

Ok, seven cages have released, around three hundred and eighty-five creatures in total. With a few from the unsecured ones. Can we get a couple of our winged friends to fly the city and count what creatures they can see dead? Also, if you can all remember the number you have killed, that will help. It is not a competition for who killed the most; it is just so we can match it up with the number released. I know you all are secretly wanting to beat my score.

Sabrina, the total from the head count of both teams is about two hundred and seventy-three. There are definitely fewer creatures to humanoids now, and they are still shooting.

Thanks Martin, I think we will have to stop the humanoids. They are doing too much damage, and we can't reason with them as they are following a set program. Have your members take them out. Ok Team, we are looking for about one hundred and twelve creatures. I want the core group to be ready to leave for Murray Bridge in a half an hour. We will leave five Vamps and two Dragons here to kill any creatures we may have missed. I will get Tarak to organize getting a representative safely in as well. I love it when one of my detailed plans works. Yes, I know, all my plans work only because you all do such an awesome job. Thank you.

Svetlana looks at Tova.

I bet she is smiling or doing one of her little quirky moves.

Yep, I am sure she is. Pity Baldy is not here to add his familiar groan.

Stella puts out an alert straight after CM's speech that there will be explosions in the compound and outside of it. Stay indoors, allowing the Mixed defenders to handle the creatures being released. They are coming to fix this cruel situation our Elite leaders have set upon us, in all our compounds, as you have seen on the news and social channels.

It is getting late in the day, and there are only two hours of daylight left. The city has long shadows that will soon fade out as dust sets in. This could be a slight advantage as fewer civilians will go out in the fading light. Also, having seen footage from Mount Gambier, they hopefully are more likely to follow the advice.

Beathan, where are we at my friend?

Sabrina, there are thirty-eight sites I know of here, all holding seventy creatures. The mix of creatures differs slightly from those in the other compounds. Ten sites are disabled, but the progress is slow because of their widespread nature. The plan intended to show rampant creatures and mixed humans in South Australia, emphasizing the need for eradication to prevent a takeover.

Back up a little there, mate. These creatures are slightly different. Care to let us all in on the slightly different bit, please?

They look different, not just one species, they are more representative of the Unhuman communities. Some can fly, as you saw in Marion, but they're all the same killing machines you've been dealing with.

Maybe lead with this type of detail next time, please Beathan, and you all complain about my plans. Ok, we have flying creatures to deal with this time and a larger number in total. Thanks for the great chat, Beathan.

So, team we have a new plan now taking Beathan's new detailed information on board. Kill anything flying, walking, or running on all fours that is not friendly. Do we all like the new plan?

Yes Sabrina.

Just one other thing.

Yes, Beathan, what's that?

No spaceship droids, or humanoids, will be released here.

Great! this makes my plan easier, and Logan won't break any pencils. Thanks, Beathan for sharing. Team let's head to Murray Bridge. Tova, load your bike in one of Beathan's shuttle pods along with those who can't fly as they are faster. Duke open the moat.

Chapter sixty-two. No Time For A Ski

They all leave for Murray Bridge, Sabrina's Hellcat leading the way, with Vamps and Dragons soaring above. As they pass over the Bordertown area, four pterodactyls Unhuman launch out of the dense foliage, expecting to capture something to eat from the passing convoy. A cauldron of Vamps and Dragons meets them, and they retreat.

As they close in on Murray Bridge, they can see smoke from sites that Beathan, Tarak and Roderick have blown up. With sunset just an hour away, the compound lights are illuminating. Darkened areas from high-rise apartments make excellent hiding spots. Beathan provides Sabrina with the location of the caged creatures, she has Dragor and Van distribute teams to circle them to watch for any release. Without Beathan, they cannot enter the area as he is literally the key to the gate.

The streets are relatively clear of people. Some reckless individuals exercise or walk. Most Bars, street restaurants, and cafes are closed or not well patronized because of the broadcast. Sabrina goes to HQ to meet Stella and get an overview of their progress. She asks her to turn on all the streetlights, park lights and building lights they have control of. Another explosion goes off. Stella tells Sabrina about the number of explosions so far.

Yes, Beathan said there are thirty-five cages holding seventy creatures each. We expect they will time the opening of the cages, just as you shut the compound gate at sunset. Trapping all the creatures, ensuring a greater effect. There could be releases outside the walls that Beathan doesn't know about. If that happens, the Vamps and Dragons will handle it. Those outside the walls will have their own protection and have lived without a moat, anyway.

It is a full moon above Murray Bridge providing enough light for the Mixed Humans and Dragons to hunt. It also will put a zest in the step of the Vamps. The comms channel fills with chatter.

Sabrina ... we... at.... Mmmm ... r...... at ... Everyone is trying to talk at once, and it is all coming out as gibberish. Sabrina waits for the team to realize their mistake and looks at Stella.

The creatures are out based on the active comms. You stay here, we will hunt them. Stella put out a warning for all citizens to stay inside wherever they are now, to let us do our job without having to save them, too.

Sabrina flashes out of HQ and into the Hellcat. Flying creatures resembling hyenas and werewolves with wings are hunting citizens, thinking they would be safe on the rooftop bars. People on rooftops capture these attacks on video and share them on media channels. Vamps swoop in, using their echo sounding to track and eliminate creatures in the darker areas.

Dragor and his team, with superior flying and strength, make quick work of any they catch in the air. Tova and Svetlana team up again and race around the city streets with a red glow under her bike. Svetlana stands up shooting. With the Harley sound thumping, it creates a menacing image for anything wanting to attack them. Shoots of blue bolts from her pulse gun light up buildings. Tova shoots with her handgun, with orange bolts flashing down the street and picking off targets.

The Hellcat, with its sphere wheels, allows Sabrina to take corners at speed, drifting around town with a green glow under it, as she shoots creatures. The whole of the compound now, with Beathan, Tarak and Roderick also joining in, has action spread all over it, lighting up buildings and the sky. Julia and Martin use their speed, strength, and agility to kill creatures in the trickier areas, with around a thousand rabid creatures released, and eight core team members doing the bulk of the work. It averages out to around one hundred and twenty-six each. The drones, extra Vamps, and Dragon's help, but lack commitment and efficiency compared to the core team. They are mostly protecting rooftops or herding the creatures towards the team and away from civilians.

Working to the team's advantage, after being caged all their lives, the creatures have a natural aversion to going into tunnels or tight places they may get trapped in. Sabrina gets out of her Cat to help an aged citizen off the middle of a wide road, when five flying hyenas spot her, attracting the attention of others, as they yelp and scream, heading towards her. She finds herself outnumbered and calls for help. Adding to her situation, two large flying creatures swoop in, larger than even the Dragon Humans. One of the creature's feathers shimmer in the moonlight and street lighting, with green metal flakes mixed in with the white and black feathers.

Sabrina is about to shoot at them but has to kill a closer creature, giving them time to get upon her before she can divert her attention back to them. Sabrina feels fear as they swoop in impressively fast, as she has no time to react. Looks straight into their open beaks, ready to bite or pick her up. They stretch out their talon-like hands and feet wide as they race in, picking up and crush the two closest threats to Sabrina. Soar up into the sky, loop around, and come back to kill the rest. Sabrina shoots the other creatures that are joining in. Unsure if they are attacking or assisting, she gives them the benefit of doubt. It lands close by, looking down at her and into her eyes. He gently flaps his wings and twisting his head, checking her out. To Sabrina's surprise, it is Eithan Hawk, and he speaks broken English.

We heard, through Hawk lines, what you do. I aware you for years Sardeena. I follow, watch, and see. We help. Do what we do in our world.

He and his mate flap their wings and get ready to take flight.

It is Sabrina Eithan. S A B R I N A and thank you for your help. I will remember. If there are more out there, that would like to help! Feel free to join in.

Increasing the flapping of their wings moves the evening air, lifting her hair. The whooshing sound echoes off buildings as they run down the road to take flight.

Sabrina contacts the entire team. The large hawks leave them be. They just saved my life.

Over time, the flashing pulses of guns reduces as the creatures become harder to find and their numbers reduce. The Vamps become the most efficient hunters, finding creatures by using their ultrasonics and thermal vision. They are doing a fantastic job of cleaning up the remaining few.

After two hours, they seem to have killed all of them. Van and Dragor arrange for a team from both species to patrol throughout the night, inside and outside the compound. Sabrina opens the comms line.

Thanks to all for a great job on a challenging day. Your efforts and compassion towards other species who have never treated you equally highlight your genuine characters and integrity. Beathan, can you please send the speed pod to pick up CM from HQ? The rest of you, my formidable team here in Murray Bridge, please join me. I will meet you outside the restaurant bar on the main street, across the road from HQ, which is lit up in all its former glory, we will address later. There is plenty of room for all my winged friends. It is called Genesis. I am parked out the front and I will book a table for us all.

Sabrina walks into the impressively large, grassed area with wine barrel chairs and tables mixed with other long benches and booths. The beer garden tables have plenty of room separating them. Decorative mood lighting gives the space a peaceful and inviting atmosphere. She sits, exhausted, in the garden's center after a challenging day.

Tova and Svetlana arrive, appearing as if they have just faced an SAS obstacle course or thrown around by a wild bull. All scratch, bruised, and weeping blood. Julia and Martin arrive next, also looking a mess, but unlike Svetlana and Tova, Sabrina is sure it is all other's blood, not theirs, that covers them. Eddy makes a surprise landing, sticking his trademark appearance in style. Sabrina flashes over to greet him.

Best one yet, Baldy, so glad to see you. You missed all the action and my new friend. He has a cool landing too, not as good as yours, but his take-off. Don't mention it to him, but it requires a lot of improvement.

I was listening to your plans and made my way over here from Yorke's at sunset. Ah yes, the Hawk, enormous with green flecks, do you know him?

Nah, not really. We've crossed paths a few times, like others who've had encounters with Sarah. He didn't seem to have any fondness for me then. He still may not, as he called me Sardeena, but I let him get away with it as he saved my life.

Well, that sounds like you, Sardeena, always making friends.

Baldy groans as he walks off to meet the others. Sabrina smiles and gives him a wave, and blows him a kiss.

Valorie and Van appear from the darkness as the owner of the bar walks out. He has his order pad open and approaches Sabrina.

I am not sure we will have what you all might like. But I am happy to arrange anything for you and your friends.

Sabrina thanks him and tells him that the HQ will pay any cost.

You will have to ask my friends what they would like. I have visited the compound many times and I have always wanted to sit in this spot, have a beer, and just feel normal. Can I have a beer, please? We would also like large jugs and buckets of water with towels, so we can clean up a bit, please.

Roderick, Beathan and Tarak arrive.

My friends here will join in with a couple of beers, as well. Thank you.

Sabrina flashes up and shoots between Dragor and Paffor to kill a creature about to attack.

Do I have to do all the work here?

She looks at Dragor and smiles as it falls.

I'm unsure what that creature will taste like, gamey I would think. Anyway, I am sure you have had enough of their taste for today. I think it was pretty even between you and the rest of the team in getting a good score, even though we outnumbered you guys. Well done, and thank you. Ask the owner for what you would like, preferably not a Pure Human though. It's possibly too soon for that sarcasm.

We'll just go talk to Eddy before you come up with your next crazy plan.

Dragor and Paffor, carefully walk in. Navigating around barrels, stools, and festoon lighting to reach a spot on the grass beside the bench. CM arrives in the Speed pod and joins the team. The owner brings out the drinks and explains he has rung his suppliers and other restaurants, and they are bringing sections for you all, our guests, to choose from.

The bar is gradually filling with the public, offering casual waves and supportive nods to the team as they enter and sit down. They order drinks, like any other night, while sitting in a bar and socializing. After a couple of hours of war stories and laughs, and with the bar full of locals who are respectfully leaving the team alone, Sabrina looks at CM.

You owe me that talk now, dad. Let's go.

She grabs him by the arm and walks to a shuttle, turning back to Beathan.

You are coming with us to my brother. You must hear this story too.

The three walk to the shuttle.

Tova, make sure you all enjoy yourselves, and anyone wanting to crash can come to my compound. We'll be there, and you're welcome.

Entering her compound, handed over to her by the upgrades Logan made before her hibernation, they move a table out to the landing bay, opening its door to admire the view over Murray Bridge. All its lights are shining and winged humans flying above it, protecting the Pure is not a sight she ever thought she would see. Sitting at a table, she turns to CM.

From the beginning please dad.

CM tells her about her mum, how she and Beathan were born. He talks about their early lives, and what living on the Moon was like. Seeing his dream become reality, his voice carries emotion and passion as his daughter finds freedom, along with the power to shape their future. It won't be easy or incident-free, but they will be safe from the Elite's extinction plan for now.

....The Sarah Project 2190......

About the Author

I am not a professional writer. I wrote this book as if it was a movie playing in my head. Having dyslexia, I just wanted to prove to myself that I could. There are people that like music, its lyrics and the story. Others hate songs or singers with a passion. Many like art that a majority think is just spilt paint. I'm sure this book falls into one of those categories.

I could not afford to have it professionally edited, so it has some warts. Hopefully, if you choose to read it, you will enjoy the story, and you can visualise the movie I see in my mind.

Thank you

Kind regards

Rob

www.ingramcontent.com/pod-product-compliance
Lightning Source LLC
Chambersburg PA
CBHW032154190626
46814CB00005BA/1991